Something blue

Something Blue

Ann Hood

BANTAM BOOKS
NEW YORK • TORONTO • LONDON •
SYDNEY • AUCKLAND

SOMETHING BLUE
A *Bantam Book* / *February 1991*

All rights reserved.
Copyright © 1991 by Ann Hood.
Book design by Maria Carella.

Library of Congress Cataloging-in-Publication Data
Hood, Ann, 1956–
    Something blue / Ann Hood.
        p.   cm.
    ISBN 0-553-07140-8
    I. Title.
PS3558.0537S58   1991   90-40047
813'.54—dc20   CIP

Published simultaneously in the United States and Canada

Bantam Books are published by Bantam Books, a division of
Bantam Doubleday Dell Publishing Group, Inc. Its trademark,
consisting of the words "Bantam Books" and the portrayal of a
rooster, is Registered in U.S. Patent and Trademark Office and
in other countries. Marca Registrada. Bantam Books, 666 Fifth
Avenue, New York, New York 10103.

PRINTED IN THE UNITED STATES OF AMERICA

RRH 0 9 8 7 6 5 4 3 2 1

For Deb

Acknowledgments

I would like to thank Lloyd and Gloria Hood, Melissa Hood, June Caycedo and Gina Gallucci, Bob Reiss, Gail Hochman, and Deb Futter for listening, reading, rereading, and always being there.

The point of no return

Jasper believes that eating turkey cures jet lag. So every time Lucy returns from a Whirlwind Weekend, she finds him in her Greenwich Village kitchen, basting or stuffing a fourteen pounder. Jasper can cure anything. Jet lag, sore feet, tension headaches. Lately, Lucy has begun to wonder if the smell of turkey roasting will make her cry someday soon, the way in high school, after she'd broken up with her boyfriend, she had to avoid hot fudge sundaes and later, when she'd had her heart broken in college, songs by the Eagles made her weep.

Whirlwind Weekends are four-day trips—two of those spent traveling—to European cities. They are for people who don't have a lot of money to spend. They stay in two-star hotels, eat prearranged meals, and Lucy talks them through every block, every step of the city. She advises them on souvenirs, she runs to their room to explain what a bidet is for, she orders for them if she has to. Most of the groups are from the midwest. Most have never been to Europe before.

This weekend she has been to London, the easiest Whirlwind trip. A short flight, standard sights, and everyone knows the language. The biggest problem on London weekends is crossing the street. Lucy always has to shout, "Look right!" before they cross. Other tour guides have had members of their groups hit by cars or double-decker buses, or scared by close calls with speeding ambulances and taxis. Whirlwind travelers are not used to foreign things. They're used to cars driving

1

on the right, shopping malls, weak coffee with Equal and skim milk. One scare can ruin their entire weekend.

When Lucy gets off the elevator she can smell the turkey. She can smell oranges too. Jasper has made his Grand Marnier–apricot stuffing. Her favorite. At that instant, she feels her heart lurch ever so slightly. She walks more quickly down the long hallway, her suitcase bumping along behind her, across the gray and black tweed carpeting that lines the halls.

For three years now, Lucy has gotten off this elevator, her eyes dry and red from jet air, and raced down this hallway to Jasper. For three years her heart has lurched like this at the thought of him in there, waiting with dinner and wine, flowers and remedies. Lucy is comforted by the feeling in her chest. Perhaps, she thinks, things are all right after all. She shifts the duty-free bag to her other hand, the bottles of Beefeater and Baileys clinking together, and searches her Whirlwind Weekends coat pocket for her keys.

But Jasper has heard her approaching and opens the door for her. He is smiling. He's wearing an apron she bought him as a gift once, a white butcher-style one with a Far Side cartoon of escaping turkeys on the front.

" 'ello, mate," Jasper says in a near-perfect Cockney accent. Jasper is good with accents. He takes her suitcase, her duty-free bag.

"Hi," Lucy says. She stands on tiptoe to kiss him.

"How was it?" he asks her.

He has set the table. Blue candles, yellow tulips, the turkey cooling on a platter surrounded by baby vegetables.

Lucy's dirty-blond hair, cut into layers, has started to fall free of the ponytail she wears for work so she removes the 1950s scarf decorated with suitcases and 707s and lets it fall free. Sometimes Jasper tells her that her hair is like lemon meringue pie, all peaks and dips down to her shoulders. He tells her that if she were blonder, she'd look like the perfect dizzy blonde, all loose hair and round blue eyes. That, she reminds him, is not a compliment.

Lucy kicks off her shoes, surveys the apartment. The good feeling has passed, replaced by that other, new one. The one that makes her want to close her eyes and cry. The one that feels like doom.

"No one hit by a bus?" Jasper asks her.

She shakes her head.

"The changing of the guard?" he says.

"Yes."

"*Cats?*"

Lucy sighs. "I've seen *Cats* twenty-two times," she says, slipping out of her coat. "Do you think that's a record?"

Jasper is unpacking the duty-free bag, lining up the goodies she's brought home on the kitchen counter like an army.

"I put in another request for a change of plays," she says. She eats one of the tiny carrots, a new potato.

"*Phantom of the Opera?*" Jasper says. Under his breath he adds, "More garbage."

Lucy doesn't answer him. She realizes he has put on classical music for her. She tries to identify the piece, but can't. She only knows it's something dark and gloomy.

"You're sighing," he tells her. "Do you know that you're sighing?"

She shrugs. "The music," she says.

Jasper looks at her, puzzled. "I thought—"

"No," she says quickly. "It's nice. Really."

He moves toward her, takes her in his arms. "What?" he whispers. "What hurts?"

Jasper is so tall that standing like this Lucy's head rests somewhere between his chest and stomach. If she listens hard enough, she can hear the steady thumping of his heart. But tonight she hears nothing beneath the layers of apron and sweater and shirt, beneath the sad music.

"I can fix it," he is saying.

Lucy's hand goes to her own chest, rests there lightly, sandwiched between them. She can feel her own heartbeat, aching against her ribs.

Jasper says, "I can. I can fix anything."

Lucy met Jasper on a flight from London to New York three years ago. Her tour group sat huddled together in the center section of the

Lockheed 1011, exhausted from their long weekend away from Ohio. A few of the men, dressed in new English riding caps from Harrods, were drunk on ale, talking loudly about England as if they'd just spent months there instead of a few hurried days.

On the flights back, Lucy always got a seat for herself far from the group. They only had questions about customs by then, and that could wait. She'd help them fill out their forms, remind them of their flight numbers, the amount of merchandise allowed in duty-free. But until then she could curl up alone and relax for the first time since she'd met them at JFK the Thursday evening before. Then they'd been a noisy group, excited and slightly confused by the hectic atmosphere and size of Kennedy Airport. They'd told her horror stories about their trip so far, stories that more seasoned travelers would not have to tell. "Hank tried to tip the stewardess," they'd say, pointing at Hank. "They made me check my suitcase!" they'd tell her. Or, "We thought we'd miss our plane because we had to circle so long here."

But on the way back, their cameras put away, their carry-on luggage filled with discounted Wedgwood and Waterford items, they slept. Lucy's seat was in the very last row. All she could see of her group were the tops of their heads. And the seat beside her was empty. She lifted her armrest, fluffed two of the small red airplane pillows, and closed her eyes.

"Sorry," a man's voice said.

She opened her eyes, looked up and up into a face that made her shiver. A chiseled and perfect face, topped with reddish brown hair. The face smiled a smile of white even teeth. Those teeth should be in a television commercial, she thought as she frowned at the man.

"You can sit in any empty seat," she told him. She sat up and looked around.

"Sorry," he said again. "This is the only one left."

Lucy stood up, searching for another seat for this man, so she could stretch out, so she could be alone for a few hours. Two women from her group saw her and waved. Their carefully sprayed and teased hair was flat now, after four days away in the London mist and drizzle. Lucy waved back and sat down quickly, before more of them spotted her.

"Friends of yours?" the man asked her.

"Sort of," she said. She rearranged her things and he settled in beside her. Keep those teeth to yourself, she thought. She would bury her head in a book. She would pretend he wasn't even there.

But he beat her to it. He'd already started on the crossword puzzle in the *International Herald Tribune*. It was the same one she'd done in the *Times* the day she'd left New York. She glanced at it, and saw that he was putting in a lot of wrong answers. In ink.

She tried to ignore his mistakes, but they were driving her crazy. He'd put MAMA instead of NANA for "Zola novel." EXAM instead of QUIZ for "surprise test." And now he put FILMORE for the clue "sixteenth U.S. president."

"He was the thirteenth president," Lucy said. She tapped on his newspaper. "And Fillmore has two l's."

"I'm awful at these," he said.

"Lincoln," she told him, and pretended to start to read her book again.

From the corner of her eye she saw he was flashing that smile. "Jasper Shaw," he said.

"No," Lucy said. She tapped on his newspaper again. "Lincoln is the answer. The sixteenth president was Abraham Lincoln."

"Oh," he said. "Right."

"And Zola wrote *Nana*." She looked away again.

"I don't want to give you the wrong idea," he began.

"You haven't."

"I've been traveling for days. From Tokyo. Maybe when I eat some turkey my mind will clear."

"Probably," Lucy said. It was difficult to ignore him. And not just because he was so perfect-looking, like a sculpture. But he was also so sincere. She almost expected him to say things like golly or gosh.

"Plus," he said, "it's hard for me to get comfortable on planes." He pointed toward his legs, all bent like pretzels to fit between the seats.

Lucy sighed. She looked right at him.

"You're really pretty," he said, and blushed slightly.

"Lucy," she told him.

"Good," he said.

She and Jasper shared the scones she'd bought that morning. He told her he was a dancer who had trouble getting jobs because he was so tall.

"What about Tommy Tune?" she asked him. "He's tall."

Jasper shook his head. "He's an exception."

"Well," she said, "are you any good?"

He nodded.

"Then something will work out," she told him.

His face brightened. "I was just in the Japanese tour of A *Chorus Line*. I played the guy who imitates his sister at ballet class. You know the one?"

"Yes."

"That was me," Jasper said. "It was so great to be working. For a while I was in the Nebraska State Ballet. But I want to really make it. So I turned thirty last month and I decided it was time. I packed up, moved to New York, and got the Japan thing. It was only for a month but I got it right away and I think that's a good sign."

"Definitely," Lucy said. "Some people wait years for something like that."

"My father hates that I'm a dancer. He thinks I should have been a basketball player instead."

They fell silent then, the sort of warm, awkward silence that comes during a first date that's going well. Lucy searched for something to say. She could talk to him about ballet. About her efforts to get freelance illustration work. About Whirlwind Weekends.

Before she could decide, the plane shook and there was a loud bang. Someone from her group screamed and the seat belt sign flashed on.

Jasper took her hand and held on, hard. She found herself thinking that it would be all right to fall from the sky with this man. To drop into the ocean with him. She felt calm, certain.

6

"I think we blew an engine," he told her softly.

"That's fine," she said.

He started to let go of her hand, but she wouldn't let him.

"That's fine," she said again.

The pilot's voice filled the plane, strong and sure. "Well, folks," he said, "it looks like we lost our number three engine."

Jasper leaned over and kissed her, quickly, on the lips. "Are you always such a wise guy?" he asked her. "I mean, do you know all the presidents, in order? All the state capitals? Things like that?"

"I'm afraid so," Lucy said.

The pilot said, "We can fly just fine without it. It just slows us down a bit. So it'll take us a little longer to get to New York."

"Good," Jasper whispered. "I still need to know who you went to your prom with. Your favorite color. Your middle name. All those important things."

"Now if we were closer to London, we might turn back and get this fixed up," the pilot said, his accent flat and midwestern.

Lucy whispered, "No one. Blue. Margaret."

"No one? I can't believe that."

"You see," the pilot said, "there's a halfway mark between the U.S. and Europe where it's equidistant from both places. So it makes no sense to turn around. And that's right where we are now. The point of no return."

Lucy has changed out of her navy blue polyester-blend Whirlwind Weekends uniform and put on Jasper's robe. He hates it. His parents sent it to him for his birthday. It's a plush black one, with his initials on the front in a curly, darker black scroll. The robe smells like Lucy's perfume.

They are sitting on the couch, drinking glasses of the Baileys she's brought from London. Slowly, Jasper takes each of her toes, one by one, in his hands, and tugs on them until they crack. This, he says, is a cure for sore feet and headaches. Lucy has both.

"Tell me about your trip," he says, pulling on her toes.

She shrugs. What is there to tell him? she thinks. Every Whirl-wind Weekend is exactly the same. In London they go for tea, they shop at Harrods, they see *Cats*. They take a sightseeing tour of the city on a double-decker bus and eat at a British pub. There is an optional tour of the Tower of London. They eat at a place called Medieval Manor, an old castle where jesters and musicians perform for them and customers have to eat with their hands. On the final night there is a sunset boat ride on the Thames, with dinner and dancing.

"What about your weekend?" Lucy asks him.

Jasper is a bartender at a place in SoHo called the Blue Painted Door. The restaurant has no real name, but the front door is painted a day-glo blue, so people call it the Blue Painted Door. Lately, it's on every magazine's HotSpot list, and is crowded with models and movie stars. Before he worked there, Jasper worked at a different hot restaurant called Betty's Bayou. When Betty's Bayou stopped being hot, Jasper started to make fifty dollars a week. Now he makes that in a good hour.

"The place," he is saying through gritted teeth, "is a madhouse. The customers are assholes. And the food stinks."

"I thought the food was good," Lucy says. She pulls her feet away from him, and curls her legs up under her.

"Angel hair pasta with sun-dried tomato pesto and blackened shrimp," he says. "Does that even make sense? I thought pesto meant made with basil. So how can it be made with sun-dried tomatoes?"

Lucy sighs. "I don't know," she says. She waits before she asks the next question. She has to prepare herself first for his reaction. She takes a breath. "Any auditions or anything while I was gone?" she says, pretending to study the new *New Yorker*'s cover.

"Give me a break," he tells her. "I work until five in the morning, making cappuccino for their seven-dollar desserts. When am I sup-posed to go to an audition? When am I supposed to even dance? A dancer has to practice every day."

Lucy tosses the magazine onto the coffee table. "So make time," she says. This litany has become as routine, as dull to her as the Whirlwind Weekend schedules.

"You know I take class on Mondays and Tuesdays."

"But that's not every day," she says. She gets up and walks over to her drafting table. Illustrating is her passion. Her newest project is the drawings for a book called *My Dolly*. First she must design the doll itself. It can't look like Raggedy Ann. It can't look like a Cabbage Patch doll. "It has to be something new. Fresh," the editor, Ashley Hayes, told her. She had whispered to Lucy over the phone. "If you do it right, it could be big. We're trying to sell rights for real My Dollys." "Well," Lucy had said, trying not to sound terrified, "nothing like a little pressure."

Now, she stares at the blank round face she drew before she left. If she keeps My Dolly bald, it is too Cabbage Patch. But somehow hair is too Raggedy Ann. She has a deadline. Behind her, Jasper is talking about his scheduling problems. He is telling her how his friend Randy got a job in the road show of *42nd Street*. Jasper rattles off Randy's destinations.

"Minneapolis," he says, "Chicago, Saint Louis."

Lucy picks up her charcoal pencil and sketches a face on the circle. She makes it a perfect face, despite the roundness. She adds cheekbones, a Roman nose, a smiling mouth with perfect teeth. She gives it ears and reddish brown hair. My Dolly has become Jasper.

He is saying, "Randy gets all the breaks."

Lucy adds a body. She is drawing quickly now. She stands My Dolly on pointe, adds a tutu, raises its arms.

Jasper says, "Six months guaranteed. Two of those in San Diego."

Lucy draws single roses at My Dolly's feet. A spotlight, the silhouette of clapping hands. She makes My Dolly a star.

Backstage

Julia stands in a line that stretches for half a block along the West Side Highway. She and fifty other women, all dressed in black leather with moussed hair and heavy makeup, are waiting to get into the pale turquoise building. There is a fluorescent mural of an old car lot painted on one side of it, the side that faces the Hudson and New Jersey. It is predawn, the sky an eerie blue-gray. The cars that pass still have their headlights turned on.

A perfect setting for a B horror movie, Julia thinks. Then she grimaces. She and these other women are in fact waiting to audition for just that, a new slasher film called *Punk Rock Nightmare*. One of them will be chosen as the heroine, the lucky punker who escapes death.

Julia moves her feet, kicking at the pavement to get warm. She surveys the competition, which is growing by the minute. The line snakes around the corner now. Everyone clutches the copy of *Back Stage* that has the ad for the audition in it. Everyone has manila envelopes with their photo and résumé tucked inside. Everyone is nervous, but trying to act cool. Some smoke cigarettes or drink coffee from take-out paper cups stamped with I Love New York. Some read *The Village Voice*.

Finally, a door opens and a man comes out, holding a notebook and looking bored. He walks down the line of women dressed like punk rockers and assigns them each a number in a slow, lazy voice.

"Time to get dehumanized again," the woman in front of Julia says, loud enough for the man to hear.

Close up, the woman looks older than most of the others. Julia tries to imagine how many times this person has risen in the dark to wait in one of these lines. How many costumes she has worn—housewife, ingenue, vampire? For Julia, this is a game. A way to be someone else for a little while and maybe even get paid for it. Like *Queen for a Day*, she has told her best friend, Lucy. Like *Sybil* or *Three Faces of Eve*. Like Halloween. Like *The Gong Show*.

Lucy doesn't really understand. But she pretends to. She is too focused, too self-aware to waste her time shopping in secondhand stores for funny costumes. She has a job and a talent and a boyfriend and a family in Massachusetts. It is difficult for her to understand, really, why Julia does this. Sometimes Lucy tells her she should put her energy into something real. "Your heart's desire," Lucy says.

But pretending *is* Julia's heart's desire. What she loves most is just this, painting her face, speaking in a fake accent, and dressing in someone else's clothes. Today it's a black leather miniskirt, thigh-high boots, a spiked dog collar around her neck and a rub-on tattoo of a rose on her arm. Who knows what it will be tomorrow? The one thing Julia is sure of, it is better not to know. It is better to pretend.

Julia is number thirty-seven.

The man with the notebook lets them in ten at a time. He yawns when he calls the first group. He glances briefly out across the highway, toward New Jersey, then goes back inside the building.

"Maybe it's good luck," the woman in front of Julia says, turning to her again. "I'm number thirty-six and I'm thirty-six years old."

Julia nods. "Maybe." She takes a mirror from her bag and reapplies her thick white lipstick. Her hair is cut really short, like a boy's, and dyed platinum blond. This morning, she spent almost an hour spiking it, tugging the short pieces, covering them in styling gel, then spraying them with heavy-duty hairspray. She looks ridiculous, all porcupine hair and eyes lined in dark black. Her own reflection makes Julia smile. She decides she will audition with a New Jersey accent.

To practice, she says to number thirty-six, "Gawd, I'm tired."

The woman frowns and turns around. A tag pokes out from the collar of her black leather jacket. Julia reads it, deciphering all the codes—class and style and manufacturer. This is a skill she acquired during a Christmas job at Bloomingdale's. During that job she told everyone she lived in Queens and was engaged to a man named Mike, who worked at a muffler place. Every night she put on long fake nails, sometimes with appliques of holly or Santa faces on the pinkie.

At Bloomingdale's, she worked as a floater, drifting from department to department, covering lunch breaks or working the big sales. She is still a whiz at reading store labels and she breaks the codes on this one easily. Julia realizes that this woman has not scoured used clothing stores for her outfit. She has bought it new, for this audition. The seriousness of that makes Julia suddenly feel sad.

She taps her on the back.

"What?" the woman says.

"Weren't you in a commercial?" Julia asks her. "For soap or something?"

The woman has sprayed a tuft of her hair orange. She is wearing an ear cuff. "I did a cereal ad a few years ago," she says.

Julia smiles. "That's what it was," she says. "Cereal."

The door opens. The man reemerges. His voice is bored. "Numbers twenty-one through thirty."

It is morning now. Rush hour traffic clogs the highway, the sky is a hazy, polluted blue.

Under the thick makeup, the woman's face softens. "You look familiar too," she says.

"I've worked here and there," Julia tells her. "You know."

"Do I ever," she says, and turns back.

Julia reads to herself: Class 06, Style 4428, Manufacturer 33.

• •

Somewhere in her heart, Julia thinks she can be a screenwriter. She dreams in movie images, tells stories like she's describing a film. "Fade in," she'll say. Or, "Close-up on high heels clicking up the stairs." That's how she thinks. But she isn't sure she will ever really do it. It is too close to her mother's work. Her mother writes young adult books, starring a Nancy Drew–like character named Vicky Valentine. Vicky Valentine is pretty, smart, and brave. She has haunted Julia forever. She is the teenager Julia never was. She is the daughter her mother always wanted. She is every teenage girl's friend. But she is Julia's archenemy.

Julia's mother lives in Brooklyn, in the same dark apartment Julia grew up in. She is everything Julia does not want to become. A woman scorned, someone slightly off-center, meek and eccentric. Her mother's best pal is a bright green parrot named Bluebeard whom Julia hates. Bluebeard and Vicky Valentine fill her mother's life. They both appeared when Julia's father left her mother for a former Miss Texas and moved away to Houston.

The last time Julia visited her mother was last Christmas. She brought her a small tree that she'd bought on a street corner. It was tabletop size, decorated with little red and white balls and ribbons. When she walked into the apartment, she saw that her mother had bought one just like it, except the ornaments were gold. She sat them side by side, like twins. The sight of those trees unsettled Julia so much, she had to sit finally with her back to them.

As usual, her mother gave her cash for Christmas. It was tucked into a card made especially for money gifts, with an oval cut from the center so Benjamin Franklin's face peered out. Julia always gave her mother a gift certificate from whichever store she had worked at that season—Tiffany or Saks or Lord & Taylor. And her mother always said, "Don't spend your money on me." The truth was that most of Julia's money was her mother's anyway, some Vicky Valentine royalties that went straight to Julia's Chemical Bank account.

Her mother put the gift certificate away with all the others, in the kitchen drawer where she kept a hammer and screwdriver and other things she would never use. Julia had seen them there, all gold and silver, embossed with season's greetings, held together with a rubber band and going back all the years since Julia had moved out.

"So tell me something," her mother always said.

It was the parrot who responded. "Snow today," he said. "Gradual clearing by morning."

Her mother laughed, but Julia couldn't even manage a smile. From somewhere outside she could hear "Jingle Bell Rock" playing.

"Any new jewelry designs?" her mother asked.

Designing jewelry was Julia's hobby, something she did to pass the time. She had learned how to do it back in camp as a teenager, and it helped her relax. Her mother always pushed her toward doing it more seriously. You could be like Paloma Picasso maybe, she liked to say.

Julia told her that she'd sold some red and green Christmas ornaments as earrings on a street corner on lower Broadway.

Her mother shook her head. "You could be another—"

"I know," Julia said.

Then they sat in a thick silence as evening approached. Julia watched the large hand on the clock move. It was the kind that dropped in big increments so that it seemed that it was stuck forever at one time, then suddenly, without warning, changed.

Finally Julia said, "I have this fascination with foreign men. They make me feel exotic or something. I keep thinking they know more than I do. That they can take me somewhere new. Somewhere far away."

Her mother cleared her throat. "That's not good, Julia," she said. "You can't trust any man, foreign or otherwise."

"It's not about trust," Julia said, knowing she could never tell her mother how far beyond fascination she had gone.

Behind her, Bluebeard said, "Small craft warnings are in effect for the rest of the day."

· ·

Sometimes, Julia wakes up afraid that she is just like her mother, that she lives with a bird and writes for a living. Then she is unable to fall back asleep. Instead, she stays up all night, planning new things to do to prove she is different. She looks in the closets for her audition costumes. She puts on a floppy black hat with a large white ostrich feather trailing down the back and slips on the highest-heeled shoes she can find. She puffs on a cigarette through a black enamel cigarette holder and imitates Bette Davis or Joan Crawford.

Prancing off-balance through the apartment she is subletting, Julia will say out loud, "Long shot of girl alone in her apartment. She is trying to become something, someone, else. Now close-up on her face. She is struggling with something. She is doing everything she can to overcome her obstacles. Hold on her eyes. On their determination. The audience knows she will eventually be triumphant."

Julia walks onto the dark stage and peers out at the three men sitting on folding chairs below it.

"Okay," one of the men says. "You're?"

She changes her mind and talks like a Cockney. "Julia Greer."

"Okay," he says again. All of the men look like accountants, but Julia assumes one must be the director of the movie, one the writer. "Basic plot," he says, adjusting his glasses. "A crazed murderer with a knife—"

"More like a machete," another man interrupts.

Julia nods. "A machete," she repeats. She imagines fields of sugarcane like she saw once in Puerto Rico when she was young and on a family vacation. Men slashed through the field with large machetes and offered the tourists fresh sugarcane to suck on.

"Whatever," the first man says. "Okay, he's like, slashing up all your friends. Your boyfriend, your roommates, etcetera. He's chasing you through some dark downtown nightclub. So. Can you give us a scream? A bloodcurdling scream?"

Julia licks her lips, clears her throat. The sugarcane image is too gentle. It ruins her concentration. She blocks it out, tries to think of

something scary. Images bubble in her head and bounce around—
that parrot, and heartbreak, and losing control. She opens her mouth
and screams at the top of her lungs.

"Okay," the man says. "Drop off your photo and résumé when
you go."

She hesitates. "That's it?"

"Right," the man says.

She steps down carefully and places her photo and résumé on a
folding table that is littered with other ones. Black-and-white posed
faces smile up at her, looking cute or seductive or perky. Her own
face floats down, settling on top. Her résumé is full of lies. She sits
down periodically and invents new lives for herself, different pasts and
experiences. This one says she studied at ACT in San Francisco, that
she understudied in *Starlight Express,* that she did summer stock upstate and made industrial films for the Navy.

Behind her, another woman in leather screams, a loud horrifying
scream.

Julia is sure this is the best scream of them all. It's a perfect
scream. She is sure she will never get the part now. So she turns and
walks as fast as she can up the aisle and out the door onto the street.

Something blue

Katherine is on the Amtrak Minuteman, heading south, from Old Lyme, Connecticut to Penn Station in New York City. It's 7:05. It's her wedding day. She has left her wedding dress, still in its protective plastic covering, hanging on her bedroom door. She has left her china and crystal and silver on her mother's dining room table, a setting of each placed there as if for company. Mostly, she has left Andy, her fiancé, asleep at his parents' house, unaware that any moment now he will get a phone call from someone telling him she is gone.

It is the first time in months, since last Christmas when Andy gave her the white gold one-carat diamond ring, that Katherine can actually breathe. She feels almost giddy. She feels like dancing. Like opening the window of the train and shouting to all the people in Connecticut and New York City that she is free. This leaving, this waking at dawn today, looking around her at all the wedding para-phernalia—seating cards, monogrammed thank-you notes, still un-opened presents, the blue garter, the old penny for her shoe, all of it—seeing it all as small and silly and wrong and actually doing some-thing about it is the bravest thing Katherine has ever done.

She is humming as she sits on the train, sipping coffee and eating a microwave-heated corn muffin. Colors seem brighter. The seats are a bright, almost blinding red. The water that is speeding past her window is a vivid blue. Her own fingernails, painted a shade of nail polish called Barely Pink, to match the hint of pink in her wedding dress, seem very pink. They seem the pink of seashells, of coral, of sunsets.

Katherine thinks about her sister, Shannon, waking up about now and finding her gone. She almost laughs out loud thinking of it. Her sister is beautiful, someone who wakes up looking good. Mascara smudges, flattened hair, blotchy skin, are all foreign to Shannon. She wakes clear-eyed and fresh.

This morning she will wake excited about the wedding. She will walk down the hall to Katherine's room to wake her. Maybe she will even bring her breakfast in bed. That's Shannon's way. "It's your day," she would say, carrying toast and coffee in on a tray. She would place a pink rose in a bud vase to keep with the day's color scheme. She would have advice for how to get through this. "Eat light. Drink decaf. Do some stretches," Shannon would say. She would say, "Leave the details to me."

Suddenly, Katherine finds herself laughing out loud. An elderly woman with a sour face glowers at her from across the aisle. The woman shakes her head. She makes a kind of tsk-tsk sound.

Katherine leans toward her. It takes all of her self-control not to tell her, "I'm running away." Katherine wants to say, "I was laughing because my sister is probably finding out I've left, right about now." Thinking this, she laughs again.

The woman's frown deepens, but she doesn't look up. So Katherine settles back in her seat, still smiling to herself.

She thinks about all the details Shannon will have to deal with now. The doorbell will begin to ring, and bridesmaids will start to appear, carrying their pink lace dresses and dyed-to-match shoes. Florists will arrive with bouquets, corsages, and boutonnieres. And all Shannon will have is the note Katherine scribbled as she left: IF I STAY HERE AND DO THIS I THINK I WILL DIE. KATHY.

No one has called her Kathy since she was a child, and now that she's signed her note that way, it seems funny that she chose it. She thinks that perhaps she should have added a PS, telling Shannon not to read what she's written to Andy. To make up some other reason. But it's too late for that now.

Katherine tries to conjure up Andy's face, sleeping, thinking that he is getting married today. But her mind comes up blank. It's as if she doesn't remember what he looks like, asleep or otherwise. As if all the years they've been together are nothing at all.

The train begins to slow. The conductor announces the station: New Haven. Katherine imagines getting off here, going to Yale, becoming an actress or playwright. Or working as a waitress, one of those women who work in small diners, who look like they have a story to tell. She startles herself. She does have a story to tell. She imagines herself, hair piled high and sprayed into a stiff beehive. A name tag that says Kaye. A cigarette in her mouth. She leans across the table of truck drivers, careful to brush her breasts against the sexiest one. She refills their coffee cups, and tells them about the day she was supposed to get married and instead boarded a train out of town.

The woman from across the aisle is gathering her things, getting off here at New Haven. The train goes dark for a few minutes, then all the lights blaze on again and the train lurches forward, toward New York City.

A week earlier, Katherine sat with her mother and sister making up the seating plan. Almost two hundred people were coming to the wedding and their names were on color-coded tags that stuck into round disks. Each disk represented one table. There were ten tags to a disk. Shannon had a master floor plan that looked like an architect's blueprints, filled with circles and squares and rectangles, all representing bars, dance floor, bandstand, head table, guests' tables.

Shannon was organized. It was her idea to color-code the tags for easier seating. Blue for his family, pink for theirs, and white for friends of Katherine and Andy. Sitting there, Katherine fought the impulse to scoop up all the tags and blueprints and disks and throw them into the air like confetti.

"We can't sit Aunt Rita with anybody," her mother said, staring through her half-glasses at the blue tags.

Shannon shook her head. "Mom, that's *his* side. We're pink."

"I know," their mother said. "Everybody on our side hates her. I'm going to have to put her with his side."

"They'll hate her too," Shannon said. "Won't they, Kat?"

Katherine said, "I don't want to marry Andy."

Shannon and her mother looked at her. Then they looked at each other.

"Premarital jitters," her mother said.

"You don't understand," Katherine said, surprised by how calm her voice sounded. "I don't care who Aunt Rita sits with. I don't care about all those people coming from Pennsylvania who I hardly know—"

"Those are your father's cousins," her mother said. "You know them."

"I haven't seen them since I was seven," Katherine said.

Her mother and Shannon looked very much alike. Katherine could see them on the golf course in matching outfits, at the country club dinner dances on Saturday nights looking almost like sisters. She was the one who had inherited her father's looks. His slightly too-thick legs, his stick-straight pale blond hair and long thin nose.

Recently, Katherine has grown her hair long, and has it professionally highlighted every ten weeks. She grows impatient, though, with blow-drying it for volume, applying sculpting foam for height, and instead pulls it back into a low ponytail tied with a ribbon, the way she did when she was a teenager, back in private school wearing plaid uniforms in kelly green and blue with matching knee socks and penny loafers. She keeps neat spools of ribbons in her bureau drawer, arranged by color and design.

Still, on a good day, when she worked very hard on herself, and in a certain favorable light, she looked a little like Meryl Streep. But Shannon and her mother, both tall and slender, with healthy auburn hair and classic features, wake looking perfect.

Her mother sighed and looked at her watch. "I have a tennis game in two hours, Missy. Do you think we can get this done?"

Shannon patted Katherine's hand. "Yes," she said, "we can. Right, Kat?"

Katherine bit down on her bottom lip. Her chest was getting tight somewhere deep inside. She tried to imagine Andy's face if she called off this wedding. She tried to imagine calling all the guests, returning all the gifts. She gulped for air, tried to breathe.

"I—"

Her mother smiled, her tanned face full of sympathy.

"I don't want to—"

Shannon shoved a glass of brandy into her hand. "Sip on this," she said. She looked over at their mother. "Will this happen to me when Rich and I get married?"

Katherine closed her eyes. She concentrated on breathing the way she had learned in a college yoga class she and her roommate Lucy had taken. There were yogis, they had been told, who were so disciplined they could breathe out of one nostril at a time, alternating back and forth, left then right, left then right.

Slowly, she inhaled. Exhaled. Inhaled. Exhaled. Then she opened her eyes again. Shannon and her mother were watching her closely. She smiled, picked up the pink tag that had Aunt Rita's name written in Shannon's perfect penmanship.

"We'll put her next to Andy's Aunt Irene. No one likes her either," Katherine said.

Andy was starting his residency in dermatology at Mass General in the fall. They had all summer to find an apartment in Boston, to choose furniture. Everything was so planned, so right. Katherine had a teaching job all lined up. She had a hope chest full of linens—all-cotton sheets, monogrammed towels, quilts and throw blankets and down pillows.

Every day, she told herself she was lucky. She woke up, feeling depressed, and made herself say it out loud. "I am the luckiest person I know," she said. It sounded as fake and hollow as she felt. The closer the wedding got, the more Katherine stayed in bed. Even though it was early June, sunny and warm, she piled blankets on top of blankets and crawled underneath them, with pillows over her head and all the windows shut.

When her mother found her that way, she opened the windows and stood over her. "You are acting like a spoiled brat, Missy," she said. "And you keep saying you can't breathe. Well, it's no wonder. It's so stuffy in here. And you've taken all the blankets out of the cedar closet. Now get up and put them all back."

But after her mother left the room, Katherine closed the windows again. Then she went over to her hope chest. It looked just like a coffin, she thought. Touching it gave her the creeps. She pulled out the five-point Hudson Bay blanket that someone had given them as an engagement gift, and wrapped herself in that before she got under all the other blankets. She stayed that way until Andy came for her.

Katherine wondered how she had gone out with him so long and never noticed before how pale his skin was. All white and pasty, like the skin of a chicken. It made her feel nauseated. In college, on the heels of Bruce Jenner winning the gold medal in the decathlon in the Olympics, everyone used to say that Andy resembled him. Lately though, with Andy's straight, even bangs and deep-set eyes, Katherine thought he looked more like Pete Rose. Or Barney Rubble. She found herself wondering more and more how she had ever found him handsome at all.

"Five days," Andy said. He was naked, on his back, his arms behind his head, staring up at the ceiling.

Katherine hoped it was dark enough that he wouldn't be able to see what she'd done up there. One night, when she couldn't sleep, she'd stood on the bed and written on the ceiling in black Magic Marker the words to all the old songs she could remember. "Operator" by Jim Croce. "Sentimental Lady" by Fleetwood Mac. All the songs from *Saturday Night Fever* and *Camelot*. There were dozens of them up there.

"Then two weeks in France," he was saying.

Katherine pulled the blankets around her more tightly. He had an annoying habit of repeating things, too. Every night that her mother went out, Andy came over and they made love, always the same way. Then he'd start this. The countdown. The two weeks in France. Next he'd map off all the areas of Boston and the rents in each. Then he'd ask her to stop wearing her diaphragm.

"Back Bay," Andy said, "is a little high but worth it. Although some of the streets—"

"Are run-down," Katherine said.

"I know we've gone over this," he told her. "I'm excited. That's all." He reached over and took her hand in his, led it down, across his stomach, to his penis. "In more ways than one," he said.

She felt like a robot. She grasped it in her hands and tugged gently, the way he liked. It took ten tugs before he'd start to moan. Twelve before he put his finger in her and kissed her breasts, very symmetrically, first one, then the other. The same number of times each. Then he'd climb on top of her and begin. She even counted how many thrusts it took before it was over.

On schedule, Andy rolled on top of her.

He pressed his lips to her ear. "Take it out," he whispered. "Don't wear it."

Katherine shivered beneath him. She shook her head.

"Don't you love me?" he whispered.

She laughed, louder than she meant to. "I just don't want to be pregnant on my wedding day," she told him.

"Is that it?" he said, smiling now. "You're just an old-fashioned girl? Is that it?"

He entered her. She tried not to count his thrusts. She stared upward, at the ceiling. In her own cramped writing she read, "Stayin' alive, stayin' alive, uh, uh, uh, uh, stayin' alive."

The train arrives at Penn Station right on schedule. 11:07. Katherine climbs the stairs, following the signs toward Seventh Avenue. She has a suitcase filled with useless items. All of her teaching aids, a framed photograph of her childhood cat Sparkle, an Ultima II makeup kit that is as big as a large box of Crayola crayons and that she has never used, some clothes and underwear, the paperbacks she had bought to read on her honeymoon in France, and an odd assortment of things like a Swiss Army knife, a pen flashlight, and a mini first aid kit. Survival things.

Katherine has a vague plan. She is going to call Lucy, even though she hasn't seen her in two years. Even though Lucy has tried very hard to ignore Katherine's overtures to continue their friendship. She is not sure why Lucy doesn't keep in touch with her, and right now, that doesn't even matter. She'll beg her to let her stay with her for a while if she has to. She'll pay her. She'll do anything Lucy wants.

Lucy returned the response card to Katherine's wedding invitation with a note that said she had to work today. But Katherine thinks Lucy was lying and that she just didn't want to come to the wedding. She's sure Lucy will be home.

Katherine passes a pay phone, takes a breath, and stops at it. She knows, however, that before she can talk to Lucy, she has to call Andy. She is surprisingly calm.

He answers right away.

"Hi," she says. Her voice is lighter and happier than it's been in a long time. She can't help it. "It's me."

Andy laughs, a little nervous laugh. "For a while there," he says, "I thought you were leaving me at the altar."

"I am," Katherine says softly.

There is a long silence during which Katherine watches them pull sheets of cookies out of the oven at a David's Cookies in front of her.

It's Andy that talks first. "What did I do?" he asks her.

"It's not you," she tells him. "It's me. I'm miserable and unhappy." And then, like a talking thesaurus, she continues. "Bleak, depressed—"

"All right," he says. "All right. But why?"

"Andy," she says. "I'm just despondent—"

"God damn it, Katherine. Stop. I feel awful enough. My Aunt

Irene is downstairs acting all indignant because she came all the way down from Portland. My father is on the phone with the tuxedo rental people trying to get a refund. My mother is in tears and I don't even know what to say to anybody."

Katherine studies the newsstand now. People are dropping change on the counter, grabbing newspapers and hurrying off. Everything is moving quickly, like an old Keystone Kops movie.

"And I love you," Andy is saying. "If you come back now we'll elope. I think that's what got to you. All this wedding stuff. Right?"

"No," Katherine says. "I'm just blue. That's all."

She hears him swallow. She is afraid he may start to cry, so she says, "I'm going now, Andy." And then she hangs up, fast. Her heart is racing. She dials the phone again and when she hears her sister's voice, she almost hangs up on her without saying anything.

Shannon sounds panic-stricken. She says, "Hello, hello, hello."

"Calm down," Katherine says. "It's me. I'm in New York and I'm fine."

"New York!" Shannon says, her voice near hysteria.

"I'm not coming back, either," Katherine adds.

"Do you know what is going on here?"

Katherine almost smiles. "Yes."

"I'll tell you what's going on here," Shannon says. "There are flowers everywhere. Bridesmaids all dressed and ready to go. Dozens of guests swarming around, drinking the champagne."

"I know," Katherine says.

She hears the doorbell ring, excited voices shouting.

"Oh, no," Shannon says. "The limo just arrived. What am I supposed to tell him?"

"The same thing you're telling everyone else," Katherine says.

"What am I supposed to tell Andy?"

"I already talked to Andy," Katherine says. She hears the doorbell again, more voices.

"Hold on a sec," Shannon tells her.

Katherine hangs up the telephone. She picks up her suitcase and buys six cookies from David's. Macadamia and white chocolate. Chocolate peanut butter. Oatmeal raisin. And three chocolate chocolate chunk. She cannot remember the last time anything tasted so good. Last night, the lobster at the rehearsal dinner tasted like cardboard.

She eats all six cookies, then goes to the newsstand and buys a handful of lottery tickets. She's never played the lottery before. The man behind the counter is from India. His voice is soft and musical as he explains how to play. He tells her the prize is eleven million dollars. She chooses her birthday, her wedding day, the train's arrival and departure time for her numbers.

As she walks away, the man calls to her, "You're a winner, miss. I can tell."

Katherine steps outside and takes her place in a taxi line. There is noise and the smell of exhaust. Around her people are shouting at each other, horns are blaring. The sky is clear and blue. There is a warm breeze. She realizes she is breathing as easy as a yogi. She realizes she is smiling.

Temps

𝕴

Lucy and Julia are watching *How to Marry a Millionaire* on Lucy's VCR when Katherine calls from Penn Station. They like to rent movies with a theme, to pretend they own a revival movie theater and plan the features. Tonight it's movies about women in New York City. By the time the telephone rings, they have already watched *Kitty Foyle* and *Hannah and Her Sisters*. They have already agreed that they really should choose the billings for a revival movie theater because they put together such great ones.

"Don't answer it!" Julia tells Lucy. "This is the part where she finds out he's just a fire ranger instead of a millionaire."

Lucy aims the remote control and freezes the movie, Betty Grable dressed like a snow bunny and smiling dreamily.

"I hate interruptions," Julia groans.

"It's probably Jasper," Lucy says. Then she picks up the phone and says hello. She keeps her eyes on Betty Grable.

"I knew you weren't working this weekend," Katherine says nervously.

Lucy frowns. She recognizes Katherine's voice immediately, but Lucy can't imagine her former best friend actually calling to check up on her on her wedding day. "Aren't you supposed to be dancing to 'What Are You Doing the Rest of Your Life' or something by now?" Lucy asks.

27

Katherine laughs and Lucy is sure there is a quiver in her voice.
"Probably I should be," Katherine is saying. "By now."

"I'm sorry I couldn't come but . . ."

Julia looks up from the *Vogue* magazine she is leafing through
and mouths "Who is it?"

But Lucy only shakes her head while Katherine says, "No, no.
It's all right. It would have been a wasted trip anyway."

Lucy hears her take a big breath.

"Want to hear something funny?" Katherine says, her voice seem-
ing suddenly small.

"Sure," Lucy says. She is sure that Katherine must be drunk.
Too much wedding champagne. She remembers that Katherine always
got maudlin and overly sentimental when she drank, even back in
college. She is probably at a pay phone in the country club, weeping
and calling all her old sorority sisters to tell them how much she loves
them, even though they didn't go to the wedding. Once she decides
this is what's happening, Lucy is ready for anything.

Julia comes and stands next to Lucy, trying to listen.

"Well," Katherine says, "for starters, I didn't get married today."

"Oops," Lucy says. "I thought it was today. The twelfth."

"It is," Katherine says. "I came here instead."

"Here?" Lucy repeats.

"Where's here?" Julia whispers too loudly.

Katherine says, "I don't have any more change. My time must
be almost up. I'm here in New York. I called off the wedding and I
came here instead."

Even though Lucy hasn't seen Katherine in a long time, she
knows her well. She knows she would never do this.

"Did Andy change his mind?" Lucy says. She thinks that Katherine will never survive being left by Andy. They have been together
forever. Once, junior year, he broke up with her briefly and she stayed
in bed for a week with the hives, large purple welts that covered her
face and chest. She imagines Katherine now, in New York, all purple-
faced and swollen and her heart almost breaks.

Julia is saying, "Who's Andy?"

And the operator is asking for more money.

Katherine says, "I'll tell you all about it when I get there."

"All right," Lucy says. "Stay calm." That is what Katherine always told her when they were roommates and Lucy had a disaster. Stay calm, Katherine would say, I'm here. Then, it was always Lucy falling apart and Katherine the one who stayed together. Lucy was the one with pregnancy scares, bad romances, or drinking too much and needing to be driven home.

They are disconnected before Lucy or Katherine can say anything else.

Lucy looks at Julia. "Shit," she says.

"Who's Andy?" Julia says again. "You never mentioned an Andy."

"Katherine's here," Lucy says.

"Connecticut Katherine?" Julia shrieks. "*The* Katherine?"

Lucy flops into the rocking chair. "I'm going to have to let her stay here," she says, groaning. "I can't not let her stay here."

"Isn't she married to a doctor or something?" Julia is saying. "Doesn't she teach first grade in somewhere awful? Like Westport? Isn't she really horrible?"

"Old Lyme," Lucy says. "And she's not horrible exactly. She's just different." Lucy is unsure why she is bothering to defend her. She does think Katherine is horrible. Sort of. They had long since grown apart. Sometimes, after college, when Lucy used to talk to Katherine, she felt like they were actually from two different countries. She would listen to Katherine and wonder how they had ever been best friends, what they could possibly have talked about all those nights side by side in their twin beds talking in the dark.

Julia is saying, "This is so great. Let's guess what she'll have on. I say a shirtdress. A pink shirtdress."

They play a version of this game sometimes with strangers. Let's guess what the next person who comes out of the elevator will be wearing. Let's guess what that guy will have on under his coat. But it feels mean doing it to Katherine.

"What am I going to do with her?" Lucy says instead.

"We could kill her and put her in the freezer. Then when the doctor-boyfriend comes looking for her we could kill him too," Julia

29

says. She opens some seltzer and drinks straight from the bottle. "We could shave her head and make her into a Hare Krishna."

Lucy takes the bottle from Julia and drinks. "She's going to be a real mess," she says. "Andy is everything to her."

Julia sighs. "I hate women who let their lives go to pot over a man."

Lucy drinks again.

"It can happen," Julia adds. "Trust me."

Julia and Lucy met at Birnbaum and Beane, an investment firm where they both spent a week working as temps. Julia used to love being a temp. She loved sitting at a stranger's desk and pretending that someone else's wedding picture was hers, that the two freckle-faced kids smiling beside it were her children, the black Lab with the Frisbee in its mouth was her dog. She loved all the goofy things people kept on their desks, things that made sense only to them. Like a windup dolphin bath toy or a small stuffed koala bear. She liked their person-alized coffee mugs—a chain of reindeer all having sex with each other, a name stamped over and over, a distant city's skyline imprinted on the front.

Lucy only lasted that one week as a temp, though. She walked around feeling disoriented and confused. She hated opening desk draw-ers and finding someone's aerobic sneakers inside. She hated not know-ing how to work the Xerox machine, not being able to find the bathroom or get an outside line on the telephone.

They hit it off immediately. "Being a temp," Julia told her, "is the greatest. You can get away with anything."

"Like?" Lucy said.

Julia showed her. They called old boyfriends on the WATS line, read fashion magazines instead of working, and took two-hour lunches at a nearby sushi restaurant. Sometimes, when Julia talked about that week, she called it the week they fell in love. She liked to remind Lucy how women's magazines were always writing about the perfect relationship. She would take the "Love IQ" tests and call Lucy with the results.

"We fit the description!" she'd say. "We're going to have to get married to each other."

"No," Lucy said. "We'd have to start having sex three times a week to be the perfect couple. And I don't want to have sex with you."

"Even without that we scored a 98 on this quiz," Julia told her. "Not even you and Jasper would score a 98."

Katherine has a way of being too friendly. Of assuming a familiarity that doesn't exist. In college, Lucy thought that was funny, how she'd go up to strangers and strike up conversations. But later it started to annoy her. And now here Katherine is, standing in the middle of Lucy's living room talking to Julia like she's known her forever.

"You look just like New York women do in the movies," Katherine is saying. "Really hip. That's great. I could never get away with hair like that."

Julia looks at Lucy for help.

"Are you all right?" Lucy asks Katherine. She doesn't see even the beginnings of hives. In fact, Katherine's skin is clear and glowing. With her hair more golden, long and pulled back with an ocean-blue ribbon, she looks like a "Before" model, a scrubbed face waiting to be made beautiful.

Katherine turns her smile on Lucy now. "Look at you," she says. "You let your hair grow so long and you've got a perm and everything. You look so sophisticated." To Julia she says, "She wouldn't even wear lipstick in college. She was always the rebel."

Katherine has been here for five minutes and already Lucy is irritated.

Julia offers the seltzer bottle to her. "Want a sip, Katherine?"

Katherine eyes it suspiciously. Then says, "Why not?" and takes a drink.

"So?" Lucy says.

Katherine sits down, looking very pleased with herself. "I know I should be feeling really awful," she says, "but I feel great. Andy—" She looks at Julia. "He's my fiancé," she says. The word seems to startle her.

She pauses and starts over. "I have been so miserable. For months now. And finally this morning I decided I couldn't go through with it. I just couldn't marry him. I mean, I couldn't go off to Boston with him and teach until I got pregnant and then spend the rest of my life having dinner parties and watching *Sesame Street*."

Lucy and Julia are sitting side by side on the couch, facing Katherine, listening.

Katherine laughs. "You two look like a jury over there," she says. She takes a breath again. "I just got on the train and came here," she says, sounding like she can hardly believe it herself.

Lucy leans forward, toward Katherine, shocked. She is sure that Katherine will go back first thing in the morning. That she will reschedule the wedding and get on with her life.

"I know what you're thinking," Katherine says, "but I'm not going back. I'm starting all over. I'm going to live in New York and go to plays and museums and have tea at The Plaza and whatever else people do here. I'm going to meet new men. Exciting men."

Julia laughs. "You're going to try to meet exciting men," she says.

But Katherine just keeps on talking. "We'll have a blast. That's all I want. I want to have fun. Everybody in the world is so mad at me right now," she says, "and I don't even care. I had to do it."

When Katherine goes to use the bathroom, Lucy tells Julia, "She's going to freak out when she realizes exactly what she's done. She's going to break out in hives and get on the first train back."

"I don't know," Julia whispers. "She seems pretty adamant."

Lucy squeezes Julia's arm. "What are we going to do with her?"

Katherine comes back into the room. She has put on pink lipstick, some mascara. "Okay," she says. "What should we do on my first day in the big city?"

Lucy says, "Katherine, I think maybe we should make a plan of some kind."

Katherine looks worried for the first time. "I'm going to find my own place," she says. "I just need something temporary. Until I get oriented. I have plenty of savings. I can even pay you."

"We were watching movies," Julia says. She motions toward Betty Grable's face on television.

Katherine wrinkles her nose. "Watching videos?" she says. "Come on. I can do that in Connecticut. This is New York City. Let's do something fun."

Julia stands up. "I've got an audition first thing tomorrow," she tells Lucy. "I'll leave you two to your fun."

"No," Lucy says, grabbing her arm. "You have to come with us. Please."

Katherine is standing alone. She is starting to look nervous. Lucy wants her to disappear. But she knows that she won't, that Katherine needs somebody right now. Maybe since she walked out on her own wedding, there is more to Katherine than Lucy gives her credit for. Maybe it won't be too bad if she stays here for a few days.

Katherine chews on her bottom lip. "Lucy and I used to have so much fun," she says. "I couldn't think of a better place to come right now."

Lucy reminds herself that they did have fun together once. She tries to focus on that, to secure some happy memory.

As they leave the apartment Julia whispers in her ear. "Temporary my ass," she says.

Whispers

෨

Lucy is on a 747 headed for Charles de Gaulle Airport in Paris. The plane is completely silent and bathed in the lights from an occasional reader's overhead and the dim red and white of the exit signs above the emergency doors. Everyone has been fed and shown a bad movie starring Judd Nelson as a lawyer. Now, with the airline's red pillows tucked under their heads, the scratchy striped blankets wrapped around them, most passengers have twisted themselves into an awkward position to sleep. To Lucy, the pillows look like oversize Chiclets, the blankets like cheap motel specials.

She can never sleep on airplanes. She is too busy running her group's itinerary through her mind, even though she knows it by heart. She is forcing their special needs into her memory—who is diabetic, who needs special assistance, who needs to place a phone call or send a package.

Beside Lucy is another Whirlwind guide named Robin. Lucy has only met Robin at the bimonthly Whirlwind meetings, held at a hotel out by Kennedy Airport. At those meetings the guides are given updated maps, names of restaurants that give group discounts, the latest money conversion charts. Whirlwind guides always work alone, so there is no need to be too friendly with each other.

In summer, two groups sometimes leave together. Like tonight, with Lucy and Robin. The groups have coded tags—LCDG for Lucy,

RCDG for Robin. CDG is the airport code for Charles de Gaulle. Airport codes are the first things Whirlwind guides have to learn. When Lucy first got her list to memorize, she was enchanted by the adventures those three letters seemed to hold. CAI, TEL, SHN, GVA, ZRH. The whole world seemed to be reduced to something manageable, something she could hold.

Beside her Robin stirs, tugs on the top of her ponytail.

"What time is it?" Robin asks, her voice hushed.

Lucy whispers back to her, "I try not to look at my watch. Makes the time go faster."

"I don't like these Paris trips," Robin tells her. "The people never wake up really. It's like a tour for *Night of the Living Dead*. The zombie special."

Lucy laughs softly. "The last time I did Paris," she says, "everyone fell asleep on the bus tour. I went running up the aisles yelling, 'Wake up! There's Notre Dame! There's the Eiffel Tower!'"

Robin sighs and pulls her blanket closer around her. She whispers, "What a mess."

"What?"

"Everything," Robin says. She presses a button on her seat and is immediately sitting upright. "Boyfriend stuff."

Lucy can hardly see Robin's face. What she sees is the high dark ponytail, a vague silhouette, the letters RCDG glowing in hot pink against her uniform. Lucy can hardly remember ever exchanging even a "Hello" with Robin before their groups converged on Gate 24 of the International Departures Terminal.

Still, in the dark 747, with the engines humming and the sounds of people sleeping around them, when Robin tells her she has boyfriend problems, Lucy turns toward her and says, "Me too." And then they talk to each other, telling a stranger things they have not told anyone else. The darkness, the low whispers of their voices, somehow make it easier.

After Robin has told her about her boyfriend Ted, about his cheating on her, his drinking too much, and Lucy has talked about her and Jasper, Robin goes back to sleep, her head resting on two red pillows pressed between her seat and the window. Far off in the distance, Lucy sees a thin line of pink. Morning is somewhere out there, she thinks. She imagines Parisians waking, making their coffee, dressing for work, while New York goes to sleep.

Lucy tries to imagine Katherine, sleeping in her apartment. She tries to will her away. What if Lucy returned from Paris and found Katherine gone, beamed back to Connecticut and Andy, a happy bride after all? She smiles at the thought. This morning on the telephone Julia had said, "Why do you let her stay? Why are you being so nice to her if you don't like her?" "I do like her," Lucy said. "She's just a pain in the ass."

Now, Lucy wonders why she really is being friendly to Katherine, long after their friendship has run its course. There used to be some things about Katherine that she liked. She presses her forehead, trying to revive those things, to call them to mind. She thinks of a spring break in Fort Lauderdale, of standing beside Katherine, their heads poking through the sun roof of someone's car, calling to boys on the sidewalk. She thinks of the way Katherine used to advise her—poorly but with great concern—about life.

How many conversations did she and Katherine have like the one she had tonight with Robin? Lucy wonders. Not on a jumbo jet, of course. But in the narrow beds of their college room, identical bright yellow ribbed bedspreads wrapped around them, the room dark except for a street light outside, the sounds of girls studying or coming in from late dates. The sounds of whispered voices in the halls.

They whispered too.

"I'm going to do something really exciting," Katherine used to tell her. "Maybe join the Peace Corps. Teach in Africa. Move to Europe."

"'Lucinda Luckinbill' will be the 'Peanuts' of the future," Lucy would say. "Lucinda Luckinbill" was the comic strip she wrote for the college paper, chronicling the woes of young women in the 1970s.

"Yes," Katherine always agreed. "You'll be famous. Definitely. You and Lucinda."

"You'll marry a sheikh. Or a duke," Lucy would say. "They'll name a small village in Somalia after you."

Katherine would sigh. "Lucy," she'd say softly, "I can't wait."

The next day, she would be the other Katherine again, dressed in her chinos and bright polo shirt, or on her way out to dinner with Andy, wearing lip gloss and Laura Ashley. But Lucy knew that underneath was a dreamer, a woman who would teach children how to read, who would, in some distant place, change the world a little bit.

Sometimes at night they imagined their futures, the way they would intertwine. Rushed meetings at JFK before Katherine left for overseas. Reunions at Lucy's New York City apartment, where they drank champagne and looked back on these late night talks. It was 1978, and they were trapped between the radical sixties and the apathetic eighties. They were either born a few years too early, or a few years too late. They weren't sure. It felt harder somehow for them to make their mark.

"But we will," Katherine used to whisper. "You'll see."

The captain announces their landing in Paris. Everyone is bleary-eyed, looking confused and disoriented.

"It's eight A.M. in Paris," the captain is saying. "Sixty-eight degrees and sunny."

Robin and Lucy do not speak. They gather their things—handbags and Whirlwind carry-on totes. When the "Fasten Seat Belt" sign dings off, they stand and search the plane for their groups.

"If your tag says RCDG, please wait for me before deplaning," Robin shouts.

Lucy studies her face in the light. She has wide lips, dark eyes with light smudges of mascara beneath them. She is very tall, very thin. She wears a diamond stud in one ear, a dangling earring in the other. She looks like a stranger. But Lucy remembers how sometime between night and now, Robin told her that she'd found used rubbers in her bathroom wastebasket when she got home from a Whirlwind Weekend in London last week. How Ted, her boyfriend, can drink a case of beer in one day. "He starts as soon as he wakes up, and drinks until there is no more." She told Lucy that after this trip, she wants

37

to not even return to their apartment at all. "I may get on a train and go home to Virginia," she'd whispered. "No more Whirlwind Weekends. No more Ted. No more Big Apple."

Lucy's group is lining up now, clutching their bags, the navy blue travel kits with WHIRLWIND WEEKENDS across the front.

"I'm so excited," she hears someone say.

Lucy takes a breath, makes herself smile. She wants a cup of coffee but it will be a long time before she gets her group through customs and baggage claim, through airport crowds and into their hotel van to the city.

Robin smiles quickly at Lucy. "Have fun," she says, without a trace of familiarity. It is what she would say to someone who did not know about Ted or what she finds when she gets back from her weekends away.

"You too," Lucy says, and turns to face her group.

Lucy stands at the entrance to the duty-free shop at the airport. The weekend is almost over. In an hour they will be on a plane back to New York. They have eaten in a real Parisian outdoor cafe, toured the city by bus, the Seine by boat at twilight. They have gone to the top of the Eiffel Tower, except for one overweight woman who was afraid of heights. Some took a side trip called "A Literary Look at Paris." Those people visited spots where Hemingway drank, Joyce wrote, and Gertrude Stein gave parties. The others shopped at a real French department store. They are all exhausted.

Lucy explains again about francs and dollars. She tells them what buys are good here.

"Grand Marnier, perfume, Chanel products," she says.

Some people take notes.

She steps aside and watches as they spill into the duty-free store, like winners on *Supermarket Sweepstakes*. She always feels sad at the end of a weekend. She feels she has cheated these people somehow, whizzing them through streets and historical monuments, shouting out facts and tidbits so fast they don't have time to register what she is saying. She always thinks they should get a refund. Or a coupon for a longer trip.

The woman who is afraid of heights taps Lucy's arm.

"You're just great," the woman tells her. She has on a T-shirt celebrating the Eiffel Tower's bicentennial. Fireworks splash across her chest. The tower climbs upward from her stomach.

"I'm glad you had fun," Lucy says.

"I did," the woman says, nodding. "I like home better. But this was good."

"Did you buy anything yet?" Lucy asks her.

"I'm on my way," the woman says. "Just wanted to tell you 'Merci boo-coop.'"

Lucy smiles. She watches the woman weave her way through the crowded shop.

Home is better, Lucy thinks, and again imagines Katherine in her apartment. She's probably cleaning, spraying lemon furniture polish on tabletops, Windexing mirrors and windows. Suddenly, that image makes Lucy feel terrible. She realizes that she does like Katherine. What she feels isn't about liking her or not. It's about disappointment. It's about all those plans they whispered to each other in the dark. Katherine is what she seemed in daylight after all.

Lucy wanders into the shop. She'll bring home champagne for her and Jasper to drink. A bottle of Grand Marnier for some late night when she is alone. Robin is beside her, dropping items into a red basket.

"How did it go?" Lucy asks her.

At first Robin frowns.

Then Lucy points to her name tag. The LCDG is a faded pink now.

Robin smiles. "Oh," she says, "Lucy. I didn't recognize you."

Before she leaves, Lucy stops at the Chanel counter. She buys a bottle of Chanel No. 19 for Katherine. She isn't sure if Katherine even wears it anymore. But suddenly she wants to bring her something. A souvenir. A reminder of another time.

Foreign bodies

Julia stands at the stove stirring risotto for her new lover, Daniel. Risotto is the only thing she knows how to cook, and she only cooks it when, like tonight, she has just made love with someone new. She always makes a different variation. An arroz con pollo with risotto. A paella. A risotto with Parmesan cheese, with marinara sauce, with clams. Tonight, she is making it with porcini mushrooms.

She tells her lovers that she lived in Italy. Or that she is actually Italian, a disowned heiress. Or that her first husband was from Milan. Milano, she calls it. Of course, none of this is true. She changes the story each time. She adds to it, she takes things away. Her lovers don't last long enough for them to know she is lying.

She chooses these men for their own foreignness. Like Ayo, the man from Somalia who sold her an umbrella one rainy day on Lexington Avenue, across the street from Bloomingdale's. And Yeorgi, the counterman at a diner on Sixth Avenue where she sometimes stopped for coffee. There was Mariano, her former downstairs neighbor from the Philippines, who boiled pig's feet for her dinner, and Andrej, the man from Poland who spoke no English at all, but who made love relentlessly.

She tells no one about these affairs. Not even Lucy. Instead, Julia pretends that she has a crush on Barry, a man in her acting class. It is unlikely that Julia would ever really like Barry. He is as American as someone can be. And as ordinary. He is a generic man—brown hair, brown eyes, a medium build. She has told him he should become a mugger, that no one would be able to identify him. That is how nondescript Barry is.

These other men are exotic. They speak with clicks and harsh c's. They slaughter w's. They are confused by VCRs, MTV, answering machines. Their penises are mostly uncircumcised, resting beneath layers of flesh like treasures. She asks them over and over about their countries, but they are usually reluctant to tell her. Instead, they think she will teach them about the United States. She doesn't want to.

Still, for a time, she takes them on what she calls her Dollar Tour of the city. They ride the Staten Island Ferry, drink egg creams, eat thick deli sandwiches of pastrami. They take the elevator to the Rainbow Room, just for a glimpse of the view, then stand and watch the ice skaters at Rockefeller Center. Julia does these things with the hope that the men will reciprocate. She wants them to show her where they are from, to call out to her in a language she cannot understand, to take her places she has never been.

Daniel emerges from the shower, naked. He is very dark, with curly hair everywhere—chest and legs and back. His eyes are so dark, they make Julia think of graves.

She met him five hours ago at a bar where she applied for a job. The bar sits way over by the West Side Highway, near the Hudson River. Almost everyone who works there is from Ireland. Daniel gave her free Guinness drafts, one after the other, until she got drunk. He had to finish filling out her application for her because she was so bleary-eyed. She rarely drinks, and cannot hold her liquor at all.

It's funny to Julia how she is never shy with these men. Their nakedness does not disturb her. Her own body does not embarrass her the way it did in high school gym classes, or even now in the open shared dressing rooms in some stores. It is not that it is such a bad body. But her breasts are too large, her hips too wide.

Yeorgi told her she had a body that was perfect for bearing children. Julia had laughed when he said that. She had shamelessly thrust her breasts toward him and said, "I'll have your children, Yeorgi. And we'll name them after gods and goddesses and live on a small island in the Aegean." "No," he said. "We will name them after all the people on *Dallas*. J.R. and Bobby. We will live in Queens."

That afternoon, her last one with Yeorgi, she had tied his arms to her bedposts until he agreed to name the children her body was meant to bear Philomena and Penelope. She does things with these secret lovers that she has never done with her two American lovers, whom she hid from under the covers in the dark.

Now, Julia studies Daniel's body as he approaches her. He is still damp from the shower. She can see tiny drops of water clinging to his black hairs. She is naked too, and she stands at the stove stirring the risotto with no shame. She is sticky from their afternoon together, but she doesn't even think about taking a shower.

"Rice?" Daniel says. He stares at her openly.

"Risotto," she corrects him. "With porcini mushrooms." She picks one of the woody mushrooms from the pan and presses it to his lips.

Daniel spits it out. "Tastes like dirt," he says.

Julia laughs at this. Sometimes she wishes that she shared these stories with Lucy. Then she would have someone to laugh with later, after the affair was over. She could say how they were both standing naked in the kitchen discussing mushrooms.

He opens the refrigerator and stares inside. He is certainly a starer, Julia thinks. Those brooding eyes study everything. Still, she is not embarrassed at what he sees when they turn back to her.

"Tell me about Ireland," she asks him.

"Ahhh," he says, cupping her buttocks in his hands. "There's nothing to tell."

"I grew up in Italy, you know," she says. "My mother was an opera singer."

He shrugs his hairy shoulders. "Ahhh," he says again. "You're a full one," he tells her.

"Full?"

He runs his hands up the length of her. "I like women full. Most women here are too skinny. Nothing to hold on to, you know?"

The risotto is done. It is creamy, perfect.

Julia smiles at him. Since she has first laid eyes on him, his five o'clock shadow has already grown in. "I thought the Irish were red-heads, fair-skinned," she says, rubbing her face against his rough one.

"I'm Black Irish," he tells her.

He pins her against the counter, takes the pan from her hand and puts it back on the stove. That's where it stays, hardening, until Daniel leaves the next morning.

Many mornings, Julia and Lucy watch television together, over the telephone. They stay on the phone through *Good Morning America* and *Live with Regis and Kathie Lee*. Sometimes, they will sit like that for hours, each in her own apartment, watching morning television with one ear pressed to the phone.

"I thought you'd vanished," Lucy tells Julia the morning Daniel leaves. "I tried calling you last night about a thousand times."

It's already past nine. Regis and Kathie Lee are telling the audience what they did the night before.

"Yeah," Julia says. "I was working on a monologue for class." She lies easily, but with Lucy she always feels a little bad.

"Which one?" Lucy asks her.

"'Uncommon Women,'" Julia says quickly. It's what Helen did in class the week before.

"Do you want to rehearse on me?" Lucy says.

Julia feels even more guilty then. "No," she says. "I'm not ready yet." She changes the subject quickly. "I can't believe we have to sit here and listen to Regis Philbin talk about his rectum."

"Listen," Lucy says, as if she senses something is wrong, "I'm going to get to work on this *My Dolly* thing. Call me later?"

"All right," Julia says. She knows she should ask about the illustrations, and about Jasper, but she doesn't. She examines the pillowcase beside her. There are almost a dozen small black hairs on it. "I've got to do laundry today," Julia says, forgetting she's still on the phone.

"Fine," Lucy says. "Then I'll talk to you tomorrow."

"I didn't mean that," Julia says. Sometimes Lucy is worse than

43

a boyfriend. She gets wounded too easily, needs too much attention. For an instant, Julia almost tells her about Daniel. To tell her about him doesn't mean she has to tell her about all of them.

But Lucy is already hanging up.

When the phone rings again right away, Julia is sure it's Lucy. So she is surprised when she hears a man's voice speaking with an Irish brogue.

She swallows hard. She does not give her foreign lovers her phone number, but somehow Daniel has found it. It takes Julia a minute to realize that this isn't Daniel. It's the owner of the bar where he works, where she left her application yesterday. He is telling her she has the job.

"But I don't want it," she blurts out. She can't go in there and work with Daniel. That's not how she does these things.

The owner is silent.

Julia frowns. She needs money. She hasn't worked in almost six weeks, since she got fired from the Tony Roma's Place for Ribs on Sixth Avenue.

"I'm not going to beg you," he says finally. "Now are you coming in tomorrow or not?"

"Yes," Julia tells him. "I meant. . . ." She can't think of a lie, so she says, "Is there a uniform?"

"I don't care what you wear," he tells her. "The day bartender is named Daniel. He'll show you the ropes."

"Right," she says.

She starts to strip the bed, then stops and calls Lucy instead.

"I got a job," she tells her. "At the Shamrock and Apple."

"Way over there?"

Julia takes a deep breath. "There're some creepy people who work there," she says.

Lucy laughs. "No kidding. This is New York."

Julia can still smell Daniel. His scent is everywhere. "I've got to go," she says.

When Julia hangs up, she goes into the bathroom and takes a long hot shower. Then, she scrubs the bathtub until it shines and there are no more black hairs anywhere.

.   .

After acting class, Julia goes to the Prince Street Bar for a drink with Barry. When the waitress takes their order, Julia orders a Diet Coke.

"Last time I had a beer," she tells Barry, "I got in trouble."

He nods. Barry works during the day for a caterer. Sometimes he brings leftovers for the class. But now he tells Julia that he's going to quit and try to get a job on a soap opera.

"No more good food," she says.

He smiles at her. "I'll cook you dinner if you want."

"No, thanks," she says. "Anyway, I'm going on a diet."

"Do you know that I used to weigh one hundred pounds more than I do now?" he asks her in a low voice.

"A hundred? How did you lose it?" She tries not to stare at him too closely. She wonders if he has stretch marks, cellulite, loose skin everywhere.

"A liquid diet," he says. "And I started swimming every day."

Julia studies his face. Suddenly, she is sure Barry is lying to her. She believes the part about his swimming, because when she stands close to him she can smell chlorine. But she doesn't believe any of the rest of it. She doesn't think someone who lost all that weight would be drinking beer. But it's something else. She recognizes something in his eyes and his voice. Something false.

Julia sips her soda. She says, "I used to be thinner. I was married once and we lived in Milano. When it ended, I kind of let myself go."

Their eyes lock for just a flash.

She says, "I'm getting back on track now, though."

Julia works with two waitresses, Flanna and Fiona. They tell her that there is only one other person there who isn't Irish. "So," Fiona says, "you're a minority here."

Daniel is behind them, slowly polishing the bar. She can feel his eyes on her, penetrating her skull and back. The four of them will be working lunch. Flanna shows her how to do setups, and where everything is. Then she sends her over to the bar so she can learn how to order drinks.

Julia doesn't look at Daniel. She straightens all the garnishes instead. She stacks the slices of orange, the wedges and twists of lemon, all the time he is explaining the bar system to her.

When he finishes, she mumbles, "Thanks," and starts to walk away.

"Not so fast," he says. He leans across the bar and tilts her face up to his. He holds her chin firmly in his hand. "Why are you acting like you don't know me?"

"I just thought it wouldn't be a good thing businesswise. You know."

"I'll take you home after the shift then," he says, dropping his hand.

Julia tries to think of an excuse, a reason for him to stay away from her. She glances quickly around the Shamrock and Apple. It's an old bar, all dark and cracked. It's the kind of place that people like to know about in New York. It makes them feel special for some reason. She thinks she will not work here long. She doesn't like to spend a lot of time with the men she picks up. She likes to use them, sleep with them until she is tired of them. Then never call them again.

Julia always makes sure the men wear condoms. Sometimes she jokes with them. She says, "Leave all weapons at the door, except Trojans and Ramses." Sometimes, she thinks of *Looking for Mr. Goodbar*, of how dangerous this could be. But mostly she goes by her gut. She protects herself from diseases and figures that's as safe as sex with strange men can be.

She looks back at Daniel. He has his arms folded across his chest, those bottomless eyes focused straight on her. She feels a shiver between her thighs. She wants him to take her home. For him to rub his rough face across her body.

Julia smiles at him. She says softly, "If you take me home, I'll keep you there all night again."

He leans closer. He presses his mouth to her ear and in his lilting voice whispers what he will do to her all night.

Julia thinks that she will have to find a new job soon. That working here could be dangerous.

Julia is in bed, the telephone pressed against her ear, watching *Live with Regis and Kathie Lee* and talking to Lucy. They are discussing Regis' former cohosts, longing for the days when he sat up there with Cyndy Garvey and Ann Abernathy.

"Back then," Julia says, "we didn't have to hear about Frank Gifford. About true love and *Monday Night Football*."

Lucy agrees. "Speaking of true love," she says.

"Jasper?" Julia asks her.

Lucy sighs. "If only he were awful. If he'd cheat on me or act like an asshole. It would be so easy to leave him then."

"I know," Julia says. Jasper is almost too perfect. He adores Lucy. He lives for her. "If he got a job," she adds. "Dancing, I mean."

Lucy doesn't answer.

So Julia says, "I quit the Shamrock and Apple yesterday."

"That didn't last long."

Julia touches the pillow beside her, almost thinking it will still be warm from Daniel's head. "The people there were too creepy," she says.

They both go back to watching Regis and Kathie Lee. They do not talk again until the show is over and Lucy says she needs to work on *My Dolly*.

"Now," she tells Julia, "they all look like Jasper."

"You can have them look like me," Julia says. "I don't mind."

Lucy laughs. She says that she will be home all weekend. She has no Whirlwind trip.

"Good," Julia says. "Let's go to three movies in a row."

"At least," Lucy says.

When she hangs up, Julia keeps the television on. Sally Jessy Raphael has on guests who had sex with the devil. Julia pulls her blankets tighter around her and listens to the women confess.

Secret ingredients

Andy calls Katherine and tells her that on Fridays he works in a clinic for people with Hansen's disease.

"Hansen's disease?" she repeats.

"Leprosy," he says. "I bet you didn't think there was leprosy in Massachusetts, did you?"

"I never thought about it," she says.

"A lot of people," Andy says, "know that the island of Molokai has a big leper colony. And there's one outside Baton Rouge. But they don't think there's leprosy in their own backyard."

Katherine says, "Thanks for sharing this with me, Andy."

He says, "Won't you come back now?"

She laughs and checks the cookies she has in the oven. "With a buildup like that, it's hard to resist. But I'm still staying here."

The cookies are oatmeal raisin. One of the women she taught with in Connecticut told her this was Mrs. Field's recipe, but Katherine can't believe that Mrs. Field's cookie recipe is so easily available. Andy has stopped talking and for an instant she thinks maybe he has hung up. But then she hears him breathing. She tries to imagine his face, but comes up with a circle as round and blank as all those *My Dolly* faces Lucy draws.

"Well," he says finally.

"Right," Katherine tells him. "Bye."

• •

Sometimes Katherine cannot believe how easily she has made the transition from doctor's fiancée to big city single woman. She has a *New Yorker* Diary datebook, with men's names and places to meet for dates neatly penned in. She gets her hair cut at Bumble & Bumble. She buys special cosmetics at Kiehl's. She buys socks on the street corner. And she is doing it all so naturally.

She feels like she is in a movie about New York and everything is passing by her in one of those whirlwind spinning collage scenes—taxi cabs, new hairstyles, handsome men. Lately, she has started to write long chatty letters to her sister Shannon and a few friends. The letters chronicle her life here. She uses lots of exclamation points and parentheses in them. And when Shannon writes back, she always starts with, "Dear Katherine, I can't believe all the great stuff you are doing!" Katherine can hardly believe it herself.

If only Lucy would warm up to her again. Katherine used to feel she knew everything there was to know about Lucy. Now, she knows nothing about her except the obvious things: there's Jasper, and Julia, and her drawing. That's it. Last night Katherine had asked her, "Are you going to marry Jasper?" and Lucy had almost bitten her head off. "That's kind of personal," she'd said.

Tonight, when Lucy returned from her Whirlwind Weekend in Paris, Katherine would try again to get her to talk. She'd give her the oatmeal raisin cookies, and wrap herself in a quilt on the couch, and tell Lucy some big secret about herself. Maybe she'd tell her something about Andy. About how she wrote those song lyrics on the ceiling. She'd talk until Lucy started to open up. Until they became friends again.

Katherine presses her finger into a cookie. The kitchen smells great, like cinnamon and raisins and brown sugar. Lucy will be able to smell these cookies before she even walks in the door.

When the phone rings, Katherine almost doesn't answer it, thinking it is Andy again. But it's impossible for her to let a telephone ring and ring.

She's surprised to hear Lucy's voice on the other end.

"I didn't want you to worry," Lucy says in that forced polite voice she uses to speak to Katherine. "I'm with Jasper at his place."

Katherine swallows hard. She glances over at the cookies cooling on the counter. "Oh," she says. She doesn't even try to hide her disappointment.

"I'll see you in the morning," Lucy says.

Katherine says, "Andy called again."

"Uh-huh."

"He's working in a leprosy clinic. Can you believe it?" Katherine picks up a cookie as she talks, and begins to break it into small pieces.

"What did he do? Move to Hawaii or something?" Lucy says.

Katherine hears music in the background. "Hawaii?" she says, trying to think of ways to keep Lucy on the phone.

"Yeah," Lucy says. "There's a leper colony on Molokai."

The cookie is a puddle of crumbs now. "Right," Katherine says. "I knew that. No, he's working at one in Boston. There's leprosy everywhere."

"Well," Lucy says, "watch who you go out with, I guess."

Katherine laughs.

"See you tomorrow," Lucy is saying.

"Wait!" Katherine says quickly. But Lucy has hung up.

Katherine holds the receiver in her hand until it starts beeping loudly. Then she wraps the cookies in tinfoil and ties a bright yellow ribbon around them. She'll go to Julia's, she decides. She'll leave the cookies on her doorstep if she's not home. Then, as if it's an appointment, Katherine writes it in her datebook, beside a Roz Chast cartoon: 7:00—Julia!

Julia does not seem pleased to find Katherine at her door.

"Cookies," Katherine tells her as an explanation, but Julia keeps her black skinny eyebrows bunched up in a frown. They are plucked slightly unevenly. They look like lopsided commas on her forehead.

It took Katherine a while to realize that the contrast in Julia's dark brows and platinum hair is an intentional one, and not meant to look at all natural. It reminds Katherine of country club women from her childhood, with their lacquered and dyed bouffants and bubble cuts, their V-shaped eyebrows and dark red or orange lips.

Julia still has not opened the door enough for Katherine to enter, and for a moment she thinks that perhaps Julia is hiding a man in there. But as quickly as the thought enters her mind, Katherine dismisses it. Julia is always talking about her lack of a love life, her crush on a man from her writing class. Or is it her acting class? Julia takes too many classes and switches jobs too many times for Katherine to keep track.

"Someone told me this is Mrs. Field's recipe," Katherine says, shrugging. "I can hardly believe that, though."

Julia steps away from the door and Katherine follows her inside. She is shocked by how beautiful the place is—an art deco–lover's dream filled with Erté-like sculptures, black and aqua furniture.

"None of it's mine," Julia says, flicking on lights as she moves toward the couch.

Katherine is almost afraid to put the cookies down on anything.

"I've never owned a thing in my life," Julia tells her. "Never had a lease. I'm like a professional apartment sitter. This guy's in Europe for three months."

"You mean they pay you to live here?" Katherine says.

Julia shakes her head. "I just live rent-free, that's all."

The black coffee table is littered with small plastic fruits, tubes of glue, and what look like fishhooks. Gingerly, Katherine sets the cookies down. Julia looks out of place in this plush room, sitting on the sofa in her green stretch capri pants and worn black sweater. Each of her toenails is painted a different color. When Katherine sees that, she feels inexplicably sad.

She says in an overly friendly voice, "I thought for a minute you were hiding a secret lover in here."

Julia seems to study her carefully. "No," she says. "My Latin lover just left."

Katherine smiles. She wonders why she wants this woman to like her so much. She doesn't come up with an answer, she just knows that she does.

"Lucy's with Jasper," she says finally.

"I know," Julia says. "She called me a little while ago."

Katherine says, "She did?" She shifts uncomfortably.

Julia nods. "She always calls me from the airport. This terrorist stuff makes me feel all weird. You know? So she calls to tell me she's back, safe and sound."

She has unwrapped the cookies and is examining one closely.

"Uh . . . there's just the usual cookie stuff in there," Katherine tells her.

Julia smiles and nods, then puts the cookie down.

They sit quietly on the sofa. Katherine is surprised at how thin Julia is. She always wears such baggy clothing, Katherine assumed she was overweight. But she is average, not unlike Katherine herself.

"No date tonight?" Julia asks her.

Katherine shakes her head. "Remember Joe?"

"The wine store guy?"

"Yes. I called him and he gave me this real runaround. Said he had out-of-town company this weekend."

"Maybe he does," Julia says.

"Maybe," Katherine says. But she knows that he did not want to see her again. It was one of the things she hoped to talk to Lucy about. Lucy had told her not to call him and she'd been right. Katherine should have just waited to see what happened naturally. She says, "Lucy is good with love advice."

Julia shrugs. "I guess so."

"I mean," Katherine says, "how could she not be? She and Jasper are so perfect together."

Julia arches her crooked eyebrows. "Mmmmm."

"Aren't they?" Katherine asks.

Julia smiles. "Isn't Jasper gorgeous?"

Katherine hesitates, then agrees. "A real hunk," she says. She points to the things on the coffee table. "Is this for a class?"

Julia laughs. "I make jewelry," she says. "Earrings. Then I take them over to Astor Place and sell them on the street. It's like a hobby."

"Oh," Katherine says. She tries to sound polite, but she can't imagine it—standing beside all those street people selling used magazines and old shoes.

"Here," Julia says, and hands her a completed earring.

It's a bunch of miniature plastic fruit, bananas and pineapples and oranges dangling from a hook.

"What I do," Julia is saying, "is sell them singly. A lot of people want just one."

"Sure," Katherine says.

Julia pulls away from her and shakes her head. "You should do something about your look, Katherine. Those little stud earrings." She shakes her head again. "It's all too young. Too—"

"I like a more classic look," Katherine says. She can't keep the chill out of her voice.

"Suit yourself," Julia says. "But you could look really great. If you got rid of the ribbons and stuff." She stands abruptly. "Well," she says, "thanks for the cookies."

"Oh." Katherine stands too. "I . . . I thought maybe you'd want to go to a movie or something. Since Lucy's the only one lucky enough to have a real date tonight."

But Julia is already urging her toward the door. "My roots are showing and I want to work on those earrings and I—"

"That's all right," Katherine says. She is surprised at how well she can mask the hurt she feels. She knows that Julia just doesn't want to spend an evening with her. "I have a ton of stuff to do myself."

She walks down the hallway toward the elevator. When it comes, a Chinese-food delivery man gets out. He is strikingly handsome, with a punk haircut and a diamond earring.

"Smells good," Katherine says, and points to his bag of food. She is surprised to see the silver foil top of a champagne bottle poking from the bag.

He smiles at her and walks down the hall. Suddenly, she has a strange thought: He is going to see Julia.

Feeling like a spy, or maybe Agent 99 from *Get Smart*, Katherine stands behind a large potted fern and watches him. He goes right to Julia's door, and when she opens it, Katherine sees the old black sweater is off, and she is wearing a lacy bustier that shows off her full breasts.

"Hi, On," Julia says with more warmth and familiarity than Katherine has ever used on a delivery boy.

She waits until On and Julia are both inside before she leaves. Out on the street, Katherine stands, unsure of which way to go, or what to do. She looks down and sees that she still has Julia's earring in her hand. Slowly, she removes her plain gold one, and places the hanging bunch of fruit in her earlobe. Then she tosses her head back and forth to feel it sway and brush against her neck. But it feels stupid, and Katherine takes the earring off, and slips it into her pocket.

Happy ribbons

"She looks like Whoopi Goldberg," Katherine tells Lucy. She holds up her hand like a traffic cop. "Not that I know anything about illustrations," she says.

Lucy looks down at her latest attempt at My Dolly. It does look like Whoopi Goldberg. But she can't admit that to Katherine because then Katherine will pat her hand sympathetically and assure her that things will turn out just fine. Lucy half expects her to break into song sometimes, the way people do in old musicals. She can see it now, Katherine dancing up the walls, her voice full of gusto and enthusiasm, singing about a brighter day.

It has been exactly one month since she appeared on Lucy's doorstep. One month since she called off her wedding to Andy and proclaimed herself a new woman. But to Lucy, Katherine is not a new person at all. She's still the same as she was back in college when they were roommates, during the years that Lucy tries very hard to forget. Now, every morning when she wakes up, Lucy is reminded of them. Katherine puts on lipstick and combs her hair as soon as she wakes up. She reminds Lucy of someone on a half-hour sitcom.

To make it all worse, Katherine cooks Lucy breakfast. She goes out early and brings home the newspaper. She writes Lucy little notes all the time. At least she doesn't sign them with a happy face, the way she did in college. But it's still awful having her here. Lucy has found herself searching the *Voice* and the *Times* real estate ads, hoping to find Katherine an apartment so she can get out already. And Lucy can return to her own life.

"I hate to ask you this," Katherine says now. "I mean, I know you're busy but I have just one little question."

Lucy keeps staring at her drawing. "What is it?" she says.

"Where's Borough Hall?" Katherine says. She thrusts a subway map in front of Lucy. "Can I take the Number Six train?"

Lucy looks at her finally. Katherine is dressed in a lightweight gray suit. The skirt is too long. And she has on a little bow tie, all pink and gray polka dots. Lucy frowns. "Where are you going?"

Katherine has on her sunniest face. She is wearing lip gloss and small pearl stud earrings. Katherine still dresses exactly the way she did in college. Chinos and polo shirts, a little Pappagallo bag, long skirts and loafers. She is an eighteen-year-old in a thirty-year-old's body.

"A job interview," she says. "I'm going to the Board of Ed to apply for a teaching position for the fall. I have to fill out forms and take a test."

To Lucy, fall is very far away. It means that, until then, if Katherine doesn't move out, she will be lurking about, all smiles and optimism.

Lucy says, "Change to the express at Brooklyn Bridge."

"Is that right across the platform?" Katherine asks. She tries to sound confident and unafraid, but Lucy knows the subways terrify her. The city terrifies her, but she insists on staying. Even when Andy calls her and tells her she is forgiven, she remains.

Lucy softens a little. "Yes," she tells her. "Express trains are always right across the platform."

Katherine shakes her head. "Not at the Bloomingdale's stop," she says.

"Almost always, then."

"And up on Eighty-sixth Street the express trains are downstairs," Katherine says.

Lucy grits her teeth. "All right. I said almost always."

"All right," Katherine says, her voice all cheery again.

It is this cheerfulness, this eternally sunny disposition, that is driving Lucy crazy most of all. There is something false in it, something almost sinister. It was that way in college too, all the girls smiling and cheerful on the surface, and different underneath. Lucy is ashamed that she acted that way too, pretending to be excited when someone got pinned, or bought a new car, or made the synchronized dance team, when really she thought it was all so silly.

"Off I go," Katherine is saying. She hesitates. "Lucy?" she says. "Wish me luck?"

That is another maddening thing about her. When Lucy went to a meeting with the *My Dolly* editor and writer, Katherine made her a big sign. "Good Luck" it said in chubby hot pink letters. And pinned to the sign was a pair of small earrings, shaped like butterflies. When Lucy spent a few days with Jasper at the beach, she came home and found a "Welcome Home" sign strung across the bedroom door-way.

"Good luck," Lucy mutters.

Lucy has a picture that she pulls out and looks at from time to time. In it, she is standing, arms linked, with Katherine and their two other college roommates, Melissa and Andrea. It was taken the summer they all worked as cocktail waitresses, and they are wearing their uni-forms—bright yellow ones with kelly green aprons. They all have the same haircuts—wedges like Dorothy Hamill wore. When Lucy looks at this picture, she cannot tell which of the girls is her, unless she studies it very closely. That's why she keeps it. To remind herself that even if she is lonely, or sad, or brokenhearted, she cannot change just to have friends.

That's what she did back then. College had frightened her. She used to sit alone at night and look out the window at the blackness, listening to the sounds of people having fun. Girls giggling, boys singing, the sounds of people running and shouting. And she would feel like she was one of those satellites, sent into space to orbit for years and years, alone, never really touching down anywhere, just watching things pass by.

Her first roommate was a transfer student named Janet. She had fifty-two pairs of shoes that she kept boxed and labeled. She had a boyfriend in Pennsylvania who called her every night. She majored in French, and sat on her bed talking to herself in that language for hours. *"Est-elle triste aujourd'hui, Mademoiselle?"* she said. Then she would answer herself, *"Oui, je le crois."*

The next semester Janet went back to Pennsylvania and Lucy had a new roommate, a girl named Pamela who sold drugs from their room and had loud sex with different boys while Lucy tried to sleep. By then Lucy had met Katherine, in an English Literature Survey class. Katherine had pledged a sorority, and had to wear something in its colors, double green and pink, every day. She had to pin double green and pink ribbons to her sweater. They were called Happy Ribbons. To Lucy, Katherine did seem happy, as if the ribbons were magical. She was always smiling, and she told Lucy funny stories about the other sorority sisters and the socials they had with fraternities. "You should pledge," Katherine told her every day. Then she'd wave good-bye to Lucy and run off to meet a group of girls, all dressed in double green and pink, those ribbons pinned to their sweaters, all smiling and happy to see her.

Back in her dorm room, Lucy would put her pillow over her head to muffle Pamela's moans, and when she'd finally fall asleep, she would dream of a world filled with smiling faces, of happy girls dressed in double green and pink. And in her dreams, she was one of them.

Lucy and Jasper glissade naked across her living room floor. Katherine is out for the evening, on a date with a man she met in the express checkout line in the supermarket. Katherine is a relentless dater. It is as if she is making up for lost time, for all the boys who smiled at her in Chem 101 or sat beside her at basketball games, all the ones she ignored because of Andy. Now, anyone in a good suit, anyone who seems disease-free and well-read, anyone who prefers Broadway musicals to prime-time television and Mozart to the Grateful Dead gets a chance to take her to dinner. Men who sit next to her on the subway. Men who swim laps beside her at the pool. Men buying milk at the Grand Union. She has only refused the ones who wore their hair in ponytails, or had unfocused gazes, or wore unpressed clothes. About everyone else she says, "You never know. He may be the One."

"No one is safe from her," Lucy tells Jasper.

He stops dancing and shakes his head. "She has got to find her own place," he says. "I never get to see you."

Lucy nods, but really the only good thing about having Katherine here is that she doesn't have to deal with what is happening between her and Jasper. Before Katherine arrived, that was all Lucy could concentrate on. How Jasper had stopped trying to get a job dancing. How he used to seem so perfect, how in love they used to be. How she had started to feel like she didn't love him, or he had changed somehow, or she had become different. With Katherine here, those things only surface sometimes.

"She got a job," Lucy tells Jasper.

"Teaching?"

"Yes."

"Now?" he asks.

Lucy sighs. "No. In September. Now she's volunteering in a soup kitchen." Lucy adds, "She's so damn good."

Jasper raises his arms and pirouettes, fast, spinning and spinning until Lucy starts to feel dizzy just watching him. She looks away, sees his reflection in the window. He is doing a whole choreographed dance, steps she cannot identify. She thinks, he's a good dancer. He will make it somehow.

When he finishes, he bows to her. She runs to him and hugs him close.

"I love you," she tells him. And in that instant it is true again.

•   •

For as long as Lucy can remember, she changed herself to fit in. She is not proud of that. She has only told Jasper and Julia how as a little girl she wanted so badly to be in the "in" group that she taped a sign on to Harriet Becker's back that said: I AM FAT. Harriet didn't know it was there, and walked around school all day like that until a teacher saw it and took it off. But the other girls loved Lucy for doing it and she spent most of her time planning new pranks. Most of them against Harriet Becker, who really was fat, and had head lice and secondhand dresses.

These things embarrassed Lucy. At night she prayed to God to forgive her for being so cruel. She started getting bad stomachaches. She threw up a lot. But she still kept torturing Harriet Becker.

"Did I tell you how I used to invite the girls who I wanted to be my friends over and I'd make crank phone calls to Harriet Becker?" Lucy asks Jasper later that night.

They are in bed by then, watching David Letterman. He has on people doing stupid people tricks.

"Forget Harriet Becker already," Jasper moans. "You were eight years old."

"But she was really homely and I told her she had won a part in a movie with Warren Beatty. I told her she was going to go to Hollywood."

Jasper says, "You've been talking about this a lot lately. Why don't you find her and apologize? Purge yourself of all this guilt."

"The next day," Lucy says, "she came to school in her best dress. It was this red velvet one, like little girls wear at Christmas. Except this was in the spring and it was already warm. She even wore her good patent leather shoes. And lace ribbons in her hair. And she told everyone she was going to be a movie star."

Jasper puts his arm around Lucy. "What is this with Harriet Becker?"

Lucy shakes her head, doesn't answer him. But she knows that it's having Katherine here that is bringing all this to mind. Katherine reminds her of how disloyal Lucy always was to herself, how cruel she could be, just to have a friend. It wasn't until after college, when she moved to New York, that she felt as if she had finally found her real self. That was why she didn't want Katherine here. She wanted to just live her own life and forget about everything else. But Katherine wouldn't let her.

"I heard she got hit by a car," Lucy says finally.

"Did she die?"

Lucy shrugs. "I thought it was my fault somehow," she says. "That I made her life so miserable—"

"Come on," he says softly.

She lets herself be kissed. Not long ago, she thought Jasper was the best kisser in the world. She tries to concentrate on that, but Harriet Becker keeps intruding, dressed in her red velvet dress and patent leather shoes. The door to the apartment opens and Lucy hears Katherine walk in. She is humming something cheery. Lucy isn't sure, but she thinks it's a song from *Annie*.

"Do you think I should call him?" Katherine asks Julia and Lucy.

They are in a Mexican restaurant on the Upper West Side. Katherine has just looked at, and turned down, an apartment on Ninety-second and Riverside. "Too small," she said. "Too far from everything." It's the fifth apartment that week she has refused.

Julia is saying, "Which one is this now?"

"Pay attention," Katherine tells her, sounding very much like a schoolteacher.

"I am," Julia mutters.

Julia and Katherine do not like each other very much, so Lucy intercedes. "Jack," she says. "The guy from Grand Union."

Katherine sips her virgin margarita. "Right," she says. "We were both in this express lane for like twenty minutes. First the cashier had to get a price on cat food for someone, then the cash register broke down, then the woman in front of me didn't have enough money." She shakes her head. "And there was Jack, right behind me, and everyone except us was getting really upset and shouting at the cashier. But we were laughing."

"Sounds hilarious," Julia says.

"It was," Katherine says.

"Look," Lucy tells her, "you just went out a few nights ago. Give him a chance to call you."

Katherine rolls her eyes. "I hate being the woman waiting by the phone, though. Women should be able to call too."

Lucy shrugs. For all the dates Katherine has had, she has used this same theory. It never works. Either the men weren't going to call her anyway and tell her so, or they feel pressured into asking her out again and have a miserable second date. If they do like her, she sends them funny cards until they stop calling her. To Katherine, though, all these subtleties go unnoticed. She thinks every date is wonderful, every man a potential boyfriend.

"I really liked Jack too," she is saying. "He's an investment banker."

Julia rolls her eyes.

"What?" Katherine asks her.

"Nothing."

Lucy says, "Just this once, wait and see what he does." She knows Katherine won't do it. The last time she promised to wait, then pretended she had called the guy by accident. "I meant to call the number right under his," she told Lucy.

Katherine points to Lucy's empty margarita glass. "Salt is really bad for you. I order mine without it. They don't mind."

Under the table Julia kicks Lucy gently.

Katherine picks up the bill. "My treat," she says. "You were both so great coming up here to look at the apartment with me."

"No," Lucy says. "I want to pay my own."

Katherine smiles. "I insist," she says.

On the sidewalk, they stop and look in a store window at shoes on sale.

"Someday," Julia tells Katherine, "you have to let me make you over."

Katherine eyes Julia and laughs. "I don't think so."

"If you're going to live in New York, you've got to look like a New Yorker," Julia tells her.

"Well," Katherine says politely. "Maybe some night for fun."

When they turn to leave, a familiar woman starts to call to them from across the street.

"Lucy! Katherine!"

Lucy freezes. It is Meryl King, a sorority sister of theirs. Lucy wants to duck into the shoe store, pretend she hasn't heard. But Katherine is already waving and shouting back at her.

"It's the King!" she's yelling. "It's the King!"

Julia grabs Lucy's arm. "The king?"

"Don't ask," Lucy says. She is starting to get a stomachache.

Meryl is beside them now, hugging Katherine, jumping up and down. Lucy moans.

"I heard about you and Andy," Meryl says. She has that false sincere voice that Lucy hates. "What happened?"

Katherine shrugs, gives a small laugh. "One of those things."

Now Meryl looks at Lucy. "And this one," she says, poking Lucy's arm. "Lives right here in New York and doesn't even pick up the phone. You know we're practically neighbors?"

Lucy nods vaguely.

"I manage that store right over there." She points across the street. "If you come in I'll give you a discount."

"Okay," Julia says.

Meryl studies her face. "Do I know you?"

Katherine squeezes Julia's arm like they're old pals. "No," she says. "She's such a cutup."

Julia gives Meryl a big fake smile that makes Lucy laugh.

Now Meryl is frowning, trying to understand the joke.

Katherine says, "Guess who else is living here in the Big Apple?"

"No!" Meryl shrieks. "No!"

Katherine nods.

Watching them, Lucy is starting to feel like no time has passed, like she is right back in school, drinking peppermint schnapps and doing line dances with these women. She places her hand on her stomach, trying to calm it.

Meryl is saying, "One of my roommates is getting married in August and we need a third."

Suddenly, Lucy becomes animated. "That is so great," she says. "What luck."

"Well," Katherine says slowly, "where is it?"

"Stuyvesant Town," Meryl says. Meryl is almost six feet tall and very thin. She is wearing large jewelry that makes loud crashing sounds when she moves. She is writing down the address on her business card. "The third has to sleep on the couch," she says. "Instead of sharing rooms. You know."

Katherine nods. "Uh-huh," she says.

Lucy says, "Katherine, you're going to love that area. This is so great."

Meryl looks at her watch. It's big too and has a hologram of a rose on it. "I've got to run," she says. "Call me, Kat." At the corner she turns, "I mean it about the discount too," she calls to them. "You too, Julie."

"Okay," Julia shouts to her. "I'll take you up on that."

They all watch as Meryl disappears into the store.

"What a coincidence," Katherine says. She is pursing her lips into small thin lines.

"An omen," Lucy says. "Definitely an omen."

It is very late at night and Lucy can't sleep. She is haunted by images of Meryl. Not the Meryl they saw on the street today, but a younger one, dressed in a lime green snowflake sweater and khaki chinos. She keeps remembering one night when she had come in from a date, a fix-up, with a Phi Sigma Kappa. Freddie was kind of nerdy. He looked like John Denver. He was majoring in agriculture. But she pretended to like this guy, just so he'd ask her to the spring weekend, and it had worked. She'd had a date like everybody else but instead of being happy, she felt miserable.

She walked down the dark corridor toward her room. Meryl's door was open and there she was, all six feet of her, stretched out on the floor, and she was saying to a group of faceless girls, "Lucy is so weird. She drives me crazy." Then Meryl started to laugh. "I even fixed her up with Freddie tonight." All the other girls laughed too. Lucy pushed the door open and walked in. "Hi!" she said as bright and cheery as she could. There was an awkward silence. "Well hello there," Meryl said. "Tell us every detail."

Lucy gets out of bed and goes into the living room. Katherine is asleep on the couch, her hair pulled into a ponytail, her face all fresh and scrubbed clean. Lucy sighs. Whatever happened to Freddie? she wonders. At Bum's Rush she had dumped him for an alumnus who had gone to the weekend alone. The older guy had been a terrific dancer, and he and Lucy had jitterbugged like mad. She'd even spent the night with him at the Holiday Inn where he was staying.

Lucy sighs. She remembers how Freddie had looked, standing alone in the corner as she had danced and twirled around the floor with the other guy. He had kept his head bent, stared down at his shoes. After a few more dances, he was gone.

At her drawing table, Lucy turns on the light. Katherine doesn't even budge, so Lucy sits down and begins to work on My Dolly. She draws carefully, the face, the hair, the dress. When she finishes, it is perfect. A sad little doll in a badly hemmed red velvet dress. She has a lace ribbon in her hair, drooping sadly against her tangle of yellow curls. To the world, she will just be My Dolly. But to Lucy, it is Harriet Becker who will get all the hugs and kisses from little girls.

Fires

Jasper hangs a string of Christmas lights shaped like chili peppers above his sofa. He spends so much time at Lucy's apartment that he has never felt the need to do much with his own. But now that Katherine is staying with Lucy, Jasper wants to make his place more homey. Lucy thinks the chili peppers are funny, but her laughter stops suddenly, and then she goes and looks sad again. This has been happening a lot lately.

She hates staying at his place. She hates the entire block with the men who stand in front of the building next door like sentries and the empty schoolyard littered with crack vials and the red and yellow bodega on the corner with the cashier sitting behind a plastic window. She even hates the name of this section of the city, Hell's Kitchen. In summer, loud music blasts unfamiliar songs from radios and the street floods with water from an open fire hydrant.

Lucy says, "How can you keep living here?"

But Jasper only shrugs. He doesn't have any answers these days. He wants to tell her things but his thoughts seem muddled, trapped in his brain.

Lucy's face brightens. "You'll be the lucky one in twenty years," she says. "This neighborhood will be *the* place to live in New York and everyone will think you're a smart real-estate guy."

He forces a laugh.

"Someone has to be a pioneer, brave the elements. Break new territory. Someone has to take risks," she says. "Right?"

"Right," Jasper says.

In the dark, the chili pepper lights blaze red, like a distant row of stop lights. Otherwise, the apartment is pitch black. Sometimes, Jasper sleeps the entire day, unaware that the sun has come out. Even though Lucy is right beside him now, he cannot even make out the vague shape of her face. There is something disorienting about this, something that makes him feel dizzy and slightly lost.

Jasper whispers into the darkness. "I've never really failed before."

She doesn't answer, but she squeezes his hand.

"I mean, I always got the parts," he says. "Always."

"But you have to try out to get them," she says. Her voice sounds weary.

"Romeo," he begins.

She squeezes his hand again. "I know," she tells him.

He says suddenly, "Where are you?"

Lucy laughs softly. "Right here," she says. "Next to you."

Jasper gropes in the darkness, trying to find her. His heart pounds and he can hear his own breathing, quick and frightened until he settles on her shoulder, her neck, feels her hair across the pillow. Then he can breathe normally again.

He tries to think of what it is he wants to tell her. He tries to organize his thoughts into some kind of story, the way in high school he used to organize term papers.

"Remember topic sentences?" he blurts.

"Topic sentences," Lucy says.

"I remember I wrote this term paper in tenth grade on national parks. And we had to hand in this outline with headings like The First National Parks. And Theodore Roosevelt and National Parks. And The Importance of Forest Fires in National Parks."

"Uh-huh," Lucy says.

"This was supposed to help us organize our thoughts. So we could write the paper, you see? So from the outline we developed topic sentences. Like, 'Yellowstone National Park was created in 1889, the first park of its kind in the United States.'"

He feels Lucy stir. He imagines that she is sitting up.

"What are you talking about?" she asks.

Jasper sighs. He knows he is looking up, toward the ceiling, but he feels like he is upside down. He decides that he will go to Star Magic tomorrow and buy the glow-in-the-dark full moon appliqué they sell. He'll stick it to the ceiling to help him feel more centered at night.

"I mean, national parks?" Lucy is saying. "Teddy Roosevelt?"

"I remember doing that paper and how surprised I was that sometimes they let forest fires burn for days. It's like a natural thing. Even though all those trees and animals die, it's good sometimes to let it burn out. Even though Smokey the Bear was telling us then how to prevent forest fires. Remember him?"

The bed sighs as she gets up from it. "I don't know anymore, Jasper," she says. "Smokey the Bear? Are you serious? I thought we were talking about us. I thought we were talking about you."

He presses his hands against the wall, to keep himself steady. He presses as hard as he can. He imagines a list in his mind. A neat outline filled with sections like Jasper Shaw: The Early Successful Years. And, The Subsequent Demoralization of Jasper in New York City. And, How Jasper Shaw Became Stuck—Terrified of Failing Even More. He searches the list for topic sentences so he can form a logical explanation for Lucy.

But the neat outline jumbles, then dissolves. He hears Lucy sigh, and walk away from him, into the bathroom where he knows she will take a bath so hot it will leave her skin bright pink, like a cooked shrimp. The bathroom door closes, and he hears water running into the tub. He imagines her in there, naked, hidden in steam. But he stays in bed, just like this, holding on.

Lucy used to kid him about being the only Hoosier she'd ever met. That was when he still believed he would be on Broadway soon.

When he went from dance class to auditions to more classes. When his thighs and hamstrings were sore from working out, and Lucy would massage them with sesame oil, rub and knead them until they became rubbery and he could hardly stand up.

Back then, Jasper used to like to tell her about what he'd done before. How in Greensburg, Indiana, where he grew up, he was such a good dancer that his teacher started to send him the hour west to Indianapolis for classes.

"Ten years old," he told Lucy, "taking a bus every afternoon to the city for class."

"You were destined to be a star," she said. She would trace the definition of his muscles then, lingering on his calves, his inner thighs.

He told her about all the parts he'd danced. He'd leap for her, spin like a skater, dance the mazurka. He used to strut his stuff.

Now Lucy says, "You don't talk about your work with me anymore." She shows him her illustrations. Brings him a piece of paper with a faceless doll on it and tells him her ideas. "Now you," she urges gently.

"Last night," Jasper says, "I made seventeen blender drinks. One guy in a Brooks Brothers suit got so drunk he passed out with his head literally in his soup."

"Not that," she says. She taps his legs lightly. "This."

Sometimes, during these conversations, Jasper takes a book of matches that is made to look like a painted blue door, and lights each match, one by one. He stares at them, holding on until he feels the heat on his thumb, then quickly shakes it until the flame dies.

For a while, he would chronicle his failures to her. He would even make jokes about the people he'd tried out for, their comments on his height. "Maybe I'll shave off a few inches here," he'd say, pointing to his knees. Or, "I have a feeling I'm not in Greensburg anymore, Toto."

But it stopped being funny. It got harder and harder to even go out there and try anymore, to listen to the dancers in his classes talk about jobs they got, to watch his friends shuffle off to Buffalo across a Broadway stage.

"Come on," Lucy would say. "Where's that fire that used to be in your eyes? Let's rekindle it."

But the best he could do lately was a slow pas de deux with her, pushing her awkwardly through the motions.

"If Katherine doesn't move in with Meryl King soon," Lucy tells him, "I'm going to crack up."

"But I've done all these home improvements," Jasper says, his arms sweeping across the room. "All for you."

Lucy wrinkles her nose.

He doesn't bother to respond. Instead, he shows her a lamp he found on the street. It looks exactly like one his parents used to have, an orange stand, loosely shaped like a figure, and a shade with geometric shapes.

"Can you believe someone was throwing this away?" he says, switching it on and off.

"Yes," Lucy says, "I can."

She has on her Whirlwind Weekends uniform, and is packing her bag for another trip to London.

"So," she asks him, "what will you do this weekend while I'm once again at the very spot where Anne Boleyn lost her head?"

"The usual," he says. "Work. You know."

"I think I'll go and see *Cats*," Lucy says. "For a change."

Jasper hesitates. Then he says, "You'll never guess what."

She is humming a song from the play, slightly off-key.

"I auditioned for that very play yesterday," he says. His throat feels dry.

Lucy looks up. She has the kind of mouth that always seems to be pouting, so he finds it hard sometimes to read her expressions.

Jasper takes a breath. He shrugs. "I gave it my best shot," he says. He thinks about all the other potential dancing cats he saw there. They were more like acrobats than dancers, tumbling and cartwheeling across the stage. He doesn't mention that to Lucy. Or that he felt stiff during his own piece, awkward and clumsy.

Her voice is eager. "What more can you do?" she is saying. "You can only give it your best and then it's out of your hands." She is beside him, putting her arms around his neck, smiling. "I can stand to see *Cats* another two hundred and fifty times if you're one of the cats."

His throat is burning now. He tries to say something but can't.

"You'd look very cute in a cat costume," she tells him.

He says, "There were a lot of good dancers there."

Even though she turns away from him, he sees her start to frown.

After he walks her to the subway, Jasper heads right back home. He pretends he isn't waiting for the phone to ring, for a message about getting at least a callback. Today is the last day to be notified, and even though he knows in his heart that he won't get another chance, there is something inside him, a flicker that says, Maybe.

When he turns the corner, he sees fire trucks, a crowd watching, and flames and smoke everywhere. The school across from his apartment is on fire, burning so fast that as he nears it, he can actually hear the flames crackle and sizzle. But he doesn't stand with the others and watch it burn. He goes inside his building, and into his apartment.

There are no messages. And the phone doesn't ring all night. Because it is so dark there, Jasper isn't sure how late he sits, pretending not to wait. He hears sirens, and more fire trucks arrive. He hears, finally, firemen telling people that the show is over and they can go home now. And he hears the radios come back on, the salsa music filling the streets again.

After a long while, he takes off his jeans and puts on a black leotard. He stretches, then goes to the barre that takes up one entire wall of the living room. Breathing deeply, he bends in a demi-plié, then another, then a grand plié. He stares straight ahead, using the glow-in-the-dark full moon to keep him centered and balanced in the darkness.

Love on the doorstep

If Katherine closes her eyes real tight at night, she can block out the distant sound of traffic below, and faintly screeching sirens, and pretend that she is back in college and that Lucy is still her best friend. She can pretend that they are in their small boxy room, the walls painted a pale mint green, the walls dotted with cheap prints—a hand holding out flowers, a Matisse cutout, some Norman Rockwell with braided girls. She can still smell the remnants of Emeraude and Charlie perfume they had spritzed on earlier. She can imagine that if she calls to Lucy, her sleepy voice will answer to her from across the room, where late into the night she sits on her bed, drawing by the beam of a small flashlight.

Katherine tries it.

She keeps her eyes shut, squeezed together as tight as she can, and says Lucy's name once.

Then again, louder. "Lucy?"

Lucy does not answer.

Katherine opens her eyes. There are lights in the courtyard six floors below. The lights burn all night on the small trim hedges and patch of grass in the courtyard's center. The super goes into that courtyard, Lucy has told her, at the turn of each season, and plants appropriate flowers—crocuses and daffodils in spring, lilies in summer, chrysanthemums in autumn, and a small Christmas tree with tiny blue pinpoint lights in winter. It is a park that no one is allowed to enter. From the window in the living room, when Katherine looks down, it seems tiny and forlorn.

Again Katherine says, "Lucy?"

There is still no answer. But Katherine thinks she hears Lucy sigh behind the closed bedroom door.

Julia often appears at Lucy's doorstep unannounced. She brings shopping bags filled with bargain clothes from Cheap Jack's or Goodwill. Oversize tuxedo jackets or seersucker blazers. Beaded sweaters, chandelier earrings, Annie Hall hats. Lucy and Julia coo over these things as if they are precious treasure.

Katherine tries to be as excited as they are, but the musty smell and mysterious stains bother her. Who wore these things? she thinks. What happened to them? She imagines the men who sleep in subway stops, the ones asking for money on street corners.

"Isn't this great?" Julia says.

Katherine quickly puts down the jacket she is holding. "Yes," she says. "Great."

Julia is here again. She appears just as Lucy and Katherine sit down to eat their deli salads. The salads come in plastic containers and are sold by weight. These too seem slightly creepy to Katherine, but she doesn't want to act overly prim or suspicious. The woman in front of her at the salad bar sniffed everything, holding a stuffed grape leaf, then a spoonful of bean salad, then a tangle of sprouts up to her nose.

Katherine tried to ignore her. She tried to be as bold as Lucy, scooping things into the container as if they were at a restaurant salad bar. Pretend you're at the Rusty Scupper, Katherine told herself. Pretend you're at the brunch buffet at the Marriott.

Now Lucy is digging into her salad while Katherine tries to get up the courage to take even one bite.

"Did you notice that woman in front of us?" Katherine is asking just before Julia knocks. "Did you notice the way she manhandled the garbanzos?"

Lucy stares at Katherine blankly, then gets up to answer the door.

When Katherine sees that Julia is here, she feels her heart sink. It's bad enough that she has to spend so much time trying to grasp the meanings of what people are talking about, searching her mind for what Tribeca means, and NoHo and Alphabet City. Her head spins sometimes with what seems like a new language. The Cloisters, Stuyvesant Town, Balducci's and South Street. And then Julia and Lucy start to talk and the language gets even harder. They throw around people's names and store names and private references without ever pausing.

Even now as Katherine thinks this Julia is saying, "You'll never believe who I saw on line at Tower. That woman Sherry who didn't have any thumbs. Remember?"

And Lucy is groaning, "Does she still have that awful perm?"

Julia nods and laughs and says, "She was buying the soundtrack to *Starlight Express.*"

They both find this incredibly funny, although Katherine can't figure out why. So she asks, "Isn't that the play where everybody is on roller skates?"

But they keep talking. America, they say. Tortilla Flats. Sugar Reef. Great Jones.

Katherine sighs and stares at her salad. It almost seems alive. She can imagine it squirming, moving. The blob that ate Manhattan. The woman who sniffed everything had on black nail polish. Who wears black nail polish? Katherine thinks. She closes the lid on the container.

Lucy touches her arm. "Come on," she says. "We'll go with Julia to Great Jones for dinner. The salads will keep."

"Okay," Katherine says. She realizes they were discussing restaurants. America, she repeats to herself. Sugar Reef. She repeats them all the way out the door and in the elevator ride downward, as Julia and Lucy start to talk about something else she doesn't understand, Ross Reports and SAG cards. She repeats them as if she is in junior high again, learning her French vocabulary words.

. .

Lucy draws Katherine a map of Manhattan. She colors it in with bright crayons. SoHo is lime green. Midtown is violet.

"I used to think Kansas was yellow," Lucy tells her. "And California was hot pink. Remember those maps when you were a kid?"

Katherine nods.

It is a hot Saturday and they are sitting on the couch in their underwear. They have cotton between each of their toes, waiting for their nails to dry. They have plastic bags on their heads, with special do-it-yourself hot oil treatments on their hair. Their faces are dark green, covered with algae facial treatments. Katherine is happy.

"I figured if you went to California, everything had a pink glow to it," Lucy is saying. "Like a haze."

The map Lucy has drawn has all the landmarks in metallic colors. The Empire State Building, the World Trade Center, all silver and copper.

"It's easy," Lucy tells her for what seems like the hundreth time. "Think grid."

Katherine sighs. "Do you believe that I learned my way around Paris in one day? That I figured out the subway in Rome?"

Lucy laughs. "No," she says, "I don't."

"Why can't Sixth Avenue be just Sixth Avenue? Why does it have to be Avenue of the Americas? And Tribeca," Katherine says, groaning, "forget Tribeca."

She feels like maybe they can become friends again after all. Last night, on the sofa—which isn't even really a sofa but a thing that resembles a sofa but unfolds into a bed—Katherine remembered visiting Lucy a long time ago at her first apartment on Sullivan Street. The apartment had been the smallest thing Katherine had ever seen. Lucy's bed was really an old door with a piece of foam on top of it. It was the worst weekend Katherine had ever had. It was hot, and they couldn't agree on anything. Lucy had looked so different, with her hair cut into a kind of punk haircut and all of her clothes black. Katherine noticed that Lucy walked fast. That's what had struck her most, the way Lucy walked fast with her head bent. The way she'd stop and sigh and tell Katherine, "Come on already." Katherine had worn the wrong shoes, new navy blue sandals, and the straps cut into her feet and pinched her toes so she couldn't keep up with Lucy's pace no matter how much she wanted to. She'd brought a new outfit too, a Gunne Sax calico skirt and white short-sleeved blouse with a sweet-heart neck that she loved. The blouse, she still remembered, had dozens of tiny buttons down the front. But when she'd put it on to go to a play, Lucy told her she looked like she was from *Little House on the Prairie* or something.

That was the last time she'd seen Lucy until she'd shown up here. Katherine had softened that memory until last night. She'd gone home and told people Lucy had become really cosmopolitan. She still called Lucy, though less and less as time went on. She sent Lucy postcards when she went on vacation. She pretended they were still good friends.

But lately, seeing Lucy with Julia, Katherine had to finally admit that she and Lucy were more like strangers than friends. She had to admit, too, that she felt jealous that Lucy had moved here and figured it all out so well—the city and how to get around it and how to make friends and live on her own. That was why, she decided last night looking down at that park no one can walk in, she remembers most how fast Lucy walked during that first and last visit here. Because even then it struck her that Lucy was somehow really passing her by.

Lucy is tapping Katherine's cheek. "Hello," she says. "Anyone in there?"

Katherine tries to smile but the stuff has hardened and she feels that if she does her face will crack.

Julia says, "If it were me, I'd want him to show up on my doorstep in the middle of the night with dozens of roses and beg me to come back."

Katherine rolls her eyes. "Andy would never do that," she says.

"If he really really really wanted you back he would," Julia insists.

Katherine cannot tell if it's Julia who's bothering her so much, or if it's this feeling of being a third wheel, of wanting to be Lucy's best friend herself. She wants Julia to move away or simply disappear. Or at least to stop dropping in like this. Then Katherine gets mad at herself for acting so petty.

"This is a guy," Lucy is explaining, "who wears boxer shorts. A guy who is still proud that he was an Eagle Scout. This is not a guy who gets drunk and drives two hundred miles to win someone back."

"A lot of interesting men wear boxer shorts," Julia says. "Lyle wore boxer shorts."

Katherine doesn't even bother to ask who Lyle is. "Andy is not. . . . " She searches for the word.

"Passionate?" Lucy offers.

"Right," Katherine says, thinking of all that mechanical sex. "Passionate." Then she adds, "He's passionate about medicine."

"If you want to see him then," Julia says, "pretend you're really sick and need immediate medical attention. Then he'll show up on the doorstep. To save your life."

"He's a dermatologist," Lucy tells her.

Julia shrugs. "You could say you have terminal acne."

She is definitely driving Katherine crazy. Katherine says in a controlled voice, "We talk on the telephone. He's made it clear he's willing to work it out. That's the way he is. Andy will not show up on the doorstep unannounced."

Katherine isn't sure, but she thinks Julia and Lucy exchange a look right then. Is it because she showed up unannounced? she thinks.

She says, "I saw a great apartment today over in Chelsea." This is a lie, but she wants to redeem herself somehow.

Now she is sure they exchanged a look.

Julia says, "You'd love Chelsea, Katherine. Maybe you should take it? Or there's that share with that King person, right?"

Lucy clears her throat. "So," she says.

Katherine reminds herself that before she came here, she had friends. Lots of them. As Lucy and Julia start to talk again about how Andy should win her back, Katherine makes a list in her mind of all the friends she had back home. There was Cindy and Marcy from college. There were some of the women she taught with, Joan and

Louise and Ellen. There were her childhood friends, both named Jessica. But then she thinks, if they were such good friends of hers, why couldn't she tell them how miserable she was? Why doesn't she call them now? Why did she leave them in their pink lace bridesmaids' dresses without even a phone call or explanation?

Julia and Lucy are laughing over something in *Spy* magazine now. Katherine does not understand what they find so funny in there ever. But they are laughing now, their heads bent close together, like Siamese twins.

For an instant, Katherine thinks she hears something at the door. She goes to it and opens it. But the hallway is empty and quiet. Still she stands there for a moment, as if she is waiting for someone to appear.

Something borrowed

Julia measures time by the apartments she sublets. The year she lived on Horatio Street, her six months on Avenue A, the time she spent in a twelve-room apartment on Riverside Drive. These apartments give order to her life. She will say, "That happened when I lived on John Street." Or, "When I lived in Chelsea I designed these great earrings from old tires." Her sublets are the framework of her life.

Julia owns next to nothing. No furniture, no futon, no coffee maker. She moves into other people's homes and lives with their things. Once, there was a real Larry Rivers painting on a living room wall. Another time she took care of three poodles. She uses their linens, reads their books, leaves herself notes under their refrigerator magnets.

Sometimes she peruses the real-estate sections of newspapers, thinking she should make a home for herself somewhere. She reads the descriptions of loft spaces, river views, junior bedrooms. She decorates an apartment in her mind, tries to decide what kind of furniture she will buy, where she will place her bed, her sofa, her bookshelves. But she never does any of it. Instead, when the real tenants return, she moves into someone else's place, and borrows pieces of their lives for a while.

Now something strange is happening to Julia. She has been in this art deco apartment for so long, surrounded by all this shiny black furniture, these Erté statues, the hints and accents of turquoise and pink, that these things are starting to feel like they are really hers. When people visit, she shows them books, plays CDs, as if it all belongs to her.

The people who live there, Darren and Frank, are in Europe. They are professional party consultants. People hire them to plan their weddings and birthday parties, their small dinners and baby showers. Darren and Frank find the perfect place, choose a theme, order flowers and food and music. They write out the invitations. They organize everything. Julia doesn't know them, but she envies their skills. They have order in their lives, an order they can impose on other people's parties. She feels like maybe, if she lives in their apartment long enough, some of this will rub off on her too.

On has brought her a pupu platter in a take-out bag.

He says in perfect English, "I am so beat. I did twenty deliveries tonight."

She chews on a sparerib and studies On's face. He is another problem. Julia likes him. She really likes him. In two weeks she has to leave this apartment and her plan would usually be to leave her lover too. No forwarding address or telephone number. But she doesn't want to leave On. He is handsome. He is smart. He plays in a band called the Copy Cats, a band that does no original music at all. They imitate other bands—the Rolling Stones, the Talking Heads. On plays the drums for them, and delivers Chinese food to make extra money.

Julia says, "Can you speak Chinese?"

He laughs. "Only words I shouldn't repeat in front of a woman," he says. He always brings champagne, and drinks most of it himself. After a few glasses, his voice gets higher, almost squeaky, and his laugh becomes a series of giggles. That is how it sounds now.

Julia stretches out on Darren and Frank's expensive rug and sighs. Everything about On is wrong. He's American, for one thing. Born and raised in San Francisco. He even went to Harvard. He only looks foreign, and although she keeps asking him to tell her stories about China, he has nothing exotic to give her.

"My grandfather only spoke Chinese," he says. "We never knew a word he was saying." Then he adds, "He lived to be one hundred and seven."

"Good genes," Julia says. She starts on another sparerib and asks, "Tell me about him."

On shrugs. "He was a mean old bastard. Always screaming at us in Mandarin."

She sits up, smiles. "Mandarin," she says, enjoying the word, the foreignness of it. She thinks of silk, of strong tea, of junks and jade and ivory.

"Yeah," On says in his squeaky champagne voice. "Like oranges."

Julia's exotic images shatter. "Mandarin oranges," she mumbles, and falls back on the rug. "How suburban. Housewives put them in salads with almonds and sugar for fancy dinner parties."

"They do?" On says. His giggles are like the champagne bubbles now. He pulls her T-shirt over her head and sighs. Then, slowly, he drips champagne on her breasts, and gently licks it off.

Julia is in the office that assigns her the house-sitting jobs. The woman she works with, Edie, has hair like Farrah Fawcett's in *Charlie's Angels*. Julia can smell the raspberry gum Edie chews and pops. It makes her feel a little queasy.

"We got three months in SoHo. Six weeks on Sutton Place."

Julia shakes her head. "I'd like somewhere a little longer."

Edie cracks her gum. Her tongue is dyed fuchsia from it. She frowns and studies her listings. "Two months on Fourteenth Street." She leans toward Julia, breathes raspberry in her ear. "I think it's Bernie Goetz's building."

"No thanks," Julia says. She is wishing that Frank and Darren stay in Europe longer, that they change their minds and don't come home, or get to plan a party for Fergie in England that will take months to organize.

Edie's face brightens. Her base makeup leaves a ragged line around her jaw and chin. "A year in Brooklyn Heights!" she says.

"No," Julia says too quickly.

Edie chews harder. "But it's a year," she says again. "And the place is right on the Promenade."

Julia shakes her head. "I'm a one-borough girl," she says.

"But it's one subway stop to Manhattan," Edie says. She sits up straighter. "I live in Forest Hills," she says. "The other boroughs are very underrated."

"No," Julia tells her.

With quick, jerky movements, Edie unwraps another piece of raspberry gum and pops it in her mouth. Her cheek bulges like a squirrel's.

"Come back next week then," Edie says finally.

"I don't have much time," Julia tells her. "Unless Darren and Frank have changed their plans?"

"You wish," Edie says. "They want you out in two weeks and the place professionally cleaned."

Julia hesitates. "Can you hold that Fourteenth Street place?"

Edie winks at her. She wears a palette of eyeshadow, all shiny shades of purple, blue, and green. "Bernie is still single, I think."

Julia rolls her eyes. "I don't think a madman is my type."

"Madman or hero?" Edie says. "Right?"

Julia takes the Number Two train to Brooklyn and gets off at Grand Army Plaza. She has not been here since Christmas. She avoids coming. She pretends she doesn't even know where this area is. But every now and then, she starts to feel guilty and she spends an afternoon in her old neighborhood.

She grew up on the top floor of a brownstone on Garfield Place, off Prospect Park West. She grew up fat and sullen, in an apartment that was always quiet except for the tapping of her mother's fingers across the typewriter keys. They had high-ceilinged rooms that made Julia feel like she lived in the Tower of London.

Sometimes, she got letters from her father in Houston, suggesting she could go and live with him and his new wife there. Then she would sit in her room and imagine riding horses, eating chili, wearing a cowboy hat. She would imagine open spaces with lots of light, flowering cactus, and roads lined with bluebonnets. She would call people in school y'all, practicing her Texas accent. Somehow it never worked out, though. His job kept him too busy, his wife was pregnant again, their house was too small. Next summer, he'd say. Next year.

At camp in upstate New York, Julia kept pictures of her father and his new family and told everyone they were hers. She would point to his wife Kelly, the former Miss Texas with honey-blond hair, and say that was her mother. She would show them the rambling house in River Oaks, with the redwood and glass and sharp angles everywhere, and say that was where she lived. She would show them her half sister and half brother, dressed in identical western outfits, and make up stories about babysitting them. When her mother, who was small and mousy, who walked with her head down and spoke in a thick New York accent, appeared to pick her up, Julia told everyone she was the family maid.

Her mother's apartment smells musty, as if the windows haven't been opened in a long time. Nothing about it ever changes—the living room furniture in harvest gold and moss green is still scratchy and stiff. The piano gathers dust, unplayed, in a corner. Julia's room still looks like it did twenty years ago, all pale peach, a small dim lamp of a ballerina holding a peach bulb upward.

"What a treat," her mother says when Julia comes in.

"For me too," Julia lies. Her words are thick, like marbles in her throat.

As a child she had always wished for a different mother—a funny, smart one with a Miss Texas trophy on the mantle and tawny hair. This mother, her real one, has a life that orbits beside Julia's, but never touches it. Their whole life together, they have sat in these awkward silences, unable to think of anything to say to each other. Julia knows her mother dreams of a braver daughter, a more beautiful one. That wish hangs in the air between them too.

Her mother adjusts her thick glasses on her nose. She looks a little like a mole, Julia thinks, squinting out beyond her small pointed face into this dark apartment. "I made some cookies," her mother says.

She pushes a plate of chocolate chip slice-and-serve cookies at Julia. As a fat teenager, Julia would eat entire rolls of these, raw. To her mother, the memory must be that they are Julia's favorites, although the truth is she can hardly stand to look at them.

Julia says, "Thanks." She starts to talk about the apartment she is living in, making it sound like it's her own. She describes everything in rich detail. Her mother nods and makes a noise in her throat something like Mmmmmhmmm. But it sounds almost painful the way she does it.

When Julia finishes, her mother says, "Who lives there? I mean really?"

Julia sighs. "These two guys. They're professional party planners."

Her mother shakes her head. "Now I've heard everything," she says. Then she adds, "Your father and Kelly probably had something like that. They had a big shindig when they got married."

"Ma," Julia says, "that was twenty years ago."

"Still," her mother says. She smooths a yellowed doily that rests on the arm of the couch. "Still."

Bluebeard, the parrot, squawks, ruffles his feathers.

Julia watches a line of pigeons outside the window. There is a small balcony there, but neither she nor her mother has ever been on it. That strikes her as odd suddenly. Her mother is telling her how her father did not seem like the type who would run off with a Miss Texas, with a woman who got manicures and facials and went off to health spas. Julia has heard this all before. She gets up and goes to the window.

"Let's go out there," she says, pushing at the latch.

Her mother jumps up. "Julia, don't. It's not sturdy enough to hold us."

"Says who?" Julia asks.

"Says the landlord. Why do you think I never go out there?"

Because you're timid, Julia thinks. Because you like to sit in the dark and feel bad. Because you like to make up stories rather than really live. Out loud she says, "I figured you never wanted to."

Her mother leads her back to the couch, her hand pressed lightly into the small of Julia's back.

"I think I have a new boyfriend," Julia says softly. She wants desperately to like her mother, to be liked by her.

Her mother's eyes are a cloudy green. They narrow. "Watch out," she says. "Men are all the same."

Julia shakes her head. "No, they aren't, Ma," she says. Her mind fills with the different sizes and shapes men come in, with the faces of her lovers, their different accents and movements. "They're all different."

Her mother touches her arm, holds it as if it's a buoy at sea. "No," she says. "Don't be fooled."

That night, she invites On to her house for dinner. She makes risotto with mushrooms, sausage, and red wine. As they eat, she studies him—his sculpted face, the high cheekbones, and black shiny eyes. Looking at him almost hurts. She realizes she will have to move, that being with On is getting dangerous. She will take the apartment in Bernhard Goetz's building. She will start over as usual, borrow someone else's life.

On refills her champagne glass. It is extra tall, with a black base cupping the glass like a tulip.

On says, "You always ask me so many questions. But you're so mysterious. Tell me where you come from."

Julia thinks of her mother, small and bent over her typewriter in that dark apartment.

She says, "Houston, actually. I come from a long line of beauty queens."

On smiles at her. "That," he says, "is easy to believe."

Nawn PAR-*lo* *ee-tah-lee-*AH-*no*

Lucy faces her tour group. They are from Edison, New Jersey, and at the start of a Whirlwind Weekend in Rome. It is the hottest day of the summer, and their sunburned faces are all turned toward Lucy. She has handed out their itineraries and name tags. HELLO MY NAME IS _____. Like a *Romper Room* teacher, Lucy thinks, I see Mabel and DeeDee. I see Freida and Stan.

Around them, regular travelers get their boarding passes, read magazines, wait to board the flight. But the Whirlwind passengers are getting their Italian lesson.

"*Non parlo Italiano,*" Lucy tells them. She holds up a large piece of poster board with the phrase spelled out phonetically: Nawn PAR-lo ee-tah-lee-AH-no.

The tour group repeats after her, "*Non parlo Italiano.*"

She is aware of non-Whirlwind passengers watching her, smirking. Lately, she has the urge at times like this to shout, "I am an illustrator! I designed *My Dolly!*" To somehow prove herself to strangers.

She tries to focus on one face in her group, the way she has heard rock singers do onstage. She chooses DeeDee, a heavily made-up woman with silver high-heeled sandals and a fake Louis Vuitton bag. DeeDee's hair is a flat red, the color of taillights on a car.

"Here's something you'll want to remember," Lucy says. She

looks right into DeeDee's eyes. *"Quanto costa?"* Her flash card says, KWAHN-toe KOE-stah? "How much does it cost?" Lucy translates.

The group laughs and repeats the phrase.

She continues until it's time to board. Hello. Good-bye. Please. You're welcome. Where is the bathroom? Thank you very much. She hands everyone flash cards with all the words spelled phonetically. According to Whirlwind rules, she must use these phrases on the flight. When someone in the group approaches her, she must say, *"Buon giorno."* She saves the phrase, *L'Italia e bellissima*, for right before landing. Italy is very beautiful.

When Lucy first dated Jasper, leaving for these weekends used to almost hurt. All she could do was think about getting home and seeing him again. But since that horrible feeling has settled in her chest, she looks forward to her trips away. It isn't even that she is able to sort things out while they're apart. It's that she doesn't think about him at all. She pretends that he doesn't exist. In New York, more and more, she can only focus on Jasper, on what went wrong.

"Do you think you're a failure?" she whispers to him at night. "Is that it?" He answers her with a heavy silence. "Are you asleep?" she asks him. He doesn't even answer. She knows that if the light were on, he would be looking away from her. *"Come va?"* she says. "What's happening?"

There is a man on the flight to Rome, a regular passenger, whose eyes follow Lucy through her routine—handing out landing forms, city maps, discount coupons. She feels him watching her and she finds herself performing for him. Making jokes, trying to sound knowledgeable. He looks as if he is from New England with his yellow tie and Brooks Brothers shirt. His eyes are green-gold. They make her think of marble.

Later he comes to her seat and brings her a split of Chianti. When he speaks to her she is surprised that he is Italian.

"I thought you were American," she tells him.

He shakes his head. "I am Antonio," he says, like a proclamation.

"Tony," Lucy says.

"No. Antonio."

"Okay. Antonio. I can't accept the wine. I can't drink while I work."

His face droops. "But it's for you," he says. "You must."

She explains about Whirlwind Weekends. His teeth have nicotine stains on them. Close up, he is older than he seemed at first. And he isn't very tall. Lucy is five four and she guesses him to be about the same.

"You cannot see Roma in a weekend," he is saying.

"I know," Lucy says. She repeats the itinerary for him. "We do the highlights," she explains. "Colosseum, Vatican, Trevi Fountain." She rolls her eyes to let him know she is somehow above all this. That she knows these few things are not what is good about Rome. She wants him to find her interesting and sophisticated.

But Antonio is ready to leave her and go back to his seat. "When you go to Trevi Fountain," he tells her, "throw in three coins. That way you will return to Roma someday."

She tries not to seem disappointed that he is leaving it at that. She says, "On Saturday the group has an afternoon free."

He turns back toward her. "Free?"

She struggles for an interpretation of what she means by free. "On their own," she says finally.

He raises his eyebrows. "Oh?"

"They can shop or go on an optional tour to Frascati. Whatever." She sees that her hands are trembling and hopes he doesn't notice.

Antonio grimaces. "*Frascati*," he says, and shakes his head.

She cannot think of anything else to say. She knows she is smiling like an idiot, all teeth and lips.

"What is your name?" Antonio asks her. He has moved closer to her.

"Lucy."

"I am not surprised," he says, his voice as soft as a lullaby. "Saint Lucia. You know her story?"

She shakes her head no.

"She was so beautiful that she drove men crazy. You know? So she pulled out her own eyes so as not to be beautiful. And she offered them to God."

Lucy is not sure what to say. It's a terrible story. All of the ones about saints are, she thinks. Pulling out eyes and shaving their hair.

Antonio is smiling at her. "*Ciao,*" he says.

"Right," Lucy calls to his back. "*Ciao.*"

Jasper is handsome. Jasper is sweet and funny. Jasper loves her. These are the things Lucy keeps telling herself on Saturday afternoon as she sits in the hotel lobby waiting for Antonio to pick her up. Right now, she thinks, Jasper is working at the Blue Painted Door. He is pouring glasses of chardonnay and Beck's draft. She imagines him in the stiff white shirt and blue bow tie that he wears at work. The cotton apron tied around his waist. Jasper has a small waist, broad shoulders, an ass that Julia describes as tight. He has a swimmer's body. She reminds herself of all of these things until she sees Antonio drive up in a small red Fiat. Then her mind goes blank and she rises from the mauve wing-back lobby chair to greet him.

Lucy and Antonio eat and eat and eat. Crispy bruschetta, pasta carbonara, saltimbocca, coda alla vaccinara, all with bottles of red wine. They are acting silly, laughing and drinking and eating. Her tongue burns from so much garlic. Antonio lifts pieces of bruschetta to her lips, wipes olive oil from her chin. He asks her to say American words. "Say baseball," he says. "Say hot dog."

He is a businessman who travels frequently to Cincinnati. This strikes Lucy as very funny, but she can't explain to him what it is that seems odd to her.

He orders fruit and espresso. His face is puzzled but he says, "I don't know what is funny but I'm glad I make you laugh." He touches her shoulder, under the thick strap of her sundress. He massages it lightly. "When I saw you, I thought you were someone who is sad."

"You were wrong," she says, leaning her face close to his. She is flirting with him shamelessly. "I go to Europe once a week," she says. "And my career as an illustrator is really starting to take off." She isn't sure who she's trying to convince that her life is so wonderful, Antonio or herself.

"Yes," he says. "But what about love? You may be happy here," he says, tapping her temple, "but what about here?"

His hand goes to her heart, and lingers there, cupping her breast. He moans slightly, and Lucy turns to see if anyone has noticed. But the trattoria is full of people enjoying their food, the sunny Saturday afternoon, each other. No one cares if there is a man sipping espresso and feeling a woman's breast.

Just as quickly as he placed it there, Antonio lifts his hand and motions to the waiter. He orders two Sambucas, *con mosca*.

Lucy's head is already spinning from the wine. But she doesn't stop him.

When the Sambuca arrives Antonio says, "*Con mosca.* You know what that means?"

She does but pretends not to.

"With flies," he says. He plucks a coffee bean from one of the glasses. "You must have three," he explains. "For luck. For love. And to ensure that you return to Roma."

She has never heard this before, about the three coffee beans. But she accepts his stories. His stories about saints and Rome are good, like little gifts. She asks him for another one.

He studies her face with his green-gold eyes. He smiles. He says, "Do we have time for a ride? I will take you somewhere for another story."

Lucy has already decided she will call the hotel and say she is sick. Tonight, her Whirlwind group has an authentic Italian meal in a villa. The hotel concierge will get them on the bus; the restaurant owner will make sure they get back on it safely after dinner. She will go with Antonio. She will listen to his stories. She wants to feel nothing except happy for this one night.

In his bright red Fiat they drive, the top down, Lucy's hair blowing about, to the Via Sacra and the Temple of Vesta.

Antonio holds her hand as they walk through the elaborate structure.

"This was built for the goddess of fire," he says.

Lucy wonders if all these double meanings are just in her head. Does he know what he is saying? she thinks. She tries to imagine him naked. She pushes Jasper out of her mind.

"The Vestal Virgins lived here," Antonio is saying. "Their job was to keep the fire burning all the time. In the center."

He must be saying these things on purpose, she thinks. She finds herself pressing closer to him.

"As long as they remained virgins," Antonio says, "they were considered the most respected and powerful women in ancient Rome."

"And if they lost their virginity?" Lucy asks him.

He pauses. His eyes twinkle wickedly. "Then they were buried alive."

Lucy's skin erupts with goosebumps. "Here?" she says.

Antonio shrugs. "In those days," he says, laughing, "maybe it was better to remain a virgin."

He leans toward her and kisses her. His moustache tickles, she tastes the sweet Sambuca on his lips. She returns the kiss with a burst of passion that she has not felt in months with Jasper. She thinks of fire, she thinks of being buried alive.

Antonio whispers, "Up ahead, on the Via Sacra, is the Basilica of Maxentius and Constantine."

She does not take her lips from his mouth.

He says, "That is the most important existing example of Roman architecture."

She moves her tongue around in his mouth. His hands have lifted her dress, and move underneath it, upward.

"And there is the Palatine hill," he says into her neck. "Where Romulus founded Rome."

She arches toward him, toward his exploring fingers.

"And there is my apartment," Antonio says. "Where no great historical event has occurred."

"That," Lucy says, "sounds the most interesting."

When Lucy gets off the elevator in her building, she smells turkey cooking. For a while, before Katherine moved in with Meryl, it was almost a relief to come home to her loud music, to the sound of her singing songs from *Camelot* or *Saturday Night Fever* at the top of her lungs.

Lucy stops and leans against the wall. Her thighs ache from her night with Antonio. He was a passionate lover; a lover of endurance. She cannot remember the last time she has felt so sexy, so wanted. It is how she used to feel with Jasper, before his jaw grew so rigid. Before he stopped talking to her about his dreams, his dancing, his thoughts.

She smells Madeira wine, wild mushrooms. It's his newest stuffing recipe. She finds herself wondering if he will be able to tell right away that she has been unfaithful. If there is something changed about her on the outside too. When she was in college, she lost her virginity with a boy named Gary. A senior. A Phi Sigma Kappa with a girlfriend back home. Gary had taken her to his room, where they drank Narragansett beer out of cans and made love all night. She was sure the next morning that everyone on campus could tell just by looking at her what she had done.

Now that same thought creeps into her mind. She closes her eyes and hugs herself hard. Then she starts to cry. That is how Jasper finds her a few minutes later.

"What?" he asks her. "What is it?"

But Lucy can't look at him. She can't answer. She just keeps crying.

Jasper puts his arm around her and leads her toward the apartment.

"That's all right," he says. "You're just tired. This Rome trip is crazy. It's too much for one weekend."

She nods, accepts his explanation.

"What you need," he tells her, "is a hot bath. With lots of bubbles."

She nods again. She thinks, *Come va?* What's happening?

What do you want to be when you grow up?

"First," Katherine tells Lucy and Julia, "I go around the room and have everyone say their name with a favorite food that starts with the same sound."

Julia and Lucy look at her blankly.

"For example," Katherine says, taking a breath, "you could be Julia Jell-O. Lucy Lemonade."

Julia nods politely and sips at her margarita, but Lucy frowns.

"Well," Katherine says, "it's first grade after all."

They are at her new apartment, the one she shares with Meryl King in Stuyvesant Town. Katherine has invited them here for dinner. She has copied exactly a menu from *Gourmet* magazine— frozen margaritas and guacamole to start, vegetarian chili and sangria for the main course, Mexican coffee and fried, sugared tortillas for dessert.

Meryl King, thank God, is away on a buying trip in Los Angeles. Meryl always wants to stay up late and sing old sorority songs. She wants to call college friends late at night and reminisce. Whenever Katherine walks in the door, Meryl greets her with a booming laugh and the old secret handshake. Katherine is embarrassed by this. She cannot believe it is worth it to put up with these things just for the pleasure of sleeping on a lumpy Castro convertible in the middle of the apartment.

The third roommate, the one who gets the small bedroom, a woman named Bianca, is at a support group meeting. Bianca is an enabler. Or so she told Katherine. She attends AA meetings, ACA meetings, meetings for women who love too much. Bianca also told Katherine she used to be bulimic and abuse narcotics. Now, she wakes Katherine early every morning with the sounds of her Jane Fonda workout tape and the whirring of the blender as it mixes her healthy protein breakfast drink.

Katherine has invited Julia and Lucy here for dinner, hoping that whatever it is about her that turns them off so much can somehow be changed. She wants them to be her friends. She wants to be able to talk to someone about things other than addictions and sorority life. Her good spirits are beginning to fade. The last time Andy called, she spent all that night suddenly remembering all the reasons she'd fallen in love with him, instead of the reasons why she'd left. She's afraid this kind of thinking could land her in Newton, the unhappy wife of a dermatologist.

"It serves two purposes," Katherine tells them. "I learn their names and see how far they are phonetically."

The armchair has her autumn classroom decorations stacked on it, construction-paper leaves in fall colors, carefully cut-out block letters that say WELCOME. Her weather and date chart is leaning against one wall, her carefully printed alphabet cards against another.

Julia says, "I hated first grade."

"You did?" Katherine says, surprised. She imagines Julia as always this cool, this with it. Someone other children would want to be friends with.

"I was so fat," she moans. Quickly she puts down a nacho dripping with guacamole, as if that one single chip could transport her back to a chubby childhood.

Katherine remembers how surprised she was when she saw Julia dressed in tighter clothes. "You're not now," she says.

"Once you're fat," Julia says, "you stay fat forever."

Lucy says, "I wasn't fat, but I hated it too."

Again Katherine is surprised. "You?"

She shrugs. "I never felt like I belonged there."

Katherine says, "I loved first grade. Maybe that's why I became a teacher." She wants all of her students to have the same memories she has of school. She thinks of it as a warm place, filled with songs and reading. When Katherine walks into her classroom, even now, she feels good. She loves the smell of chalk and new pencils, the shiny wooden floors and worn books.

But Julia and Lucy are still looking so miserable, she says, "Maybe you remember it differently than it really was. Maybe it wasn't really so bad."

Now Julia laughs. "Trust me," she says. "It was awful."

Lucy says, "What else do you do the first day, Katherine? Give us a positive experience this time around."

"I read them a story. I have them paint a picture of their family—"

Julia groans. "I always hated that. My family was miserable. A typical broken home, you know? Once the teacher even called my mother in. She was all worried because I drew myself as a princess and my mother as a little tiny person. I always drew my mother like an ant."

Katherine sighs. "That's significant," she says.

Then she cannot think of anything else to say. She feels exhausted. Tomorrow is her first day at school and her usual techniques seem all wrong now. Maybe New York schools are different. Maybe she will have a classroom full of kids like Julia, dressed in clothes that are funkier than hers, their hair dyed platinum blond, tiny bunches of plastic fruit hanging from their ears. Maybe none of them will like her either.

"My students always like me," she says, surprising herself that she says it out loud. "I mean," she adds, "I'm a good teacher."

Lucy says, "You're the perfect first-grade teacher."

And Julia agrees.

Katherine sighs again. She isn't sure if Lucy has complimented her or insulted her. She finds herself wanting to prove that she really is a good teacher. If only she'd brought all the clumsy cards and cheap perfume her students have given her in the past. But all those things were back in Connecticut with the other remnants of her old life.

"What else will you do tomorrow?" Lucy is asking her.

Katherine relaxes a little. Lucy's eyes seem kinder than they have in a long while. "I ask them what they want to be when they grow up."

"There's a sign of the times," Julia says. "Six years old and they need to claim their career goals."

"No," Katherine says, her voice defensive now. "I learn a lot about them that way."

"I thought every little girl wanted to be a princess," Julia says.

"Or a mommy," Lucy says, groaning.

Katherine realizes that they are not really attacking her, or her teaching plan. Like her, they are just trying to figure out their own lives. "Or Vicky Valentine," Katherine says.

Lucy laughs. "Definitely."

Julia looks at them both and for an instant Katherine thinks she is frightened. But then she asks calmly, "Who's Vicky Valentine?"

Katherine and Lucy both talk at once.

"She's a teenager by day, a detective by night."

"An urban Nancy Drew."

"She lives in Manhattan—"

"On Park Avenue—"

"With her perfect parents. The rich lawyer father, the sophisticated but loving mother. The cute freckle-faced brother."

"But at night she and her two friends solve mysteries and save lives."

Julia begins to eat some guacamole and chips. She nods as they talk.

"How could you have lived all these years and never read a Vicky Valentine mystery?" Katherine asks her.

"There are thousands of them," Lucy says, still smiling at the memory of those books. "Much better than Nancy Drew."

"I don't know," Julia says. "I missed them somehow."

Katherine says, "I used to play Vicky Valentine with my sister all the time. We'd take our flashlights and look for clues in the garage."

Lucy is nodding. "Vicky Valentine had the best life you can imagine," she says.

97

. .

It is a warm night and it seems to Julia and Lucy as they walk home from Katherine's that the streets are filled with people in love. Everyone is holding hands, kissing on street corners, clinging to each other.

"This is so depressing," Julia says.

Lucy suggests they walk downtown to the Blue Painted Door, where Jasper will give them free drinks. When they were crazy in love with each other, she used to meet him at closing time at the bars where he worked and they would drink free cognac while he closed up. She hasn't done that in a long time.

"Katherine's not so bad," Julia is saying. "She tries so hard."

"Too hard," Lucy mumbles.

"Why doesn't she go home?" Julia asks her.

Lucy shrugs. She too has been thinking those things, that Katherine isn't as bad as she makes her out to be. That she should go back home. "Who knows?"

The Blue Painted Door is not very crowded, and they find seats at the bar right away. Jasper grins when he sees them, but when he takes their drink orders the grin has already faded. He complains about how few tips he's made, how rude the customers are, how tired he is.

When he walks away, Julia whispers, "Remember when he used to smile?"

Lucy nods. She watches him, frowning toward a man at the bar. She tries to give him a break. The customers are all dressed in black clothes, a room full of trendy vampirelike people. The women have on miniskirts and Lycra, the men boxy Japanese suits. There is an unpleasant atmosphere here, she tells herself.

Then Julia whispers, "Remember when he was a dancer?"

Lucy keeps her eye on Jasper. She wonders how different things would be if he were still trying to dance. She is afraid she is going to cry. She leans closer to Julia. "I feel really terrible about something," she whispers.

"About Jasper?" Julia asks her.

"No," Lucy says. "Well, sort of. I had an affair." She laughs at the word. "A fling is more appropriate."

Julia's eyes widen. "When?"

"In Rome," Lucy says. She is carefully shredding a bright blue napkin.

Jasper winks at her from the end of the bar.

"God," Lucy moans, unable to even smile at him in return.

"With an Italian guy?" Julia is saying.

Lucy nods. "The worse part," she says, "is I enjoyed it. It felt good being with someone other than Jasper."

"Someone who wasn't so gloomy," Julia reminds her.

"I feel awful," Lucy says. She cannot look at Julia. Her fling with Antonio seems worse now that she's said it out loud.

Julia tries to cheer her up. "Did he want to know all about America?" she asks.

"No. He told me everything you want to know about Rome but were afraid to ask."

Julia frowns. "No kidding."

Jasper brings them their drinks. "You look pretty," he says to Lucy.

She keeps shredding her napkin. "Thanks," she says softly.

When he walks away again, Julia says, "Maybe we should leave."

Lucy nods but doesn't get up.

"Let's walk somewhere else. Shoot everyone out there in love."

"Okay," Lucy says.

"Let's walk over the Brooklyn Bridge," Julia says.

"What's in Brooklyn?" Lucy asks her.

Julia hesitates. "My mother."

Lucy is taken aback. She has known Julia for almost three years and she thought, all this time, that she was from Houston. That her mother lived in Milan. She sees that there is something important in Julia telling her this. Her friend's face seems expectant somehow. But Lucy says, "I can't believe you never told me that."

Julia's eyes are searching Lucy's face, but Lucy can't tell what it is she's hoping to find there.

"What does she do in Brooklyn?" Lucy says.

"She's a writer," Julia tells her.

"Your mother is a writer living in Brooklyn?" Lucy repeats.

Julia laughs a short sad laugh. "Yes."

"What does she write? For a magazine or something?"

Julia takes a breath. "She writes Vicky Valentine," she says. Her eyes still travel over Lucy's face.

Lucy laughs then. "Come on," she says. "You just told me you never even heard of Vicky Valentine."

Julia's voice is calm. She looks Lucy right in the eye. "I know," she says. "I lied."

Lucy doesn't talk much as they walk uptown from the Blue Painted Door. Julia's heart is pounding. She knows Lucy is angry at her, but she feels elated. She is glad to have told her friend something true about herself, something she usually keeps hidden. Sitting at that bar, feeling Lucy's sadness, her desperation, Julia had wanted to give her something of herself. When Lucy told her she'd slept with a stranger in Italy, Julia knew she would admit something too.

They reach Lucy's apartment first.

"Listen," Julia says, "I'm sorry."

But Lucy just shakes her head. She looks hurt.

"It's something I don't tell people," Julia starts to explain. "I hated growing up with the shadow of Vicky Valentine, Girl Wonder, around me. It made me feel bad."

Lucy stops her. "Never mind," she says.

Julia watches her unlock the door.

"Hey!" Julia calls to Lucy. When Lucy turns around, Julia says, "You know, there are things that seem worse when you say them out loud. So you keep them to yourself and hope that maybe they'll go away."

The doorman is peering over his *New York Post* at them. He always lets Julia up without buzzing Lucy first. He winks at her, and calls her "*amiga*," slapping her palms when she comes in. But tonight he is pretending he doesn't know her. Tonight he is just glancing up through his heavy dark eyes.

"I told you about Italy," Lucy says.

Julia looks at Miguel nervously. He drops his eyes.

"Not at first," she says.

"I told you," Lucy insists. Her keys dangle from a key chain shaped like the stub of a theater ticket. From where she is standing, Julia can make out the word *Cats* on it.

"I never told anybody before," Julia says. She can feel Miguel watching again, but she keeps staring at that key chain, at the writing on it. *Cats*. "Even in school when all the kids toted around Vicky Valentine books and read them during homeroom and study period, I never said a word."

Julia has a heavy feeling in her chest, and she thinks that maybe it is the weight of her other secret, of all those men she takes home with her. She is afraid she might start to cry, to sit down right here on the sidewalk and cry.

"Call me tomorrow?" she manages to say.

Lucy seems to be deciding something. She nods in a way that makes Julia know that she won't call her in the morning, then she waves goodnight, and disappears inside.

Julia stands there, staring at the door, for a while longer. She does not really expect Lucy to come back out, but she waits anyway. She has an urge to follow her upstairs. To tell her everything—about why she lied, about the dark apartment in Brooklyn, even about her lovers. But she does nothing. She feels all exhausted and empty inside. She finally walks the rest of the way home. When she gets there, On is sitting on the stoop, waiting for her.

He starts to kiss her right there, while she fumbles for her keys. She whispers to him but he does not hear her. "I'm afraid," she tells him again.

He pulls away from her. "Of what?"

She tries to say it, to put it in words.

"Of me," she says at last. "Of me."

• •

Katherine tries to adjust her body to the thin mattress on the pull-out bed. She tells herself she has to get to sleep, she tries to will sleep on herself, but all she can do is toss. When she first came to New York, she slept solidly, long dreamless sleeps. Lately though, she has trouble falling asleep and when she finally does, her dreams are vivid and frightening.

An all-night talk radio show is on in Bianca's room. Katherine hears the callers' screechy voices, pleading. She sighs and puts on the light. It is after four o'clock. She picks up the phone and stretches its cord so she can take it back to bed with her. Then she dials Andy's number in Boston. It rings and rings. After twenty she stops counting and just listens for a while. Then she hangs up.

Jasper calls Lucy.

"I know it's really late," he says, "but can I come over and spend the night?"

She doesn't want him there but she says yes.

Later, after he has come in slightly drunk and made clumsy love to her, after he is asleep, she starts to cry. She cannot remember the last time she felt this lonely. She doesn't have Jasper anymore, she doesn't have Julia. She lies there in bed thinking of all the people in the city, millions and millions of them. She tries to give them faces, feelings, to connect with even one of them. But all she does is feel more alone.

Jasper stirs. He moans and rubs his eyes. "I drank too much tonight," he says. Then he sees she is crying. "Lucy," he says, putting his arm around her.

He smells like old booze. This makes her cry even harder.

"You don't love me anymore," he says. "Do you?"

"I don't know," she tells him.

He gasps slightly. An intake of breath that sounds like it hurts.

"If I got a job dancing," he says, "would you love me again?"

"I don't know," she says again.

He is hugging her hard now. He says, "You want me to talk about things. But I don't know what to say. My whole life, all I wanted to do was dance. Be onstage."

"Your life isn't over," she says. "Is it?"

But he doesn't answer.

Best friends 4 ever

"I keep thinking about Carrie Campbell," Lucy tells Jasper.

"Carrie Campbell," he repeats.

She sees him searching to put a face with the name.

"You don't know her," she says. "She was my best friend in seventh grade."

Jasper groans. "First it's this Harriet kid, now Carrie Campbell."

"This," Lucy tells him, "is completely different."

They are at the Corner Bistro, eating hamburgers and drinking sangria, watching the Mets beat the Cubs on television. In one hour, Jasper will go to work at the Blue Painted Door and Lucy will start to meander through the Village and SoHo alone. She will try on dozens of pairs of jeans and not buy any. She will go to a late movie. She will browse in bookstores and card stores. She will do anything not to call Julia.

Lucy sighs. "This is worse than almost anything."

Jasper is watching the game. It is eleven to three in the bottom of the seventh. She is sure he cannot be that interested at this point. But when she points that out to him, he says, "It ain't over till—"

"Spare me," Lucy says.

During the commercial she asks him, "How could she not tell me something that important?"

Jasper crumples his napkin and leans back. "I don't know a lot of things about a lot of my friends," he says. "If I found out one of them was in the CIA, I wouldn't care."

Lucy doesn't answer him. She feels as if she is twelve years old again and Carrie Campbell has stopped being her best friend. There is that same sense of having lost something important, not by being careless, but by fate itself. She cannot even stand to watch Regis and Kathie Lee. She cannot bear to talk to Katherine, to admit that this has happened.

"We used to sign yearbooks AFA," Lucy says. "A friend always."

Jasper says, "Why don't you just call her? Have a big knock-down-drag-out fight?"

"She should call me," Lucy says.

The game is ending. The final score is twelve–eleven, Cubs.

Carrie Campbell was one of the first girls in school to develop breasts and wear a bra. Her parents both worked the late shift in factories, so she and Lucy would spend every afternoon alone together in the Campbells' house. It was not a new house, like Lucy's. It was old and tilted, with linoleum that was worn in spots and a constant smell of fried foods. Carrie's older brother, Hank, spent every afternoon upstairs in his bedroom with his girlfriend. They had both dropped out of high school and worked the graveyard shift at the factory.

Lucy and Carrie used to sit in the small hallway outside Hank's room and listen. Lucy was never sure what it was they were listening for, but every now and then there would be a creak or a grunt and Carrie would smile at her, triumphant. Sometimes, Hank would hear them out there and he would come into the hall in his underwear and socks and kick Carrie. Sometimes, Carrie and Lucy would go into his room after Hank and the girlfriend had left and search his bed for pubic hairs and hard Kleenex.

But mostly, Lucy and Carrie talked about what it would be like to go somewhere exotic. Carrie had a pen pal in Scotland and she was sure she would go and visit her there someday. "I'll fall in love

with a man named Angus and we'll pick heather and drink Dewar's."
Lucy used to be amazed by the specificity of this fantasy. And so
she believed in it completely. Her own plans were more vague. She
cut pictures out of the travel sections of magazines and pasted them
in a notebook that she and Carrie always studied. Thai women in
gold headdresses, lovers strolling by the Seine, the Aztec ruins of
Mexico. "And you'll come and visit me and Angus in Edinburgh.
Right?" Carrie would ask. "Angus and me," Lucy would tell her.
"Not me and Angus."

It amazes Lucy now how much she remembers all the details of
that friendship. She can smell the Campbell house, see the brother's
dingy underwear, her own scrapbook of faraway places. She even
remembers Carrie's pen pal's name. Mary MacIvyre.

She remembers, too, how for weeks Carrie made excuses about
seeing her. How in the corridors at school, Lucy would pass her
hanging around the radiator with a group of other girls. How those
girls would giggle when Lucy passed by. The last day of school, signing
yearbooks, Lucy saw that in Franny Cook's, Carrie had written, "Your
best friend 4 ever!!!! AFA, Carrie (CC)."

Even thinking of that all these years later, Lucy feels sick to her
stomach. It is as clear as if she is looking at it right now. Carrie's left-
handed writing. The purple ink. The realization that she did not have
a best friend anymore.

She calls her mother and asks her if Carrie Campbell still lives
in town.

"Three kids," her mother says. "And none of them with the same
father."

"I used to like going over her house after school," she tells her
mother. She doesn't mention the search for pubic hair and hardened
Kleenex.

"I was much happier when you started to hang around with
Jilly and Nancy," her mother says. "They weren't as wild as that
Campbell girl."

· ·

Jasper says, "Call her already."

But Lucy refuses.

She keeps wandering the streets alone. She lies to Katherine and tells her Julia is away for a while. She goes to bookstores and reads the backs of Vicky Valentine books, as if they hold some secret information. VICKY HELPS FIND A SERUM FOR A DEADLY DISEASE! VICKY HELPS STOP SECRET INFORMATION FROM REACHING THE RUSSIANS! VICKY GOES UNDER-COVER AT AN ICE CREAM SHOPPE TO HELP FIND A KID-NAPPER!

There is danger and intrigue and happy endings, but nothing more.

"Call her already," Jasper insists.

And then one night, while he is asleep, Lucy goes into the kitchen and dials the telephone. But it isn't Julia that she calls. It's Carrie Campbell.

Even though it is almost one in the morning, Carrie sounds wide-awake. She has a smoker's voice, but still Lucy recognizes it imme-diately.

"Carrie?" Lucy says. "This is Lucy Wilcox. I don't know if you remember—"

"Lucy? How are you?" She does not sound surprised, even though they have not really spoken for almost twenty years.

"I've been thinking a lot about you lately. I know that must sound odd, but—"

"The funny thing is, your name just came up the other day. Hank—remember my brother Hank?"

"Yes." Lucy wonders if Carrie remembers them searching his sheets, listening at his door.

"He said just the other day that he heard you had this job where you go to all these exotic places. I said, that sounds like Lucy."

"You did?" Lucy asks.

"Sure. You used to have that book full of magazine pictures."

Lucy is smiling. "Yes," she says again.

"Now me," Carrie says, "I got three rug rats. One nastier than the other. Plus I got Hank's girl and her twins living here—"

"Hank's girlfriend?"

Carrie laughs. "His *daughter*. Tiffany." She lowers her voice. "Sixteen years old with twins. What a mess."

"Well," Lucy says.

"I suspect you don't have any," Carrie is saying.

"Any?"

"Kids," Carrie says, laughing again.

"Oh," Lucy says. "No. I'm not even married."

Carrie laughs even harder.

Lucy feels herself blush. She stammers, "I was wondering," she begins. Then, "This may seem very odd but I was thinking about you and how we used to spend all that time at your house and, well . . . whatever happened?"

Carrie says, "When?"

"Why did we stop being friends?" Lucy blurts.

"I don't know. Seems like you started to hang around with that Jilly and Nancy. Going to parties at the lake and getting a charm bracelet and things like that."

"Me?" Lucy says. "You and Franny used to laugh at me when I walked past you."

Carrie sighs. "I remember it the other way around. But I did always like you. I still have a picture you drew me. A starry sky, all big swirls and great colors."

Lucy is blushing again. She had copied Van Gogh's "Starry Night" and given it to Carrie for her thirteenth birthday.

"I saw that and I thought, that Lucy's going somewhere," Carrie says.

Lucy tells Jasper that she called Carrie Campbell.

"No," he says. "You called someone you haven't talked to all these years, since you were a kid, and you won't call Julia?"

"I know," Lucy says. "It doesn't make any sense at all."

The next morning, during Regis and Kathie Lee's opening, the phone rings.

When Lucy answers, Julia says, "I can't believe the way she rubs her stomach on national TV. It's disgusting."

Lucy watches as Regis locates Omaha on a map of the United States.

"I miss you," Julia says.

"I thought we were friends," Lucy tells her. "And now I feel like I don't even know you."

Julia says, "I've been so sad."

"Me too."

"You don't forgive me yet, do you?" she asks Lucy.

"Not exactly," Lucy says.

She hears Julia take several deep breaths.

Then Julia says, "There are things I hide even from myself. I'm a hider. When I was a kid, I hid behind fat. Now I hide behind costumes. Funny hats and weird makeup."

Lucy doesn't say anything.

"How can I show you what I can't even show myself?" Julia says softly.

"I know," Lucy says.

Then, quiet again, Julia asks, "Do you hate me?"

"No," Lucy says.

"Can we go steady again? You can wear my high school ring?"

Lucy laughs. "It's nine-thirty," she says. "Can you make it here in half an hour?"

"I'll bring the bagels."

"Good. Sally Jessy Raphael is going to have on women whose brothers-in-law are the real fathers of their children."

Julia says, "I'll be right there."

After she hangs up, Lucy doesn't get out of bed to dress. Her hair is in a loose ponytail. She is wearing her glasses. And she has on a T-shirt that turned pink in the wash. But Julia will not mind. Lucy smiles and watches as Paul Prudhomme teaches Regis how to eat crawfish. For the first time in weeks, even though she still feels mad at Julia, Lucy feels centered again.

When she hears Julia knock on the door, Lucy calls, "Come in."

One wheelbarrow

Nathaniel Jones is famous. He is a genius, the boy wonder of children's book publishing. He rules from a townhouse on Beacon Hill in Boston. At thirty-three years old, Nathaniel Jones has won every award, traveled to every continent, dated every beautiful woman. In pictures, he looks a little like Don Johnson on *Miami Vice*—unshaven, sexy smile, casual pale pink linen suit. His face is in magazines and subway posters selling Scotch and T-shirts.

Nathaniel Jones is all of these things, and he has summoned Lucy to Boston for a meeting. On the telephone, he sounded like a Hollywood producer. He called her babe. He said he'd send a car to meet her at Logan Airport. In the background, Lucy heard phones ringing and a song playing, over and over, about the wonderful world of children. The song reminded Lucy of the ride at Disney World where you float through canals and dancing dolls sing, in wooden shoes, kimonos, grass skirts, the same song, nonstop.

That is the song, "It's a Small World," that plays in Lucy's mind all the way to La Guardia to catch her flight to Boston. When she got out of bed this morning, Jasper had clung to her. "Don't run off with this guy," he said, pretending to joke.

Now, at the ticket counter, she pushes away images of doing that very thing. Perhaps this is fate, she thinks. Nathaniel Jones sees the drawings for *My Dolly* and falls in love with the artist. "I must have this woman!" he decides. He calls, pretending to have a new project for her. He talks her into coming to Boston, where he will sweep her off her feet.

Lucy starts to laugh at her own imagination. Nathaniel Jones needs an illustrator, she tells herself. Not a girlfriend. She fights back thoughts of Jasper's face as he watched her getting dressed this morning. She tries to keep her chest from aching so much. She worries, standing there in her black miniskirt and tuxedo jacket, that she is staying with Jasper because the alternative—being alone—is even worse.

She has thought of herself as independent, as self-assured, as brave. Didn't she move to New York City all alone, knowing no one here? Hasn't she hustled for these illustrating jobs? Once, she went mountain climbing. She has scuba dived. Can she really be afraid of life without a man? The thought frightens her. It is what she suspects is true of Katherine, who bravely left Andy and moved to Manhattan but desperately hands out her telephone number to any man who seems even remotely normal. Lucy still finds messages on her answering machine for Katherine: "Hi, I was sitting next to you on the A train. You said I should call." "My name is Don. I bumped into you on Broadway. Literally. Remember? You dropped all those Magic Markers?" "Katherine, this is Vance from the bank machine. The one at Chem Bank? On University?" Lucy is suddenly worried that she is no farther along than Katherine. That she is clinging to someone she no longer loves just to avoid being alone. Just to avoid handing out her phone number to strangers, hoping they will rescue her.

The reservationist says "Next" in a way that lets Lucy know she has called her already.

"Sorry," Lucy says, stepping up to the counter.

She is afraid that there will be no ticket waiting for her. That Nathaniel Jones decided he wasn't interested in her, as an illustrator or a lover.

She says, "There's supposed to be a ticket here for me." She rolls her eyes, as if the idea is ridiculous.

The woman's fingers hover over the computer keyboard. "Name," she says. Her lipstick is magenta, her eyeshadow violet.

Lucy's eyes settle on the woman's ring finger, where a diamond ring and a wedding band sit nestled together.

"Name," the woman says again, sighing.

"Lucy Wilcox." Lucy forces a smile. "It's probably not even there," she says.

The computer starts clicking and printing, and the woman holds a ticket out to Lucy.

Lucy says to herself, "Nathaniel Jones has really sent for me." Then, because the woman is bothering her somehow, Lucy says it out loud. "Nathaniel Jones has sent for me."

The woman looks up, right through Lucy. "Next," she says.

In person, Nathaniel Jones is smaller, heavier, more like a man in the garment business than Don Johnson. Lucy is disappointed. Then she reminds herself why she is here. For a job.

The writer is also there. Her name is Fawn MacIntyre. She is tall and cool, with alabaster skin and flaming red hair pulled back in a ponytail and tied with a shimmery plaid ribbon. Fawn MacIntyre manages to be both hot and cold at once. When she turns her blue eyes on Lucy, she is an iceberg. But they melt when they gaze at Nathaniel. Gaze adoringly, Lucy adds to herself. She decides Fawn MacIntyre is having an affair with Nathaniel Jones.

"Fawn," Nathaniel says. "Fawn. Tell Lucy your great idea. Your brainstorm."

Fawn's voice could chill a corpse. "I believe," she says, "that children's books often talk down to children. A is for apple. B is for boy. That sort of thing."

Nathaniel is too impatient to wait for Fawn to finish. Telephones are ringing all through the townhouse. That song is playing repeatedly. Lucy hears people running, doors slamming, harried voices.

Nathaniel says, "It's a counting book. With bigger words in it than the basic books have." He starts shuffling through some papers on his desk. "Like, One wheelbarrow. Two tutus." He looks up and smiles at Fawn. "I like that one."

Fawn says, "Lucy, may I hear a concept for one of those from you?"

"Right now?" Lucy says. Her head is spinning from the noise here.

"Well, if you can't come up with something now," Fawn says. She shakes her head, opens her hands. Her fingers are long, the kind of fingers that play the piano.

"Two tutus," Lucy says. "Maybe something like two little ballerinas, pirouetting. But really fast so they're basically a blur. But we see the tutus, all sparkly and pretty, very clearly."

Nathaniel Jones leans closer to her. Now his face has settled somewhere between the magazine photos of him and Lucy's initial reaction to it. He is all-right looking. He is even a little sexy.

"I love it," he says. He pronounces each word like it's its own sentence. I. Love. It.

Fawn does not warm any. She says, in her icy voice, "Not bad."

Nathaniel starts talking about a contract. He thrusts papers at Lucy. The top one says:

One Wheelbarrow
Two Tutus
Three Thistles
Four Friends
Five Fireworks
Six Snowflakes
Seven Seashells
Eight Elephants
Nine Nutcrackers
Ten Tornadoes

Lucy thinks, This woman is a genius?

"Number ten is up for debate," Nathaniel says.

"No," Fawn says. "I like the image of destruction and chaos."

"What do you think, Lucy?" he asks. "I was leaning toward tomatoes myself."

"Tomatoes are good," she hears herself saying. She wants to burst out laughing. She wants to know what is so complex about four friends? Or seven seashells?

"We'll let you know," Nathaniel says. He is putting on a pale pink linen blazer. He is not wearing socks. Around his middle there is the very beginning of a paunch.

He says, "So let's grab some lunch and get you back to New York." He points at Fawn, who is smoking a cigarette. "You can't join us, right?"

She flicks her ashes into a gray marble ashtray. "Right," she says. She looks directly at Lucy, like she's warning her.

Lucy says, "Gee, my boyfriend will be happy I'm getting home so early." She can't believe she has just said "Gee." But there's something about Fawn that makes Lucy feel very young and unsophisticated.

"That's sweet," Fawn says.

"All right, all right, all right," Nathaniel is saying. "Let's hustle."

Everyone at the restaurant knows Nathaniel Jones. It's like being out with a movie star. Or the president. He waves and smiles, moves from table to table easily. He introduces Lucy as a fabulous new artist. It's all she can do not to jump up and down with excitement. It's all she can do not to run away from this scene.

Finally, they take their seats in a cracked red banquette. The restaurant is very old, comfortably elegant, with stiff linens and gas lamps overhead. Lucy feels like she's in a Henry James novel. She tries to memorize every detail to tell Julia later.

Nathaniel Jones is saying, "*This* is a restaurant. I am so sick and tired of pasta with nuts in it. Of arugula. Of blackened food."

Lucy finds herself nodding, agreeing with him even though she really disagrees. She likes arugula. She likes Cajun food. She and Jasper go to the Great Jones Cafe for blackened redfish once a week. Yet she keeps nodding and agreeing as Nathaniel goes on and on about all that's wrong with food like that.

When a waiter in a red jacket and bow tie approaches, Nathaniel asks her if she likes beer.

"As a matter of fact I love beer," she says. She doesn't tell him that she hasn't had any since college, when she could drink an entire pitcher of Narragansett by herself along with shots of peppermint schnapps.

"All right, John," Nathaniel tells the waiter. "Here's what we want. Two Sam Adams. Two chowders. And the pork roast."

Lucy feels like she's in an old movie, having a man order for her. Something tells her she should be offended but a bigger part leans back against the banquette and relaxes.

"Very good," John the waiter says.

And Lucy imagines that he clicks his heels before he walks away.

"Where was I?" Nathaniel says. He rubs his temples, as if his fingertips can read information inside.

"Cajun food," Lucy says.

"It sucks," Nathaniel tells her. "Let's talk about this book."

And then, over beer and chowder and pork roast and real strawberry shortcake and coffee he does just that. He talks about this book and his other projects while Lucy sits and nods and smiles the entire time. She thinks that by the end of lunch she has said twenty words. Tops. And after months of Jasper's hard silence, these two hours seem wonderful. She barely tastes the food. Instead, she settles into Nathaniel Jones's words and lets herself be wrapped up in them.

There is a limousine waiting outside the restaurant and Nathaniel puts her in it. "I always walk back from here," he explains. "It's going to be fun working together." He closes the door and the car pulls away and Lucy feels like she has been on a date instead of a job interview. On the plane back to New York, she tries to study the book. One wheelbarrow. Two tutus. Three thistles. But she can't concentrate. She can't wipe away the gauzy feeling of her lunch with Nathaniel Jones. Even after she's back home, settled on her own couch with a cup of coffee, hoping the caffeine will snap her out of this dreamlike state.

•   •

On the phone later she tells Julia everything. She describes Fawn MacIntyre. She reads the ten items in the book to her. She repeats all she can remember about the lunch.

When Lucy finishes Julia groans, "He sounds awful."

"Awful?" Lucy says.

"Like a real pig. Like a sexist. I mean, he ordered your food? He ordered pork roast?"

Lucy hesitates. She knows she should feel more offended. If today really had been a date, she would think he was all wrong for her. So why is she feeling the opposite?

"He sounds obnoxious," Julia says.

"You're right," Lucy says. "He does sound that way. But he wasn't at all."

"Look," Julia laughs, "you're not Doris Day. This is not 1950. Women just aren't treated that way anymore."

"You're right," Lucy says again. She thinks, It didn't feel so bad. It felt good. It felt like a relief.

"And another thing," Julia is saying, "what the hell is a thistle?"

"I think it's like a flower," Lucy says. "A long purple flower."

"He is definitely sleeping with Bambi."

"Fawn."

"Whatever."

Lucy laughs. She doesn't want him to be sleeping with Fawn. Suddenly, she isn't sure of anything. "Why do I feel so mixed-up?" she says out loud.

From across town, Julia says, "Who doesn't?"

"Nine Noriegas," Jasper whispers. "Ten Tiananmen Squares."

"Very funny," Lucy says.

They are in bed, not touching. Jasper has brought a bottle of champagne to celebrate her new assignment. But all it has done is make her feel cranky.

"I want you to go on auditions again," Lucy says into the darkness.

"You do," Jasper says.

"I want you to get a job dancing."

This time he doesn't answer.

"I mean," she continues, "that's what's wrong, isn't it? That's what's making you so sullen."

"Am I sullen?" he says. Then, as if to prove her wrong, he croons, "Am I blue?"

Lucy sighs. "You're something," she says. "You just won't tell me what it is."

She waits. But Jasper still doesn't answer, and she is left alone in the quiet darkness.

Something new

Every day Katherine stays at school late. She breaks dates. She skips dinner. Lucy tells her she has a classic case of depression, but she cannot figure out its source. She asks herself if she would rather have married Andy, moved to Boston, and hosted dinner parties every week-end. The answer is always the same—no.

Katherine reminds herself that soon she will have enough money to get a little studio apartment here in Chelsea where she teaches. She tells herself she has dates lined up for almost every night, that one of those men could be IT, Mr. Right, her knight in shining armor. Still, she feels the same. The bulletin board outside her classroom is the best in the school because she spends every afternoon working on it. Her classroom is the neatest one, her papers graded and starred and hung at right angles on one wall. The desks are in perfect rows, the erasers are dust-free, her plan book up-to-date.

Yet here she is again, at four o'clock, standing in the nearly empty school, trying to think of one more thing to do so she won't have to leave this room. She has a date with a man named Ben whom she met at the bakery around the corner last week. They had stood, pressed close together in the small bakery, each waiting their turn in line. Katherine could tell he was wearing Polo, he was that close. She had felt the cool air on his trench coat. And so she had smiled up at him, and rolled her eyes in fake exasperation at the crowd. "All this for an oat bran muffin," she'd said. He had a nice laugh, she'd thought. He's a lawyer, tall and not bad looking. But she is thinking about canceling their dinner at the Chelsea Trattoria.

Spencer Barrow, the fifth-grade teacher, pokes his head in the doorway.

"Still here?" he asks.

Spencer, Katherine thinks, looks like a Weeble, one of those children's toys that wobble about without falling down. He is the kind of man that mothers and old ladies love, all round baby face and boy-next-door personality. She can picture him as a Boy Scout, in green shorts and knee socks, helping the elderly cross streets. To Katherine he is too friendly, too helpful, always offering her a ride home or advice on the school's staff.

He lives somewhere in Queens, which bothers her for a reason she can't identify. And, worse, he idolizes Elvis Presley. So much so that his own hair is cut into a ducktail in the back and he wears, on occasion, blue suede shoes. He has told her he wears them only when he feels especially happy.

"Want a lift home?" Spencer says, all cheery and full of a toothy smile.

"No thanks," Katherine tells him. "I like to walk." She wonders how many times she will have to tell him that before he gets the message.

"Even in this?" Spencer says, pointing toward the window.

Katherine follows his finger. Without her realizing it, it has started to rain. A real downpour. Now that she is aware of it, the rain seems to pick up speed and bang noisily against the windows.

"Shit," she says.

Spencer giggles.

"I have this date tonight," Katherine says, frowning. She notices Spencer is wearing brown pants with black socks. "I still have to go home and change and then come back here." She leans against her squeaky-clean blackboards that she has just finished wiping down. "What's the point?"

"Tell you what," he says. "Let me take care of you. Put yourself in my hands." He opens his palms toward her.

She is surprised by what nice hands he has. No, she corrects herself, she is surprised how rugged they seem, large and masculine. This gesture, the sweetness of it, makes her smile. Maybe Spencer himself is full of surprises, too.

"You don't know what you're getting yourself into," she says. "I'm clinically depressed."

"You are? How so?"

Katherine shrugs. "I don't know. However one is clinically depressed, that's how I am."

She squirms slightly. She has let Lucy and Julia talk her into buying some new clothes. She spent a lot of money on them and she hates everything she bought. Black stirrup pants, a tapestry vest, ugly clunky black shoes, a Betsey Johnson floral bodysuit. It's that bodysuit she has on now, with a skirt that makes her hips look too big, and she feels uncomfortable suddenly.

"I hate what I'm wearing," she tells Spencer.

He nods. "It's pretty ugly."

Spencer is like that. He says exactly what comes into his mind. "There's a direct path," he has told Katherine. He tapped his head, then drew a straight line to his mouth. "From here, to here. No editing." Sometimes, the things he comes out with make Katherine shudder. She finds herself wondering where he is from, who raised him. But this afternoon, he makes her laugh.

"You know what?" she says. "I'll take you up on that offer."

He looks surprised. "Really?"

"I'm yours," she says.

At least, she thinks as she gathers her things, he makes her smile.

Katherine is surprised by Spencer's neighborhood. His street is a quiet suburban one, lined with large leafy trees and two-family houses. The leaves are vivid reds and yellows. They make her think of New England, and make her a little homesick.

There is something both sweet and repulsive about Spencer, and Katherine decides that she should try to focus on the sweet part as much as possible. This is sometimes difficult. His manners are terrible—he splashes through puddles and sends sprays of water on her, he doesn't hold the door open for her, and when they arrive upstairs at his apartment he disappears, leaving her alone in the living room. Katherine decides he isn't rude exactly; he's naive, socially ignorant. He needs a date with Miss Manners, she thinks. For an instant, she even imagines herself as his teacher. Spencer playing Eliza Doolittle to her Henry Higgins.

There is a scrap of fabric in a glass case on another wall. That is what Katherine is studying when Spencer reappears.

"Las Vegas," Spencer says.

She turns toward him. He is drinking something and has changed into jeans and a flannel shirt, both of which look brand-new, all stiff and bright. She sees that he has put on his blue suede shoes.

"I ripped it from a jacket Elvis threw in the audience," Spencer is saying. "A woman next to me caught it and let me tear off that little piece there." His voice is almost reverential.

"How fascinating," Katherine says, not even trying to hide the sarcasm.

Spencer seems not to notice. "I figured the glass would keep it from fading," he says.

He goes over to the television and turns it on.

"You get cable?" he asks her.

She is very aware that the repulsive side of him is dominating right now. Katherine thinks again of *My Fair Lady*, of a triumphant Eliza and a smug Professor Higgins. "The rain in Spain," Katherine repeats to herself, "stays mainly in the plain."

"You know," she tells him, "maybe I would like something to drink, too."

He looks puzzled.

"I mean," she says, "you should have offered me something."

"This is a Coke," he says. "You want one?"

"No, thank you."

Spencer laughs shyly. "I'm not a big ladies' man. I've had three girlfriends, each for two years. That's about it. No dates in between to speak of. No one-night stands." He laughs and blushes. "I admit it," he says, "I'm a mensch. But I'm loyal. I'm a nice guy. I like dogs. I like old ladies. Babies. Roses. George Gershwin. The works."

Katherine feels herself warming to him again. " 'S wonderful," she says.

Spencer blushes even more. " 'S marvelous." Quickly, he looks into his glass of soda. "I broke up with my last girlfriend, Gloria, about a year ago. She moved to Denver. That was a tough one." Suddenly he looks up, right at Katherine. "I don't entertain much, you know? In fact, you're the first girl I've had here since Gloria left."

"That's all right," Katherine tells him.

He smiles. "Yeah?"

She nods.

His confidence is back. He tilts his head. "Hey," he says, "I'm a great cook. You'll see. I have all the teachers over for a Christmas party every year and I do all the cooking myself. I even make homemade eggnog and Christmas cookies. Little bells and stars with those silver candy balls."

"I love those," Katherine says.

Spencer smiles at her and she thinks that, really, he is almost cute. Almost.

"Tonight, though," he says, "I'm taking you out to Mama Rose's Italian Garden. It's right in this neighborhood and it's so fantastic. You'll love it."

Katherine says, "That sounds great."

He nods. "First, we'll watch *Taxi*. Then we'll go."

"*Taxi?*"

"I never miss it," he says, and flops into the chair under Elvis's cloak scrap.

Katherine stands awkwardly for a minute, then settles onto the couch.

Mama Rose's Italian Garden is too tacky for words. There are plastic grapes clinging to plastic vines on the walls. There's a mural too, an ornate map of Italy in clashing colors, all reds and pinks and oranges. And a man roams around the room playing "Santa Lucia" and "O! Solo Mio" slightly off-key on an accordion.

Katherine cannot tell if Spencer appreciates how awful this place is. He's too busy talking about his trip to Graceland last summer for her to ask.

A waiter appears at their table, looking bored. He reminds Katherine of John Travolta in *Saturday Night Fever*—tight pants, a gold chain nestling somewhere in his shirt, pointed shoes.

Spencer leans toward her. "Let's get the Mama Rose special," he says. He counts off on his fingers all the food it includes. "Antipasto," he says, "minestrone, spaghetti with clam sauce, veal Parmesan, a glass of Chianti, ice cream and coffee." He smiles proudly as if he is somehow responsible for the menu.

"That sounds like an awful lot of food," Katherine says. She tries to push away thoughts about the quiet candlelit restaurant she was supposed to be eating in tonight, of the tall lawyer who was supposed to be beside her. She is beginning to wonder if she will ever make a good decision again.

The waiter clears his throat.

Spencer adds, "All that is only thirty-two dollars. For two!"

On top of everything else, Katherine thinks, he's cheap too. "Fine," she says.

The waiter slides a basket of bread toward her. She looks up at him and he winks one of his droopy blue eyes. Bedroom eyes. Katherine gives him a dirty look, and he slinks off in his tight pants and polyester shirt.

Already Spencer has started talking again, this time about an Elvis concert he saw. Katherine is having trouble focusing on what he is telling her. All the colors and ornamentation are making her dizzy. She hopes that Ben, her real date, got the confused message she left on his answering machine, breaking the date, blaming work and rain. She hopes he calls her again.

"They say," Spencer is saying, "that there are two words known in every country in the world. Everywhere. The Sudan. Australia.

Ecuador." He smiles proudly again. "Coca-Cola," he says. "And Elvis."

"What is this fascination with Elvis Presley?" Katherine says. "I mean, it's an obsession. It's crazy."

Spencer's smile does not fade quickly. Instead, it seems to crack and fade like old wallpaper.

"I'm sorry," Katherine says. "It's just too much."

He nods. "Everybody has to have something," he says. His voice is soft and sad. "Some people collect stamps. Or coins. Some people buy shoes. Mine is Elvis. It could just as easily be Abraham Lincoln or Amelia Earhart or Hitler." He shrugs. "It keeps me busy," he says. "It keeps me company."

The waiter arrives again and gives them each a plate with salami, peppericini, one black olive, and some iceberg lettuce on it. The plate and the food are ice cold.

The sight of it, and the things Spencer has said, become too much for Katherine and she begins, without warning, to sob.

"Oh, no," Spencer says. He jumps up and looks around, as if he could find someone to make her stop.

She keeps saying, "I don't know why I'm crying like this."

"You must know," Spencer tells her. "People don't just cry for no reason."

She lifts her head. He's right, she thinks. "Since I moved here I've been so busy trying to act like I like it and like I did the right thing, that I've been"—she pauses, searching for the right word— "denying everything."

"Like what?"

"Like I hate sleeping in a living room on a pull-out sofa. And I hate my roommates. And sometimes—" she pauses again and swallows hard, "sometimes I miss Andy."

Spencer's frowning face floats in front of her, through her tears, like a watercolor.

"Who's Andy?" he asks.

"My fiancé. I mean my ex-fiancé. For a long time all I could think about was how miserable I was and how rigid and predictable he was and I forgot how once, at a carnival, he won me a big blue stuffed tyrannosaurus." The memory of that blue dinosaur makes her start crying again. "And," she says through her sobs, "we used to sit down and draw blueprints of our dream house. Where the kitchen would be. And the den."

The waiter removes the uneaten food in one motion, and deposits, just as quickly, two bowls of soup.

"Andy used to even watch beauty contests with me on TV. Like Miss Universe and Miss America. Not a lot of guys would do that."

Spencer says softly, "I watch them sometimes."

"You do?"

He nods.

She has stopped crying again and is sniffling and wiping at her eyes. "I must have mascara everywhere," she says.

"You do," he tells her. "You look like a raccoon."

"You don't mince words," she says, "do you?"

"Why don't we have a nice dinner now?" Spencer says. "If you want, you can have more than one glass of wine, even though only one is included in the price."

Katherine takes a deep breath. "One will be fine," she says.

He pats her hand. "You're going to be okay," he says with great conviction. "Just you wait and see."

The next day, when Katherine walks into her classroom, there is a large bouquet of daisies in a vase on her desk. "Gracie for a lovely evening," the card says. It is signed with a fancy, curled S. Katherine smiles. She touches the flowers lightly with her fingertips. He's an odd one, she tells herself. After they left the restaurant, he had simply pointed her in the direction of the subway and waved goodnight, leaving her to find her own way home. Still, he had made her feel better somehow.

She begins to write new words on the blackboard. CAT. BAT. RAT. She makes each letter big and perfect. Somewhere in the distance she hears a bell ring. In a few minutes, her students will file in, two by two. They will hang their coats, stand by their desks, and greet her with a loud "Good morning, Miss Bedford." Katherine decides that she will get an Elvis CD for Spencer.

She hears her class's footsteps approaching and she wipes the chalk dust from her hands. On her big felt board, Katherine sticks a bright yellow sun in the weather square.

Katherine goes to Tower Records and buys a CD of Elvis singing Christmas songs. Then she goes to meet Lucy for cappuccino at Bruno's Bakery. Since Katherine moved out of Lucy's, they don't see each other very much. Even though Katherine knows Lucy prefers it this way, she wishes they got together more. Lucy has a pragmatic approach to things that Katherine needs sometimes. Tonight, she will tell Lucy all about Spencer. As she rushes across Bleecker, Katherine knows exactly what she will ask Lucy: Have you ever been attracted to a guy who's completely wrong for you?

But when Lucy asks her about her date last night, Katherine hears herself say, "It was awful." She laughs. "Unless you like Weebles," she adds. Then, in great detail and with much exaggeration, she describes everything—Mama Rose's Italian Garden, her trip alone down unfamiliar streets to the subway.

Lucy laughs throughout the story. She laughs so hard, tears roll down her cheeks.

Katherine traces the outline of the CD through her bag. She knows she should feel guilty making fun of Spencer this way. But she can't stop herself. Now she is describing his clothes, his framed scrap of Elvis's jacket. What she leaves out are the little things that stayed with her too, the sweet things. Spencer, she reminds herself, is all wrong for her. He's not tall enough, interesting enough, ambitious or handsome enough. She pushes back an impulse to tell Lucy that his hands were nice and manly.

Instead she thinks that she will go right back to Tower Records and return the CD. She'll exchange it for something for herself. The new Linda Ronstadt maybe. She'll call Ben and apologize for breaking their date. She'll call the man she met last week in the elevator. She'll call the accountant from New Jersey she went out with once a while back and ask him to dinner.

"Even the name," Katherine hears herself say, "Spencer. I mean, really."

On

Julia moves into a loft in Tribeca, on North Moore Street. It is spare, with a bright blue fireplace on one wall and multicolored wooden chairs everywhere. There is no couch, which Julia finds disconcerting. She wants to stretch out with a book or magazine, but there is nowhere to do it. The loft is very big. Her voice echoes when she talks.

Her first night there, after pacing the length of the place for an hour, she goes to a bar around the corner. The neighborhood is recently chic, but this bar seems friendly and old. She hears, immediately, an unfamiliar accent.

"Australian," the man tells her when she asks.

Julia thinks of the redness of Ayers Rock, of kangaroos and koala, of long lonely stretches of nothingness.

She smiles at the man, who is younger than she, with longish blond hair and a deep tan. He tells her he is traveling around the world. He has already been to Singapore, Fiji, Hawaii, and San Francisco. He stopped in Chicago and Miami.

"These are places I've heard of," he says. "Places I thought I should see."

Julia nods. "And what did you think of them?" she asks him.

He seems puzzled by this. He frowns and shakes his head. "I

thought in Fiji people would walk around naked. That everyone in San Francisco would be a hippie. I thought Chicago would be full of gangsters. And everything in Miami would be pink."

Julia nods again. This makes sense to her. She, after all, always lives in an illusion. She says to him, "I apartment-sit for people who are away. I use all of their things. Their phone number, their beds. Even the messages on their answering machines."

She isn't sure he understands the connection but she doesn't mind.

He tells her that he is supposed to go to Paris and Greece before he goes home, but he might just stay in New York a while longer. "I can't take too much more disappointment," he says, sounding very sad.

His name is Timothy, and naked he seems still younger. His body is smooth and hairless, tanned without any tan lines. They do not speak when they enter the loft. They haven't touched yet, but once inside his hands are everywhere. He is rough. He is eager. He has her down on the cold tiled floor and still they have not spoken a word to each other.

Julia has to fight very hard to not think of On, whom she has left without telling him where to find her. Still, his dark eyes seem to be etched in her mind. It's as if On is there, watching her. As this man from Sydney pushes into her, hard, she is thinking of On, and she suddenly has an orgasm like she has never had before. She thinks, later, that she blacked out from its intensity.

But still Timothy does not talk. All night this goes on. He never tires. And she never stops thinking of On. Finally, it's morning and she stumbles around the unfamiliar apartment searching for a coffee-pot, a toaster. She can't find either, so she returns to the bed, a platform with a thin foam mattress.

Her voice sounds dry and hoarse. "These people apparently don't eat breakfast," she says, standing beside him. She feels aware of her breasts, of their fullness, in a way she never has with her lovers before.

She reaches one arm across them. "There's no toaster or anything," she adds.

"I'll take you out for breakfast," Timothy says. He stretches like a lion, with his blond mane and muscled legs. "I've never seen a bird come like that," he says, grinning.

She feels herself blush.

Timothy lifts his arm, and points to five small new bruises. "You're a wild thing," he says.

Julia kneels on the bed, letting her arm drop, her breasts fall free. She doesn't want him to touch her again. She wants him to go. But she says, almost desperately, "Tell me about Sydney."

"All right," he says. He describes it in great detail—the Opera House, the beach, the pubs. He tells her that at Christmas, they have Santa's sleigh pulled by kangaroos. He tells her about a city that is cosmopolitan and modern.

Julia feels herself grow cold. "No," she says. "It can't be that way."

"It's like me and Chicago," he says, laughing. "I kept looking for Al Capone. You want me to tell you about Crocodile Dundee. Right?"

She feels like she is upside down. She doesn't want him to touch her, so she touches him. She wants him to go, so she makes him stay. Nothing makes sense. This time, and all the rest of the day, he talks. He makes up stories for her, about aborigines and kangaroos and Alice Springs. And each time he enters her she tries not to think about On. She makes him talk instead, tries to focus on the foreign sound of his words, on his descriptions of things she does not know.

That night at acting class, Barry announces that he has a part as a doctor in a soap opera in L.A. The class applauds, but falsely. Julia knows that they are all wishing they had that part instead of Barry. She almost can't believe it's true. Dull Barry has won a role on a soap opera.

"It's a small part," he adds with great modesty. "The brother of one of the regulars. But if it works out, they may make me a Vietnam vet who has been impotent and hospitalized until now."

Suddenly Julia stands up too and makes an announcement. "I won't be back either," she says. "I got a role in an off-Broadway show. As one of the Chiffons." The Chiffons are a female trio who sing fifties music. The lie surprises even her.

Natalie, a curly-haired blond who thinks she looks and acts like Jessica Lange, narrows her eyes at Julia. "Which role?" she asks. Natalie goes on auditions every day. She knows everything that's casting.

Julia doesn't even blink. "As Bunny," she says.

"There is no Bunny," Natalie says.

Julia shrugs. "Suit yourself."

No one knows quite what to do. They look at the floor and shuffle their feet.

"Come to my place," Julia tells Barry after class. "We'll celebrate."

His ordinary brown eyes widen. "All right."

On the way, they stop for some Great Western champagne. They link arms and sing "We're Off to See the Wizard." They start to skip after Canal Street, and skip all the way into her apartment.

"This is a weird place," Barry says. His voice echoes too.

"I'm a minimalist," Julia tells him.

"I guess so," he says.

She takes his hand and leads him into the bedroom, where the sheets are still rumpled from Timothy. There is a bright white light somewhere outside, and it lights this room sufficiently so they do not need to turn one on inside.

"Julia," Barry says, "I don't know if this is a good idea."

Julia lifts her sweater over her head, unclasps her bra. She is thinking that she should do this. That something has changed in her. She no longer can have her strange lovers. Perhaps what she needs is this, someone ordinary and familiar. He is staring wide-eyed at her breasts. She pulls off her boots, her jeans, and now Barry groans, still fully clothed.

"Listen," she says, "you're going off to L.A., to stardom. This way, you'll never forget me." She knows she doesn't really care if Barry forgets her or not.

Barry reaches out and touches her, but with just his fingertips. She feels her nipples grow hard.

Julia leans close to him. She stares straight into his eyes. He is a liar, like her. She knows this. She does not even believe that he is going to L.A.

"I don't think we should," Barry says, although he doesn't stop touching her.

She tells him the truth. She says, still staring at him, "I spent all day in this bed with a man from Australia. I pick up strange men from foreign countries. That's my hobby. That's what I do for fun."

Barry's hand stops long enough for him to unzip his pants.

"I don't tell anyone," Julia says as she opens a packet of condoms. "I just do it. I take them to whatever apartment I am living in and I have sex with them until I hate them. Or myself. Whichever comes first."

His pants are hardly off but she mounts him. On's face drifts in front of her eyes but she fights it.

"I'm not with the Chiffons," she says. Barry is small, only half-hard. But she doesn't stop. "I just felt like saying that."

She expects Barry to confess to her. To tell her he was never fat, that he is not on a soap opera, that he understands. But he just keeps staring at her, wide-eyed, and she keeps talking, telling him everything like a priest.

Finally, he whispers up at her, "I don't know what to believe. I feel like you've taken me on this incredible journey."

He is still soft.

She says, "Do you want to leave?"

"I'm just so overwhelmed," he tells her. He does not seem embarrassed.

"Do you want to go to Conran's with me to buy a sofa?"

"What about this?" he asks her, indicating her nakedness, his own half-nakedness, all with a sweep of his hand.

"I'd rather buy a couch," she says.

"All right," Barry says.

• •

Julia's couch is navy blue, flecked with white. It is the first thing she has ever owned, and she makes Barry move it from place to place, first against the window, then facing out, then facing the fireplace. He does all this good-naturedly, giving her his opinion of where it looks best.

Finally, they leave it facing the fireplace. Julia imagines adding more things to the room—a bookshelf, knickknacks on the mantel. When she was young, she used to collect things from the ocean. She had brightly colored starfish from a trip to northern California, sea glass from Cape Cod, sand dollars and seashells and bits of coral. She could start to collect something else now, something new. And she could line the mantel with whatever she chose—cats or angels or tacky salt and pepper shakers.

Julia hears a soft pop. When she turns, Barry is standing with the champagne opened, bubbles flowing from it like a mini-volcano.

"We never chilled it," he says.

"Maybe we should have broken the bottle over the couch," she tells him. "The way they christen ships."

Barry has had better luck finding things than she has. He sits beside her and hands her a fluted glass filled with champagne.

She starts to take a sip, but he stops her. "We have to have a toast," he says.

"To the couch!" Julia says.

Barry seems disappointed but clinks his glass against hers anyway.

"Boy," he says, "you know how to tell a good story."

"What do you mean?"

He shrugs. "You know. Back there." He nods his head toward the bedroom.

Julia hesitates. Then she says, "It's an erotic tool. I read it a long time ago in the *Sensuous Woman*. She also says it's very sexy to wrap yourself in Saran Wrap."

"Only if the guy likes sandwiches," Barry says.

• •

Barry leaves after one glass of champagne. At the door, she shakes his hand and wishes him luck in Los Angeles. He sticks to his story, but Julia still does not believe him. When he is gone, she stretches out on her new couch, and pours herself another glass of warm champagne.

In her mind, she adds a rug to the large room, a rocking chair, a museum poster.

Still, On seems to be there, following her, watching her. So Julia picks up the phone and calls him.

He sounds relieved to hear her voice.

"I didn't know what to think," he tells her.

"I know," Julia says. "Everything happened so fast."

"What happened so fast?"

She runs her fingers across the fabric of the couch. The white flecks look almost like birds in flight.

"I got a small role," she says, "on a soap opera."

"Wow. That's great."

"It's in L.A., though," Julia says. "That's where I am now. It all happened so fast."

There is a brief silence, then On says, "Well, you had to go. It's such an opportunity."

"Yes," Julia says. She feels she may start to cry, so she adds quickly, "This isn't my phone, so I'd better go. I'll call you when I'm settled."

As she hangs up, she hears his voice, sounding very faraway. "I miss you," he is saying.

Six snowflakes

꒳

It is the first December 6 in four years that Lucy and Jasper do not spend together. It is the date that they use to celebrate their anniversary, the day when they met on that flight. It is the day they fell madly, love-at-first-sight, in love.

This year, Lucy pretends it's just a day like any other day. She pretends that she did not, two weeks earlier, break up with Jasper. Instead, she calls Julia and watches Regis and Kathie Lee, on the telephone. She buys a *New York Times* and reads it from cover to cover. She reads every article. She reads the classifieds. She does the crossword puzzle. Then she takes herself out for lunch at a place she usually avoids because it's too expensive.

When she gets off the elevator back on her floor, she notices that two apartments have already hung wreaths on their doors. She pauses in the hallway, staring at those wreaths and wishing that, as if by surprise, or magic, Jasper has returned in his old incarnation—alive and full of hope. As if there really will be a turkey roasting in her oven, wine chilling, a vase full of flowers on the table.

Lucy sighs. It is hard to pretend that December 6 is an ordinary day, or that today isn't really December 6, when there are fresh evergreen wreaths with red velvet bows, when the halls smell like Christmas and the air outside smells like snow. Lucy continues down the hall and into her apartment. At first she is struck by how empty it feels there. She remembers the way Jasper used to fill it somehow.

Her answering machine is blinking green. A message. She lets herself think that it could be him. As it rewinds, she tries, unsuccessfully, to conjure his voice. Somewhere, Lucy has read that faces linger in the mind, but voices are the first thing to be forgotten, the hardest to re-create.

She pushes the button marked PLAY and holds her breath.

It's Nathaniel Jones.

"Babe," his voice says, "these snowflakes look like doilies. Call me and let's rethink this."

Now Lucy lets disappointment flood her. She has found these past few weeks that it's easier to put her emotions on something else instead of her life without Jasper, to blame crying on an AT&T commercial instead of on a broken heart, to blame sleeplessness on jet lag instead of on the empty half of her bed.

And now, to blame disappointment on six snowflakes. She has worked hard on these snowflakes. She made them pure white against a midnight-blue sky, drifting, almost dancing downward to a blanket of white fallen snow. Each of her snowflakes is unique, six-pointed, delicate and lacy. They are like the ones Katherine has her first-graders cut from a folded piece of construction paper, full of curves and alleys and points like a Russian church.

It will be good to work on this all day, she tells herself, as she begins to dial the 617 of Nathaniel's phone number.

His secretary puts her on hold, and while she waits, she wonders what Jasper is doing today, right now. Could she, by sheer willpower, force him into changing back? Into talking to her the way he used to? Into a dancer leaping across a Broadway stage?

"Babe, babe," Nathaniel's voice shouts into her ear, freezing Jasper mid-jeté.

"Those snowflakes are beautiful," Lucy says.

"All business," he laughs. "Not even a how are you?"

Lucy closes her eyes. As graceful as snow, she imagines Jasper completing his jump, landing on pointe, getting applause.

.   .

He didn't talk when she broke up with him either. He just stood there, nodding, in his satin jacket that said A *Chorus Line* across the back in Japanese while Lucy cried and screamed at him for ruining what they had.

"And you have to make some decisions," she told him. "What are you doing with your life? You're a dancer, aren't you? Aren't you?"

He stopped nodding then, and stared past her, at a blank spot on the wall, as if it held a greater fascination than what she was saying.

"I need time alone," she told him, calmer then. "I need time to think."

He said, "I understand."

And then he had started to leave. At the door, he turned to her. "Lucy?"

She didn't look at him. She didn't answer.

"I love you," he said.

She hadn't stopped crying all that night. Long after she'd heard the elevator arrive and take him away from her, she kept on crying.

That next day, she left on a special Whirlwind Week, three cities in three days. Paris, London, and Dublin. She wished she could stay gone forever, that she could disappear down one of Dublin's cobble-stoned streets, or into the Paris night, and transform into someone new. Someone who didn't ache inside.

In a way, after that first week, she felt renewed. When she walked into her apartment, she didn't have a sense of dread, of wondering what she could say or how she could help. It seemed lighter, airier, as if Jasper's dark mood had closed in the walls somehow. It was then that Lucy worked on her snowflakes. Hours by the window, mixing paint and thinking about nothing except snow.

She spent more time with Julia. And Katherine. She developed a one-line answer to why she broke up with Jasper. "He was a great boyfriend but he'd make a lousy husband." That seemed to say it all—he was a bartender without hopes of being a dancer. He was fun but not serious. He was immature. He was wonderful, but just for a while.

None of that was quite true, but Lucy couldn't bring herself to say what was stuck in her heart like a rock. That she had imagined, had known really, that they would be married, that no matter what, they would be together. She couldn't believe she had been so wrong about them.

Every day, she found small bundles from Katherine at her mailbox. Oatmeal cookies and Toll House cookies and brownies, all neatly wrapped in plastic wrap and tied with bright ribbon. Her freezer was lined with Katherine's baked goods, in neat colorful rows. Katherine still believed cookies and milk could cure anything.

Lucy signed up for a special Christmas Whirlwind Week to Bethlehem and Jerusalem. She signed up for tap dancing classes. She bought two hundred dollars' worth of books. She did everything not to call him. Not to remember how his voice had sounded, what he'd told her, as he'd left that last time.

She drew her six beautiful snowflakes, and pretended everything was exactly as it should be.

"Babe," Nathaniel Jones says, "they look like they belong over the arms of a couch in an old lady's house."

"Snowflakes," Lucy tells him, "are all unique. They have six points and—"

"Hon," he cuts in, "this isn't about science. This isn't about meteorology. It's about a mood. Catching the right mood for this book."

Lucy doesn't reply. She stares out the window, at the gray day, the low-hanging clouds that seem about to drop on the city.

"You know the eight elephants you did?" Nathaniel says. "I love those elephants."

She is drawing the pictures out of numerical sequence. She is drawing them, instead, by inspiration. As much inspiration as she can get for the subjects. She drew one red wheelbarrow, as stark and real as an Edward Hopper painting. She drew eight elephants in a huddle, trunks resting on heads and ears wide and alert. They are like a big happy elephant family.

Nathaniel is saying, "Now you know and I know that elephants are mammals. They have hair, right? But you didn't draw a bunch of stiff black elephant hair. Did you?"

"No."

"You didn't need to. You drew beautiful elephants."

"I drew beautiful snowflakes," Lucy says.

"The snowflakes are all wrong," he says. "Tell you what. I'm coming to New York next week. We'll have dinner and you'll bring me some new snowflakes."

Lucy agrees, although she can't imagine there is another way to draw a damn snowflake.

"And maybe you'll have another drawing too?" Nathaniel says. "The thistles or something?"

"I'll have something," she says.

"Babe," Nathaniel tells her. "You're great. You are. Fawn can be difficult. Just remember, I'm on your side."

It is like Jasper vanished. Like he never even existed. Lucy finds herself walking past the Blue Painted Door, peering in for just a glimpse of him, but there is always someone else behind the bar. She runs errands in his neighborhood, expecting that he too, as if by mental telepathy, will be buying produce on his corner, or wine at Astor Wines. She stops short of actually calling him. She doesn't know what it is she wants to say to him. Or what she wants to hear him say. So she goes for cappuccino at Veniero's, sitting by the window to watch passersby. She goes to Pete's Spice and buys basmati rice and whole cloves and currants, lingering, watching everyone who walks in or walks by. But Jasper never appears.

She spends too much money on a new dress for her dinner with Nathaniel Jones. She buys a strapless black velvet minidress, a rope of fake pearls. She sits at her drawing table, hour after hour, trying to imagine snowflakes that catch a mood. But they all look like doilies to her now.

And then, one day the grayness changes, and it starts to snow. Small frenzied flurries chase each other to the ground. Lucy stands by her window and watches them. They are blurred and frantic, these snowflakes. When she finally draws, the night before her dinner with Nathaniel, she draws just the tops of buildings, a grayish white background, a blur of snow. And then, she chooses six spots, and paints them silver. A silver that glistens, that stands out against her sky.

Nathaniel Jones knows everyone even here in New York. He can hardly get through the crowded restaurant there are so many people shaking his hand, wanting to say hello. Lucy follows behind him, in her new dress, clutching her snowflake drawing, until finally they are at their table, on a small balcony that hangs over the restaurant.

"I feel like Juliet," Lucy says, peering down at the crowd.

"Let me tell you something," Nathaniel says. He leans way back in his chair. "You're a knockout."

Lucy feels her heart speed up.

"I mean, you are a knockout," he says.

She mumbles thanks.

Nathaniel slaps his hands together. "So we'll order some champagne. And you've got to have the grilled tuna. Done very nouveau with ginger and plums. And we'll need oysters."

She starts to smile. There is something about Nathaniel that she knows should offend her, but instead she likes it. She likes having him decide everything. Now she sits back in her chair, and lets him do all the talking.

Lucy knows she should not, cannot, go to bed with Nathaniel Jones. She works for him. He's a playboy. He's a male chauvinist.

So, at the door to her apartment, when he places the key in its lock, she says, "Thanks for a lovely evening. I'm glad you like my new snowflakes."

She even extends her hand for him to shake.

But Nathaniel just walks right in, gropes for the light, and flicks it on.

"I'm always amazed at how small apartments in this city can be," he says, looking around and shaking his head.

"Tomorrow," Lucy says, still standing by the door, "I have to leave for a week. To Israel."

"One of these Whirlwind things?" he says.

"Yes, it's—"

He turns to her. "You have any cognac?"

She studies him. He looks very out of place here in her apartment. Clumsy and big when really he isn't big at all. He's much shorter than Jasper. Yet he seems to cover so much more space. Lucy is convinced that Nathaniel is one of the sexiest men she has ever met. Not handsome. Not cute. Sexy. She wants him out of here before it's too late.

"Listen," she says, still not moving away from the door, "I think you should go."

Nathaniel looks amused. "You do," he says.

"I mean, we have a working relationship and I think it should stay that way."

His amusement seems to grow. "Absolutely," he says.

"Why is that funny?"

"I only asked for some cognac," he tells her.

"That's all you said," Lucy says, "but I feel these vibes coming from you—"

"Sex vibes."

She feels her face getting red. "Sexual. Yes."

He takes a step toward her. "Well, you're very perceptive."

She holds up both hands, as if to ward him off, and he laughs.

"No," he says. "I'm going to leave."

Lucy frowns. She reminds herself it's for the best. That he should go as fast as possible. "Good," she says a little too enthusiastically.

Nathaniel laughs again. His eyes crinkle nicely when he laughs.

"And thanks again," Lucy says. She sounds as if she's at the end of a Whirlwind Weekend.

"Have fun in Italy," he says.

He walks past her without touching her at all. Still, goosebumps rise up her arms.

"Israel," she says.

"Israel." He doesn't even pause. He just walks right down the hall and into the elevator.

But Lucy stands there, frozen, for a long time.

Truth or dare

༄

Julia has filled the loft with new things. At first she feels guilty for spending so much of her Vicky Valentine royalties on decorating an apartment that isn't even hers. But the more she buys, the more right it feels. She has bought and hung prints—Warhol's "Marilyn," a chubby Botero orchestra, a Georgia O'Keeffe flower. She has added a coffee table, a desk, bookshelves. Every day she goes out shopping for something else. She goes to flea markets and buys odd pieces of Fiesta Ware—platters, cups, bowls. When she returns to the apartment, she is always amazed. She walks around it, touching each item.

The bed has blue and pink striped sheets and a quilt of the Manhattan skyline. She has a Krups coffee maker, a toaster oven, a juicer, all lined up on the counter. She put a round, boldfaced clock on the kitchen wall. She has throw rugs scattered across the tiled floor—geometric designs and fat red roses.

Julia invites Katherine and Lucy over for a post-Christmas get-together. She buys forged iron candlesticks and twisted red and green candles, striped like candy canes. She buys coasters and a coatrack and a lazy Susan. On the big windows, she stencils stars and a slice of a moon in gold.

When they come in, they gasp. Her home is that beautiful.

Katherine is holding a loaf of cranberry bread. Her nose is very red from the cold, her hair shiny with snow.

"This is great," Katherine says, looking around.

"Who lives here anyway?" Lucy says.

Julia laughs. "I do," she says. "Who do you think? Santa Claus?" She takes their coats and hangs them on the new coatrack, letting her fingers pause to rub the smooth wood.

"No," Lucy says, "I mean who really lives here?"

Although she knows it shouldn't, the question jars her. Julia says, "I . . . I don't know."

Lucy is watching her face too carefully.

"Well," Katherine says, smoothing the pleats of her forest green wool skirt, "whoever they are, they have good taste."

Julia smiles weakly. "Yeah," she says.

It is Lucy who changes the subject. She has just been to Bethlehem and Jerusalem and she has brought postcards in lieu of pictures to show them. "A Whirlwind Week is the worst," she tells them.

Julia brings out her new hammered silver ice bucket and a bottle of wine. She has filled the lazy Susan with nuts and bought antique nutcrackers and nutpicks.

Katherine says, "Everything looks so nice, Julia."

Again, she is aware of Lucy watching her closely, so she shrugs off the compliment and starts to ask questions about the trip.

It's Katherine who asks the real question. "How are things without Jasper?" she says.

Lucy smiles falsely. "Just fine."

"Liar," Julia says.

"No," Katherine says quickly. "It's like Andy and me. When it's time to break up, you know."

Lucy shakes her head. "No," she says. "I am lying. It's awful. And he hasn't called or anything."

"Andy calls me all the time," Katherine says. "I wish he wouldn't."

"Why don't you call him?" Julia asks Lucy.

But Lucy shakes her head again.

Katherine says, in her best schoolteacher's voice, "Let's pretend we can have any man in the world. Who would you choose?"

Lucy groans. "You and your sorority games." She turns toward

Julia, who is cracking walnuts. "This is what we did in college. Night after night. We talked about men. Their penises. Their smells. Every word they said. It was so unhealthy."

"You did it too," Katherine says. Her face has crumpled slightly with hurt.

"But I hated it," Lucy says.

Katherine focuses on the hard shell of a hazelnut. Somewhere in the building, someone is playing "Heart and Soul," slow and clumsy, on the piano.

"I'm sorry," Lucy says, although there is not even a hint of apology in her voice. "That's how I feel."

Katherine looks up. "You used to draw that comic strip for the school paper. Lucinda Luckinbill."

"Who?" Julia says.

"Lucinda Luckinbill," Katherine repeats. Her face has relaxed again.

Julia notices for the first time that Katherine's smile is a little lopsided. It makes her seem more real, that smile.

She's saying, "She was sort of like 'Cathy.' Someone everybody could relate to. I remember this one, right before finals, Lucinda Luckinbill is like falling asleep at her desk. And she's saying stuff like, 'I must finish this paper. I must.' And she's slapping herself in the face. Then she goes for a cup of coffee and spends all night gabbing with her girlfriends wide-awake."

"My claim to fame," Lucy says. She is smiling now too.

"Lucinda Luckinbill was great," Katherine says, still remembering.

Lucy thinks a minute and says, "I'd choose Jasper. My old Jasper."

"I thought you'd choose Nathaniel Jones," Julia says.

"Ugh," Lucy says. But she blushes as she says it.

"I think you're hiding something from me," Julia tells her.

Katherine is caught up in the game already. "I would choose someone I haven't met yet. He's handsome and kind and funny and exciting."

"He rides a white horse and wears shining armor too, I bet," Julia says.

"No," Lucy says. "He's make-believe. He goes out with people like Cinderella and Snow White."

Katherine stiffens. "Ha-ha."

For a while they go back to Lucy's pictures and she tells them more about her trip.

But then Julia says, "What else are you hiding from me?"

"What do you mean?" Lucy says. She avoids Julia's eyes.

"I think something happened between you and Mr. Jones."

Katherine wrinkles her nose. "Isn't he really creepy though?"

"He's not creepy," Lucy says, gathering up the postcards. "And nothing happened."

"Uh-huh," Julia says.

Katherine gets excited. "Ooooh," she says. "This is like Truth or Dare."

"Please," Lucy groans.

Katherine turns her attention on Julia. "In Truth or Dare, we get to each ask a question and the person has to tell the truth or take a dare."

Lucy stands up as if she might leave. "It is a stupid game. 'How many times did you have sex with that Phi Sigma Kappa?' 'Have you ever given a blow job?' And if you won't answer, you have to run outside in your underwear or eat cat food or something."

"It's fun," Katherine insists.

Julia pulls Lucy back onto the couch. "Truth or Dare," she says. "Did you have sex with Nathaniel Jones?"

"The man has never even touched me," Lucy says.

Katherine looks at Lucy and says, "My turn. Why don't you like me anymore?"

"I like you."

But Katherine shakes her head.

"This is ridiculous," Lucy says.

"We used to be so close, though," Katherine adds softly.

Lucy stands again. "This is not how I want to spend my evening."

"It's a fair question," Katherine mutters.

"How's this?" Lucy says. "You don't know me. That's all. I hate that my whole life I always pretended to be someone else just to have friends. I'm embarrassed by that. And it wasn't until I moved here and made new friends and had my own life that I realized how embarrassed I was. Then you show up with your cookies and cakes and false sisterly love and I don't want it. Are you happy now?"

Katherine is staring, wide-eyed. "No," she says.

Lucy pulls her coat on roughly. "And you want to play this game so bad, Miss Vicky Valentine, why don't you start telling the truth?"

Julia has moved toward her friend, to stop her from leaving, but now she stops. "I told you the truth about that," she says.

Katherine says, "Lucy, where are you going?"

"Home. So I don't have to run around Tribeca in my underwear."

"Running around," Julia says. "It's more like running away."

Katherine nods. "Here I go," she says, holding up three fingers like a Girl Scout about to take an oath. "The truth. I'm afraid what I really want, more than anything, is to be a doctor's wife and live in Newton, Massachusetts. To drive a Volvo and have four children and a golden retriever. But I'm afraid that I shouldn't want that. That it's wrong somehow to want that."

Lucy laughs. "I don't want to bare my soul here, guys. Sorry."

It is Julia who takes Lucy's arm, feels her stiffen under her touch. "I know you miss Jasper."

But Lucy shakes her head. "Aren't I supposed to end up with a successful guy?"

"Like Nathaniel Jones?" Julia says. "Ha!"

Again Lucy says, "I don't want to do this."

The three of them stand in an awkward silence, Julia still gripping Lucy's arm, as if to hold her there in place.

When Katherine speaks, her voice sounds very small. "God," she says. "Do you really feel about me the same way I feel about Meryl? Tell me I'm not that bad."

Julia feels Lucy relax finally.

"You're not that bad," Lucy says.

The entire apartment seems to sigh in relief.

Julia says, "What do you say we go out dancing? Celebrate the holidays right."

Katherine looks down at her wool skirt, her cable-knit sweater, and wrinkles her nose. "I'm not dressed for a club."

"Sure you are," Julia says, laughing. "You're dressed like a suburban housewife."

"Where to?" Lucy asks her, as Julia wraps a leopard-pattern scarf around her neck.

"The truth?" Julia says. "This guy I like is playing in a band tonight in the Village."

"Barry?" Lucy says, surprised.

"No."

Katherine narrows her eyes. She buttons her camel hair coat slowly, ties her red plaid scarf. "Let me look into your future," she says. "This man is exotic. He is handsome. I see him riding. No! Pedaling a bicycle."

Julia doesn't say anything at first. She thinks over what Katherine says, can make no sense of her guess about On. Suddenly, it doesn't matter. "Not bad," she says.

She holds the door open for Lucy and Katherine to pass.

"You like a man on a bike?" Lucy is saying. "What is he? A messenger?"

Julia slips the keys into the locks. "He's a musician," she says. "Primarily."

She feels Katherine still watching her, waiting.

"Since I don't want to run around in my underwear either," Julia says, "he also works for his uncle. Delivering Chinese food." She hesitates, then adds, "And I'm absolutely nuts about him."

The nightclub is smoky, filled mostly with NYU students drinking neon blue drinks in tall glasses. Julia chooses a table in the back, unsure if she really wants to have On see her. His band is already playing a set of songs by the Rolling Stones and the Beatles, and couples fill the dance floor, shaking and doing the twist.

149

"Which one?" Lucy whispers.

"The drummer," Julia tells her. She keeps her eyes on him. There isn't the usual disappointment that comes after not seeing someone for a while. He hasn't turned more handsome in her imagination. Instead, here in the flesh, he is exactly as she remembers him. All the nights she felt him with her, all the time with Timothy that she felt On watching, he is just the same here in front of her.

"Cute," Lucy whispers.

Julia nods.

Katherine is smiling at her, saying how much she loves these old songs. "This is great," she says.

Something in Julia tells her to leave before On spots her. It is the thing that always enables her to walk away. Her foreign lovers, she knows, are just another way to keep herself from getting too involved. It is, Julia decides, easier to leave strangers, and odd apartments, than to face things, to put herself on the line.

That thing inside her is saying, "Leave. Leave." She imagines walking out of here and going to a bar somewhere to find a man who cannot understand her. A man from someplace very far away. A man whose eyes will not haunt her.

She halfway stands, as if to go. The band starts a slow song. It is something Julia imagines teenagers at a high school prom might slow-dance to. She can't place the song, but it keeps her there, holding the sticky edge of the table. Underneath her fingertips she feels initials someone has carved there. The song, the rough letters, all make her strangely blue. They make her feel that she has lost something. Something she can't identify.

On the dance floor, couples are swaying, their arms around each other's waists and necks. Suddenly Julia remembers the song that's playing. It's "Color My World." At Friday night school dances it was always the last song played, the one where couples danced too close, holding on to each other for dear life. The song that Julia always heard from the ladies' room down the hall, where she hid until the last dance was over and everyone started to leave. Now without her noticing, Katherine has asked someone to dance. She is out there, smiling up at a stranger in a gray pin-striped suit.

Lucy is saying, "Does this guy know what he's in for? Two point five children. A woman who likes to bake."

Julia thinks about hiding in the ladies' room now, but she knows she will stay right here instead. That after this set, she will approach the band, and call to On. Later, she will tell him the truth. She will tell him that she has never even been to L.A., ever. She will tell him that she is afraid of things like love, and secrets told.

Now she swallows hard as the song draws to a close. She feels both frightened and daring. Julia sits back down, slowly, but she doesn't let go of the table. Instead, her fingers clutch the letters she cannot see, and her heart beats hard and fast against her ribs.

Bedford and barrow

❧

"That guy Spencer is so weird," Katherine tells Lucy over leftover Christmas cookies and eggnog in Meryl King's apartment. That is how Katherine still thinks of the place where she lives—Meryl's apartment.

"Why do you keep hanging around with him then?" Lucy says.

"I don't know," Katherine says. "He tries so hard."

The cookies are shortbread ones, cut into the shape of stars. Lucy breaks off each of the five points before she eats one.

"Anyway," Katherine says, "for the holiday talent show, what do you think he did?"

Lucy shrugs.

"Imitated Elvis," Katherine says, laughing. "What else?"

Lucy laughs too. "Is he for real?"

"He lip-synched 'I Ain't Nothing But a Hound Dog,'" she continues. "Complete with rotating hips." Katherine jumps to her feet and imitates Spencer imitating Elvis.

Lucy is laughing hard now. "Stop," she says.

"It's like he's possessed by Elvis's spirit or something. I swear, he would name his son Elvis."

Lucy groans. "What was your talent?"

Katherine hesitates. In college, she had been a Ramette, part of a synchronized dance team that wore short skirts and go-go boots and danced on the football field at halftime. Lucy used to make fun of her uniform, of all the practicing it took to learn the steps and choreograph new ones.

As if she has read Katherine's mind, Lucy says, "Don't tell me."

"I didn't pull out the uniform," Katherine says. She wants to be able to laugh at herself. But she had loved being a Ramette. She used to love the way the cold autumn air felt on her bare legs as she danced, the way the sparkling blue fringe on the vest swayed when she moved. She liked being a part of something.

When she danced to the theme from *Rocky* for the school talent show, remembering all the right steps and doing it again had made her feel good. It had made her think back to the way she used to search the stands for Andy and his friends. It used to seem that his face might burst when he watched her, his pride was that evident.

Lucy is gentler with her than Katherine expects. "Well," she says, "if that's your talent."

Katherine frowns, unsure if Lucy has meant to put her down again. "Remember how nervous I was when I tried out?" she asks her.

But Lucy waves off the question. "Not more nostalgia for the good old days. Please."

"They weren't that bad, were they?" Katherine asks, really hoping for Lucy to say something good about their time together then.

But Lucy doesn't. "I like the present a lot better," she says.

Katherine wonders how her memories can be so much warmer, so much better than her friend's. She looks at Lucy, carefully breaking apart another star, and wonders what it is she sees when she remembers.

These are the things that Katherine used to know: that she loved Andy more than anything in the world; that she would teach first-graders the wonders of spelling their names, of opening a book and recognizing what was written there, of knowing that $1 + 1 = 2$; that the world—her world—was a safe and good one; that she could make a perfect soufflé, coq au vin, vegetarian lasagna; that she would have children and a house with quilts on the beds and fireplaces and shelves of good books.

Now, Katherine knew none of these things any longer. She is thirty years old and sleeps on a pull-out sofabed in someone else's apartment. She dates men who don't know her, who don't even take the time to know her, who talk about investment banking and the price of co-ops and summer shares in the Hamptons until she gets dizzy and asks to go home. Her six-year-old students give her subway information, tell her she should carry an extra twenty dollars to give to a mugger if she gets held up, and ask her for detailed descriptions of lambs, bats, and cows.

She feels she knows nothing. At night, she talks to Andy on the telephone, his voice sounding unreasonably close, like he is on the couch beside her. He tells her about his patients, the ones with gangrene, with AIDS, with burns. He tells her he took another resident to the hospital Christmas party, a woman named Shelly from Long Island who is an ophthalmologist. He doesn't tell Katherine he loves her anymore. He has stopped asking her to come home.

"Do you like this woman?" Katherine asks him. "This Shelly?"

"Sure," he says casually. "I like her."

"Good," Katherine lies. "That's good."

More and more, her reasons for being here are blurring. She tries to recall those months of sleepless nights but they seem small and distant. She tries to remember why she lay on her back like Michelangelo and wrote all those lyrics on her bedroom ceiling. But that too seems insignificant. Instead, she remembers Andy's face at football games when she danced. She thinks of the way he hid her engagement ring at the bottom of a champagne glass to surprise her. She relives their long drives on back roads in Vermont, buying old tables and chairs and bureaus to refinish and put in their home someday.

"Where is our furniture?" she asks Andy one night.

"What furniture?"

"Our antiques," she says. "All the things we collected together."

He pauses. "Shelly's helping me fix them up. She's real good at design."

Katherine feels a lump swell in her throat. She is afraid she will not be able to get the words out. "Design?" she says in a choked voice. "What's there to design? They just need to be stripped and refinished."

Andy pauses again. "Shelly thought—"

"Those are my chairs!" Katherine says, nearly shouting. "I picked out that table with the funny legs."

Meryl sticks her head into the living room. She is wearing a flannel nightgown littered with yellow rosettes. Her face is shiny from a night moisturizer and there are smears of mascara under her eyes. She has orange juice cans in her hair. She uses them as curlers.

"You all right?" she asks Katherine.

Katherine nods at her. When Meryl disappears into her bedroom again, Katherine says in a hushed voice, "I'm the one who loved that old rocking chair. The one we got in Maine."

Andy sighs. "I know," he says.

"When I get my own apartment, I'll want some of those things, you know. I'll want you to send them to me."

"I know," he says again.

Spencer says, "This is a big surprise."

Katherine smiles weakly. She tries to get up some enthusiasm for her post-Christmas date with Spencer. But all she can think about is how silly he looked imitating Elvis.

"I can't wait," she tells him.

They walk downtown from school toward the Village. Spencer is so excited that he is bouncing slightly as he walks, like a stuck jack-in-the-box.

Katherine says, "Andy has a new girlfriend. And she's painting all of our antique furniture."

Spencer nods.

"Her name is Shelly," Katherine says. Then she adds, "She's an ophthalmologist."

Spencer brightens. "That's one of the most commonly misspelled words," he says. "Everyone forgets there's an H after the P. Oph."

"How can it be one of the most commonly misspelled words?" Katherine says. "Who ever spells the damn thing?"

Spencer stops walking. "Ooooh," he tells her. "You're jealous."

155

"Of an ophthalmologist?" she laughs. "Hardly."

"Uh-huh."

"I just don't want to see all that good furniture ruined." She starts to head down Seventh Avenue again, walking faster so that Spencer has to hurry to keep up.

"Prerogative is another one," he says, grabbing her elbow.

"Prerogative."

"A lot of people spell it P-E-R instead of P-R-E."

"Fascinating," Katherine mumbles.

"Like, it's a woman's prerogative to change her mind and not get married to someone she doesn't want to marry," he says.

"Uh-huh," Katherine says.

Spencer starts bouncing along beside her again. "That's what I like about fifth-graders," he says. "Improving their spelling and vocabulary. I'm real tough on them when it comes to spelling."

Katherine glances over at him. His face is relaxed and happy. She softens a little. Spencer is a teacher like her. They share the same joy in giving children knowledge. That is, after all, something special between them. She tries not to think about how Andy and Shelly are both doctors.

"It starts with you," Spencer is saying. "Right in first grade good spelling habits begin."

When he tries to take her arm in his, Katherine lets him.

"Here we are!" Spencer announces.

He points upward.

Katherine stares into the sky. It is a gray December late afternoon, the sky full of clouds, the moon a smudge of white.

"What?" Katherine says.

Spencer stands on tiptoe to reach her face, then slants it downward slightly. "There," he says. He holds her chin in his gloved hands.

She sees it then. They are on the corner of Bedford and Barrow.

"Our names intersect," Spencer says. He is grinning as if he is responsible for this juncture. "Katherine Bedford. Spencer Barrow."

Katherine nods. "That's really something," she says.

Spencer starts to bounce across the street. "Chumley's," he says. "We'll eat here, on our corner. This will be our place from now on."

Katherine does not know why she does it, but she does. Later, she blames it on too much red wine, the warmth of the restaurant, the shepherd's pie and Spencer's face softened in the dim light. But after they eat, even though it is late, when Spencer asks her to go back to his apartment in Queens with him, Katherine goes. On the E train, their two gloved hands hold each other. They stare straight ahead and don't speak until they are in his apartment.

He pours them each a glass of brandy.

He lights candles and puts on a jazz album.

"Miles Davis," he tells her.

Katherine nods. She has not slept with anyone except Andy in her whole life. This is not something she has ever told anyone. She even sometimes pretends that she's had a few flings, one on a cruise she took with her sister, one in Greece the summer after she graduated from college. If she were to choose a different lover, she would not choose Spencer. He is too short. His clothes don't really match. His manners are poor.

But here she is on a sofa somewhere in Queens, letting Spencer undress her, letting him touch her. Her mind races. She thinks of all the men she has dated since she came to New York. Handsome ones. Successful ones. But she has not let them do what she is letting Spencer do to her. And she feels oddly detached from the action, the way she feels when she thinks back to college and it appears in her mind like a home movie.

She watches in that way as his mouth circles her breasts, as he undresses himself and leads her down the hallway to his bedroom. She registers his naked body as if from a distance, as if she can't smell his carefully splashed Aramis, as if she cannot see his surprisingly compact body, his strong arms and flat stomach. She knows he plays racquetball before school every morning and guesses that accounts for his good muscle tone. On the outside, Spencer looks like the guy who gets sand kicked in his face by the bully, but underneath, Katherine notes, he is well-built, almost sexy. But still all of it seems like it's happening to someone else.

When it's over, Katherine starts to sob. She feels all wrong suddenly. She has kept this act private, as something between Andy and her. Now she is with a man who reveres Elvis Presley, and she imagines that Andy is in bed in Boston with an ophthalmologist.

Spencer, looking dreamy and satisfied, pats her back as if he's trying to burp her. "I know," he whispers. "I know."

In the morning, Katherine wakes up to the feeling of Spencer's mouth settling between her legs. She feels herself stiffen. She and Andy did not do this. He used to beg her to take him in her mouth, but she thought it was too disgusting. "But everyone does it," he told her. "You pee out of there," she said. "No way."

Katherine tries to lift Spencer's head, to pull it away, but he is persistent. She thinks about too many things—how she must smell and taste, why she didn't shave her legs yesterday—until somewhere in her center she goes completely soft. Her mind goes blank. She hears heavy breathing and doesn't realize for an instant that it is her own.

When Spencer finally does move, and slides into her, Katherine feels as if she is starting to fall, the way she feels sometimes in dreams when she is on a cliff or stairway, beginning to lose her footing.

She manages to start to say something about it to Spencer, to warn him, but then it's too late and she is lost in that feeling.

When she catches her breath, she opens her eyes and sees Spencer, still on top of her, watching her closely.

"I've never . . ." she begins. She remembers how she used to ask Lucy to describe an orgasm to her and Lucy telling her it was impossible to describe. "But I don't know if I've ever had one," Katherine told her. Lucy used to laugh. "When you have one, you'll know. You won't have to ask me."

"Never?" Spencer says.

She shakes her head.

"Really?"

"Don't go getting a swollen head," she tells him. She is waiting for her mind to clear, for her energy to come back.

He is smiling at her like crazy. She sees a bit of bread caught in his teeth. Katherine cannot believe what has happened, what is happening. She sits up quickly. She wants to leave, but can't think where to go. She can't face Meryl right now. And Lucy is on a Whirlwind Weekend. She feels lost.

Spencer is gently pushing her back down onto the bed.

"I'll make you breakfast," he whispers. "Stay here."

She turns her head from his nakedness as he pads out of the room. Outside the window, fat snowflakes are falling, all slow and lazy. Katherine pulls the sheets and blankets around her tightly, and tries to figure it all out.

Snugglys

Sometimes Lucy wakes up in the middle of the night and thinks, Even if I walk out of my apartment right now and meet someone, I wouldn't marry him for a couple of years. It would be another couple of years before we had a child. The numbers begin to click off in her mind, the years add up and she realizes that would make her thirty-five years old. *If* she meets someone today, when she walks out the door.

Lucy wishes she had been born ten years earlier or ten years later. Either way, things would have been simpler. She would have fallen in love and gotten married without all the questions that fill her now. Or she would have been more sure of her place in the world and tried to have it all. As it is, she's caught somewhere between those two places. She feels she has missed out. There is no certainty for her. She wonders how Katherine, embarrassed as she is by her admission, knows what she wants. She wonders how Julia gets along without these questions plaguing her.

It's three A.M. and Lucy has looked into a fictional crystal ball once again. There she is, the only gray-haired mother at the kindergarten PTA. Or with her young daughter being mistaken for her granddaughter. Or worse, there she is in this very spot five years from now, still calculating what will happen if she walks out the door and falls in love.

That is when she calls Jasper. She doesn't even think about it. She just picks up the phone and dials his number, her fingers banging out the familiar beeps and tones by memory.

Even though it's the middle of the night, Jasper's voice sounds wide-awake. He is still a night owl, Lucy thinks. She remembers how he would pad around the apartment long after she'd fall asleep. She used to hear him eating in the kitchen, or the sounds of late night television coming from the living room.

Lucy thinks all this when she hears his voice, so that is just what she says.

"Still up and around while the rest of the city sleeps," she says. She tries to make her voice sound lighter than she feels.

There is a loud silence before Jasper speaks. "Lucy," he says. His voice cracks.

"I thought you might want to have some breakfast," she says, thinking of the idea just then.

"Okay," Jasper says quickly. "The place on your corner?"

"Okay." Her hands are trembling as she hangs up the phone.

Lucy's mother is a walking dictionary of clichés, and right now she would be saying this one: "You can't teach an old dog new tricks, Lucy." Lucy thinks that too. In the past, she has given that same advice to friends who return to old lovers who drank too much, or had affairs. "You'd be crazy to go back with them," she has said.

As she dresses, she tries to figure out what it is about Jasper that needs changing. He needs to communicate with her, she decides. He needs to dance. No. He needs to get that fire back in his eyes. There is a feeling in her that is bigger than logic. It is telling her that she and Jasper are meant for each other. It is saying that when she walks out the door, the man she will meet will be the right one after all.

·   ·

Although he has come from uptown to see her, he has arrived first. When Lucy walks in, there he is, sipping coffee, frowning, waiting.

"Hi," she says. She can't stop smiling. That other part of her has her almost convinced that Jasper is back to his old self.

When he raises his eyes to her, they are sad. They break her heart.

"What?" she asks him. "What?"

"I feel like I'm split in two," he says. "I feel like I've lost my arms or my legs. My heart."

"Me too," she says. She slides beside him in the booth. "But it'll be different now," she tells him. "You'll see."

Jasper shakes his head. "What if it isn't?"

"It has to be," Lucy says.

He sits there, looking into his coffee cup, and shaking his head.

"Don't you think we can make it better?" she asks him. She thinks of all his cures. Turkey for jet lag. Sea salt baths for tired feet.

He doesn't answer her.

"Come on," she says. "Talk to me."

But he doesn't.

Lucy sinks back against the booth. She is suddenly very tired. So tired that she thinks she could rest her head here on the shiny blue Formica table and sleep, despite the fluorescent diner lights, the crashing of plates and cups against saucers, despite the sinking feeling that is enveloping her.

Instead, she stands, her legs all shaky, and she says, "If you think of a way to fix this, let me know."

He smiles up at her. "I could make you a turkey," he says.

She has not even taken her coat off yet. Her fingers tug on the big black buttons. "Does that cure broken hearts?" she asks him.

"It's worth a try," he says.

"Call me when you want to try it then," she says.

He nods. He watches her walk away. Lucy wants him to jump up and come running after her. She wants a movie ending to this. Jasper wet from rain, coming to her, fixing it all. She wants love to win out. At the corner she stops. She waits for the door to open, for him to come out to her. She waits and waits but he doesn't appear. As she walks back to her apartment, a group of laughing teenagers pass her. A man walking his dog smiles at her. But Lucy feels like she is the only person in the world.

Lucy is from a small town in western Massachusetts. The town is rimmed with mountains and factories. When she goes back there, everyone complains about developers moving in and cutting down trees. They talk about night shifts and layoffs, Nintendo and sitcoms. Sometimes she feels like she has arrived here from outer space. She does not even speak the same language as her relatives anymore.

She doesn't go back often. But lately, Lucy has felt a great need to get away from the city, from the street corners and restaurants that remind her of Jasper. So she accepts an invitation to her cousin Jackie's baby shower, for no other reason than to hide from her hurt.

Her parents' house is in the middle of a development of nearly identical homes built in the late fifties. The lawns are scattered with ornaments—badly painted elves or smiling plaster rabbits. There are small flower gardens with wooden decorations of Pilgrims who churn butter when the wind blows. To Lucy, it all seems so busy. The fake kittens climbing the side of a house, the hedges cut into geometric shapes, the mailbox that looks like a barn door. She supposes it is a way to claim their individuality in a neighborhood of small square ranch houses. But it all makes her dizzy and she is relieved when she arrives in her rented car at her parents' own moss green and brick house.

The living room is already filled with people—relatives and friends. There is a fire blazing in the fireplace, and a folding table set up with cold cuts and breads, store-bought potato salad and coleslaw. These are the parties that Lucy grew up with, and the familiarity of it makes her glad to be here, in the middle of the Berkshires on a cold March Sunday afternoon.

Jackie sits in the center of everyone, round and swollen, dressed in a horizontally striped dress that makes her look even larger.

"I can't get up too easy," she laughs.

So Lucy goes to her cousin and hugs her. Jackie is five years younger than Lucy, and in Lucy's memory she is a chubby little girl with a pixie cut, always trying to play with the older girls.

Everyone starts to talk to Lucy at once. "Where's your boyfriend?" they ask. "When are we going to dance at your wedding?"

She finds her mother in the crowd and smiles over at her.

"Lucy wants a career," her mother says. She tries to sound proud, but everyone knows she isn't. Of the cousins her age, Lucy is the only one not married. The others, all here today, have two, three, even four children already. They own houses just like this one. They eat dinner with their parents every Sunday, and rent houses on the lake for the summer.

"Big city girl," someone mumbles.

Lucy knows how to avoid this. She turns to Jackie. "How do you feel?" she asks her.

Jackie rolls her eyes. There is nothing of the little girl Lucy remembers in this woman.

The other women laugh.

"You'll know soon enough," her Aunt Rhoda says.

Paula, Jackie's older sister, says, "Not if she doesn't hurry up. Lucy's the same age as me. It's almost too late to start a family now."

Paula rubs her own pregnant belly. Lucy has lost track, but knows Paula already has a few children. She has been married for as long as Lucy has lived in New York.

"Don't make Lucy feel bad," Aunt Rhoda says. "Your Great-aunt Tess never had children."

"She couldn't though," someone says.

Lucy swallows hard. "So, when are you due?"

"Two weeks," Jackie says. "Thank God."

This time it works. Everyone launches into their own stories of childbirth. Late babies, forceps babies, C-sections, preemies. Lucy steps back. Coming here was wrong, she thinks, watching them. She counts four more pregnant women her own age. These are the same people who, as children, she tried to be like. The ones she wanted as friends. This could have been her baby shower. She could be sitting here, happy, not worrying about illustrating children's books, or trying to figure out what lies ahead. But instead, knowing exactly what comes next.

Her mother comes over to her, with a pale blue paper plate heaped with food.

"She knows it's a boy," her mother says. "They have this test now. Jackie told me all about it. They made her drink a lot of water, then before she peed they took an X ray of her stomach—"

"A sonogram," Lucy says.

Her mother looks at her, surprised. "She told you about it?"

"Everybody has them," she says. She doesn't add that she had one herself for an ovarian cyst scare a few years back. In this room, sonograms are unusual. Abortions are not mentioned. The women here could be from another generation.

"She showed me the picture," her mother says. She laughs. "It's a boy all right."

Lucy nods.

Her mother pats her shoulder. "It's not too late for you," she says.

"Ma," Lucy says, "women today have babies into their forties. I've got a long way to go before it's too late."

"Forties?" Her mother laughs again. "You watch too much *Donahue*. All those women starting families when they're old."

"I didn't see it on *Donahue*," Lucy mumbles.

Aunt Rhoda has joined them, and is nodding her head with great enthusiasm. "I saw that one," she says. "That one woman, the one with the dyed blond hair? Had her first baby when she was forty-four and her second when she was forty-six. Crazy."

Aunt Rhoda is wearing a bright blue polyester dress that is shiny and ruffled. Lucy supposes she is wearing blue in honor of this baby boy.

"And that lady who said people who have babies young are making a mistake?" Aunt Rhoda is saying.

Lucy's mother says, "She was the one wearing blue jeans, right? Can you imagine? Wearing jeans on *Donahue*?"

Lucy walks away from them. She circles the crowded living room. Nothing in it has changed since she was a child. The aqua Danish furniture is the same, the bleached wood end tables, the lampshades with racing covered wagons. Above the fireplace are her mother's Lladro statues, expensive porcelain cased in glass. Lucy buys them for her in Europe. She knows that every Saturday her mother opens the case and dusts each figurine carefully. The little girl with a basket of kittens. The bride and groom. The three nuns. The geese.

"We're still fighting about it," Jackie is saying. "I want Justin James and Jimmy wants Jeremy Justin."

"All J's," another pregnant woman whom Lucy doesn't recognize says. "That's cute."

Lucy wanders the hallway. She peeks into the bathroom. Her mother has hung out the mauve monogrammed towels that she uses for company. She passes her brother Keith's room and goes inside. It is the room of a teenager—posters of scantily clad women hang beside pictures of Ted Williams and Yaz. She sits on his twin bed. The brown corduroy spread is wearing thin. Keith went to Georgetown for college and never came back to Massachusetts again, except for Christmases. Now, he lives in St. Louis and works for Budweiser. He sends Lucy short notes on postcards of Clydesdale horses. For her birthday he sends her a case of Bud Light.

She supposes her mother feels odd here too. The only one whose children have left town and moved to cities, who haven't married or given her grandchildren. Her mother smiles when people ask her about that. She makes excuses. But Lucy knows she wishes it were different.

Her mother pokes her head in the doorway. Her hair is still brown. None of the women her age are gray. They go to the beauty parlor once a week to have their hair washed and dyed, set and sprayed.

"What are you doing in here?" she asks.

The rules are you stay in the party room. Lucy knows that. She knows too that this embarrasses her mother.

"Rhoda thinks you're upset," her mother adds.

"I just drove three and a half hours," Lucy says. "I need a rest."

"Now?"

Lucy sighs. "I'll go back in there."

Her mother's face relaxes. It is smooth and unlined, an attribute she credits to Oil of Olay. She used to write to them, hoping she'd be in one of their ads. But all she got were notes of thanks and coupons for discounts on the product.

Thinking of this, and of her mother spending Saturday mornings dusting those figurines, touches Lucy and she gets up and hugs her.

"How are things with Jasper?" her mother asks her.

"They're not," Lucy says.

Her mother nods. "I know you're upset, Lu, but it's for the best. You need a man who can take care of you."

Lucy sighs. "I can take care of myself."

"That's not right," her mother says sadly. "Look how Daddy takes care of me. That's what you need."

"Come on," Lucy says. "Let's go back to the party."

"What did you get her?"

"A Snuggly. Like you told me."

Her mother squeezes her waist. "Good girl," she says.

Lucy is asleep, surrounded by her childhood dolls and stuffed animals, when her mother comes into her room the next morning.

"Honey," her mother says, shaking her arm lightly. "There's a man on the phone for you. He sounds very important."

Lucy opens her eyes and struggles to orient herself. There is the *Gone With the Wind* poster of Clark Gable staring into Vivien Leigh's eyes while Atlanta burns behind them. There is the bureau top covered with old cosmetics and atomizers. The bookshelf lined with adolescent books—*Joy in the Morning, Marjorie Morningstar, Mr. and Mrs. Bojo Jones*. And there is her mother leaning over her, dressed in a quilted pink bathrobe, a curl on either side of her face held down with hair tape.

"Mom," Lucy says, sitting up. "What?"

Her mother shrugs. "Some man needs to talk to you."

Lucy gets out of bed and her mother's eyes widen. "No pajamas? No nothing?"

167

Lucy frowns and reaches for her old worn terry-cloth robe.

"We will go to Pittsfield today and get you a nightgown, young lady," her mother says.

"I don't want to go to Pittsfield," Lucy says, following her mother to the telephone.

It is an old black rotary dial phone, and Lucy is surprised by its weight, how heavy it feels in her hand. When she was younger, they had a party line, and she would pick up this phone and listen in on strangers' conversations.

"Hello?" she says.

"Hey, doll," Nathaniel Jones says. "Four-one-three? You're right down the Mass Pike from me and you don't let me know? I have to hear it on your answering machine?"

Lucy shrugs as if he can see her.

"How about I drive there and we go to dinner? You ever been to Wheatleigh's? It's amazing."

"No," Lucy says. "I'm here visiting."

"I can be there in no time," Nathaniel says.

"I don't think so," she says.

Her mother is standing in the doorway, watching. Lucy turns away from her. There is light blue confetti on the rug, like icing on a birthday cake.

"You have to celebrate," he says.

"I do?"

"Inside scoop, babe. *My Dolly* sold to Calico. They want you to do clothes. A boy version. A sister. Coloring books. The works. Your agent will call you on Monday."

Lucy feels her heart pick up, start to race slightly. "Are you sure?"

Nathaniel laughs. "What do you think?"

"I don't believe it," she says. Her voice barely comes out.

"Don't faint on me, babe." He is laughing softly.

Nathaniel Jones, Lucy thinks, has a very sexy laugh.

"I'm glad I got to tell you," he says. "I wish I could see your beautiful face right now."

Lucy touches her tangled hair, her old bathrobe, and smiles.

"So what do you say?" he asks her.

"Let's wait until I hear it officially," she says. "Then I promise we'll celebrate."

It's difficult to say no to Nathaniel Jones, but when Lucy finally manages to hang up, she turns to her mother again. Her father is there too, in a flannel shirt and stiff Levis. They are waiting.

"I think," she says slowly, "that I made it." Her mind is racing as fast as her heart now. No more Whirlwind Weekends, she thinks. No more unpaid MasterCard bills.

"What?" her mother says. "Was that Jasper? It didn't sound like Jasper."

"My Dolly," Lucy says.

"What?" her mother says again. "That drawing you did?"

Lucy takes a deep breath. "Wow," she says. "Wow."

Something old

෯

Meryl King has wonderful news for Katherine. She stands there, flushed and excited in her Italian suede pumps and Donna Karan outfit.

"Bianca is moving out!" Meryl practically screams. "She's going to live in Alaska!"

Katherine smiles, unsure of why this news is so great. "Alaska," she says. "Well."

Meryl leans toward her in a cloud of Carolina Herrera perfume. "Katherine, darling, sweetheart. This means you get her bedroom. All we have to do is find someone to take your place on the couch!"

Katherine feels her smile freeze. "Well," she says again.

"She says her move has nothing to do with those Alaska men who are always on TV looking for wives," Meryl says, lowering her voice as if Bianca could hear them, even though Bianca is not at home. "She says she went to this kind of psychic who takes a world map and draws these grids on it. Every person has a different reading, and certain points indicate bad environments and others are good environments. Bianca says New York came out her worst place to live. Along with Columbus, Ohio, and Leningrad. Alaska is numero uno."

"That's amazing," Katherine says.

Meryl tosses her head back and laughs. "She thinks I don't know she's been writing to one of those guys. I see the letters with the Alaska postmark. Can you imagine moving all the way to Alaska just to get married?"

Katherine sees something in Meryl's eyes. Something that tells her Meryl would indeed move to Alaska, or Columbus, or Leningrad, to get married.

"Maybe we should write to those men," Katherine says softly.

"Right," Meryl says.

Katherine walks over to Bianca's room and looks inside. It's a small room, a room that Bianca refers to as her space. Now, Katherine thinks, this will be her space. She shivers.

"Remember Leslie Walker?" Meryl is saying. "Her little sister Laurie is moving to New York in the spring. She pledged after we graduated. Plus, she's a nurse and will probably work weekends and stuff, which is great."

Katherine nods, not really listening. Bianca has painted the room a muddy lilac. She has also painted a rainbow on the closet door.

Meryl peeks over her shoulder. "Remember our motto?"

"No."

Meryl slaps her on the back. "If you said that to one of the sisters when we were pledges, they'd have you doing push-ups on the lawn at Phi Sig."

"After the rain, the rainbow," Katherine says.

"I painted that rainbow on the closet door when I had this room," Meryl says proudly. "It made me feel less lonely."

"Do you think we can find someone else?" Katherine says, turning away from the room. "Someone besides Leslie Walker's sister?"

Meryl looks surprised. "Are you kidding?" she says.

Katherine tries to smile. She remembers Leslie Walker as one of the party girls. She used to get drunk and sleep in her car in parking lots of bars in town. Time to get the Walkman, people used to say on Sunday mornings, and a posse would go out to find her and bring her back. They used to tell her she had done crazy things like dance top-less on a tabletop or kiss someone nerdy. She always believed them too. Katherine tries to convince herself that a nurse wouldn't be that bad. She and Shannon aren't exactly alike. Sisters aren't always the same. But still, she doesn't want to live with Leslie Walker's sister.

171

"Leslie's married," Meryl is saying. "She lives in Pennsylvania. She married that bartender from Willows. Remember him?"

Katherine wants to go somewhere to hide from Meryl, but her bedroom is still the living room, and there is nowhere else to go.

Katherine has started to tell everyone how wonderful Spencer is. She brags about his cooking, about the sweet things he does to surprise her. She has even made him handsome. Somehow, this seems almost true to her. She is embarrassed that sex can make her see him so differently.

Lucy, however, keeps asking her about the other things.

"I thought he had no class," Lucy says, frowning. "I thought he worshiped Elvis Presley."

"He likes Elvis Presley," Katherine tells her. "Just like you like David Byrne."

Lucy doesn't buy any of it. And Katherine can almost read her mind—she thinks she will do anything just to have a boyfriend, to have someone to love. What bothers Katherine is her own fear that Lucy may be right.

At night, Katherine reminds herself of all the things that are wrong with Spencer. The things that used to make her cringe. The new things that should be bothering her now, like the way he refuses to talk about serious things. Or the way he still sends her off alone to the subway on mornings after she has stayed at his apartment. Or the fact that during Easter vacation, he is going to drive to Graceland. But none of it matters when they are alone and the lights are out. She wonders if Andy is experiencing things like this with Shelly, the ophthalmologist.

To everyone at PS 15, she and Spencer are an item. His class always giggles when they see her. In school, when she is bringing her first-graders inside from recess and she passes Spencer's class on its way out, Katherine blushes, thinking about what they do together. She tries to remember all the things that are wrong with him, to remind herself why he's all wrong for her. She sees his round boyish face.

Those dumb blue suede shoes that he wears more and more. But all she can think of is his mouth and tongue. Then the other things fade completely away.

Katherine dials Andy's number in Boston. He is living in an apartment in the North End. It's a renovated warehouse, with a glass elevator and a doorman. His apartment is a duplex, with a bath and a half. He can walk to Faneuil Hall, to the Aquarium, to the subway. Boston, he tells her, is heaven.

She has not been able to reach him for days. But finally, tonight, he answers.

"I was worried about you," Katherine tells him.

"Why?"

His voice is full of accusation. Katherine fills in the blanks. You weren't worried when you left me at the altar, he is thinking.

"Because I've been calling you for three days," she says.

"Oh. I was in Maine."

"Maine?" Katherine says.

"Ogunquit."

Katherine and Andy used to go there for romantic weekends. They had a routine—a bed and breakfast by the ocean, a special stretch of beach to walk on, a place for lobsters, a place for ice cream.

"It's always nice there in March," she says.

"Mmmmm," he says. "It is. Anyway, what can I do for you?"

"Did you. . . ." Katherine hesitates, tries to adjust her voice to a tone of mild curiosity. "Did you go there with Shelly?"

He doesn't hesitate. "Yes," he says.

"You took Shelly to our place?"

"Katherine," Andy says, sighing. "It's not 'our place' anymore."

"I guess not," she says. "Now it's yours and Shelly's."

He doesn't answer.

"Fine," she says finally. "I want some of the furniture. I'm moving into another room and there's nothing in it."

"I don't know—"

"And I need it before Easter," she continues, talking quickly now, "because I'm going to Memphis that week and I'd like to be settled before I leave." Her lie comes out easily. Hell, she thinks, maybe I will go with Spencer.

"Memphis?" he says.

"Yes."

"Tennessee?"

"Yes, Andy. Memphis, Tennessee."

Andy starts to laugh. "What are you going to do?" he says. "Visit Graceland?" He laughs even harder. "I'm sorry," he adds. "I'm just joking."

Katherine says, "Very funny."

Andy calls Katherine again the very next day from the hospital. She can hear the familiar sounds of doctors being paged, bells ringing, people rushing past. Those sounds used to be a big part of her life, and she strains to hear them better. She almost wants Andy to stop talking, so she can forget for a minute how different everything is now, but he is in a hurry.

"I'll bring the stuff next weekend," he says. "The sleigh bed, a bureau, and what else?"

She tries to think, but her mind feels muddled.

"One of the quilts," she says. "Any one."

"I'm going to rent a U-Haul," he tells her. "Shelly is picking stuff up at her parents' place on the Island so I'll drop your stuff off and then pick her stuff up."

Katherine says, "Shelly again?"

"If you think of anything else," he says.

She doesn't want to hang up. She hears him being paged, hears a loud beeping sound.

"That's me," he says. "Bye."

"Wait," Katherine says. But the connection is already broken.

• •

It is Friday night and she and Spencer are at Mama Rose's Italian Garden. Katherine picks at her veal Parmesan. The meat is too heavily breaded, the sauce too sweet, like bottled sauces.

"The food here isn't good," she tells Spencer. "Do you know that?"

"What's wrong with you?" he says. He leans back in his chair to get a better look at her.

"It's not me. It's the food here."

"We came here on our first date," Spencer says. His voice is quiet and firm, as if that is the only thing that matters.

Katherine doesn't look at him. She twirls some spaghetti around and around her fork. She thinks about Andy and their first date. They went to see a duo called Aztec Two Step in Edward's Auditorium in college. He smuggled a bottle of wine in a paper bag. She was so nervous, so excited, that she can't remember any of the songs the band sang. It was Andy who chose one of their songs to be played at their wedding.

Spencer pushes his chair closer to the table.

"Is this about Andy again?" he asks.

"This," Katherine says, "is about the quality of the food here." She pounds the table lightly. "At this restaurant."

He glances around. "Calm down," he says.

At noon tomorrow, Andy will appear at Katherine's apartment. He will have the things she asked for. She wonders if Shelly will wait for him in the rented U-Haul. Or if he will come alone. She wonders how he will look, what he will say when he sees her.

Spencer's face has fallen. He looks frightened, as if he is about to go into battle.

Katherine reaches over and takes his hand in hers. "Hey," she says. "Do you want some company when you go to Memphis?"

He doesn't seem to trust the question, to trust her.

"Why?"

"I've never been there. I've never been to the south at all," Katherine says. "Unless you count Florida."

"Would you like to see Graceland?" he asks.

Now he is softening, his face is open and eager. Katherine can't help thinking of a puppy, a cocker spaniel or golden retriever. She thinks too of Andy laughing on the telephone about this very thing. It is silly, she tells herself. Going to Graceland is silly.

But she tells Spencer, "Maybe."

Andy holds the American flag quilt in his hands. It is navy blue, with small flags patched haphazardly across it. When she sees him on her doorstep, holding something they bought together in Vermont last year, Katherine does not get all weak-kneed and weepy the way she had anticipated. Instead, she feels calm. And being beside Andy after all this time is not exciting, but normal somehow.

When he walks in, she holds the door open and peers into the hallway. No ophthalmologist waiting there.

"Where's the U-Haul?" Katherine asks.

"I parked it in a garage," Andy says.

He seems nervous. His jaw muscles are twitching slightly, the way they used to before he took a big exam, or first performed surgery.

"I thought maybe we could have some lunch first," he says.

"Great," Katherine says, leading him to the couch. When he sits, she adds, "Can you believe this was my bed?"

He blushes slightly, and shrugs.

"It'll be good to have a real one," she continues.

"A real one?"

"Bed," Katherine says.

"Oh. Right," Andy says, and blushes again.

Just when she thought it never would, the awkwardness passes, and Katherine finds herself telling Andy everything she can think of to tell him. She talks about Lucy. She tells him about Julia, and the Chinese delivery boy—drummer. She talks about the way here in New York, you can buy socks and earrings and 100 percent wool scarves right on the street corner.

He is talking too. She has long ago forgotten his enthusiasm for medicine. But now she remembers. He describes patients and treatments in loving detail, and Katherine finds herself warmed somehow by this, by sitting here beside him and listening to his voice.

What she wonders as he talks is whether it is worth giving up this familiarity, this ease and comfort, for passion. All those dinners when she sat across the table from strangers, she was waiting for a lightning bolt to strike, for Fourth of July to begin, for that feeling she gets now in the dark with Spencer. But, she keeps thinking, is it worth losing this?

Andy is saying, "I know you would love the food there, Kat. The menu changes every night. It's like getting surprised, you know?"

"Yes," she says. "I know."

Andy stops talking and smiles at her. "Of course you do," he says.

There are no lightning bolts, no fireworks. It's the same. She can predict where he will touch her next, how many times he will move inside her before he's finished. Whatever Andy has been doing with Shelly, these things have not changed. But still, Katherine feels happier than she has since she first came here filled with satisfaction and courage.

What he says when he catches his breath again is, "I must be nuts."

"Why?"

He strokes her cheek. "Because I would go right now, this very minute, down to city hall and marry you."

Katherine turns to face him. Their eyes are very close. She can feel his breath on her. It smells like Scope. "You would?" she whispers.

Andy nods. "I guess that makes me the biggest pushover ever."

"What about Shelly?" Katherine asks him.

"I don't love Shelly," he says. "I love you."

They did not bother to open up the couch. Instead, Andy opened the quilt he had brought her and spread it on the floor. Now, he pulls it over them both, wraps them in it like a cocoon. Katherine smells detergent, and knows he had it washed before he brought it to her. She knows that he tightened the nails in the furniture, and polished the wood. She moves still closer to him, until she is pressed against him completely. Andy sighs softly when their bodies touch.

"Are you still blue?" he whispers to her.

She is, but it is different now. She knows there are no right answers, no true things to do. She thinks about passion and the way her insides seem to melt when she and Spencer make love. She thinks about this very instant, how right it feels to have Andy here with her.

"Right now," she says finally, "I couldn't be happier."

Andy hugs her. "Really?" he says. "Really?"

Katherine nods. For this instant, that's the truth.

Aliens and
other invasions

Before her father ran off with Miss Texas, Julia can remember a different childhood. In it, she does not yet have to buy her clothes in the big girls' department. Her mother boldly ventures out, not only around their own neighborhood, but frequently into Manhattan, where she eats lunch in restaurants and goes to theater matinees on Wednesday afternoons. Her father is in those memories too. Not as a blur the way he lives in her mind today, but as a man who stood in the middle of Garfield Place and played catch with her. He wears a sweatshirt and faded blue jeans. And her mother cheers them on from the stoop. Everyone, in these images, is smiling—Julia, her mother, her father, even passersby.

Can it really be that the warm Saturday morning when Julia's father left them was the last time her mother smiled? That it was in that instant that the apartment grew dark and airless? That Julia ballooned into a fat, lonely child and her mother stopped going out? Julia isn't sure. But she knows there were months of dinners from restaurants that delivered. Pizza, Chinese, and BBQ chicken. She knows there were months when she dressed herself for school, did the laundry, brought her mother meals in bed; when her mother did not open the shades on the windows or even leave her bedroom.

When Julia started doing the grocery shopping, she used to eat her way through the aisles, pushing pink iced cupcakes into her mouth, small bags of Fritos, Scooter Pies. Her mother sent her for tests on her thyroid. "How can you be so fat when we hardly keep any food in the house?" she used to say. But her thyroid was fine. At school she started to pay other kids for their lunch desserts. Oreos and Twinkies and homemade brownies. There seemed to be a spot inside her that Julia could not fill up, no matter how hard she tried.

On tells her that she is not fat. But she can't see that. She tells him about all the food she used to eat. "But Julia," he says, "that was a long time ago." Still, she looks in the mirror and sees a fat person.

What Julia wants to know is if her memories are real. She wants to know if her mother really stood on that stoop cheering and smiling, if her father played catch with her. She wants to know what is true and what isn't.

Her mother is not exactly agoraphobic. She sometimes takes a cab into Manhattan and meets with her editor or agent. She goes to the movies on Flatbush Avenue on Sunday afternoons by herself. It is just that she doesn't want to go anywhere or do anything. But On tells Julia that she should clear things up with her mother. That she should spend some time with her. "You never know," he says. And Julia agrees.

She fills the loft with fresh flowers. Spring flowers. She puts them in old jars that she buys at a flea market in SoHo. She sells her earrings at that flea market too. Her new designs are made from nuts and bolts and screws. She shops in hardware stores on Canal Street. She is amazed by the varieties of these things, by all the possibilities there are.

On does not work for his uncle anymore. Instead, his band keeps getting more and more gigs all over town. Julia spends her nights watching them. Most nights, On goes home with her. She tells Lucy that she feels an order to things that she has never felt before. She tells Lucy her own life is becoming clearer and that she wants to go to film school. She has so many ideas. She wants to write screenplays, and she outlines them in great detail for Lucy and Katherine.

Sometimes, when she is alone at the loft in the late afternoon, and the light comes through the large windows, Julia almost gasps out loud. The light shifts and spills, and she cannot believe that all of this—these flowers bursting from jars, On's shirt tossed across a chair, this furniture and these nut-and-bolt earrings, are all her doing.

It is on one of these late afternoons, just before the sky turns violet, that Julia calls her mother and says, "Tomorrow I'm taking you to lunch."

"Oh," her mother says. "I don't think so, Julia. Not tomorrow."

"Yes. Tomorrow. I want you to get in a cab and meet me in the city."

Her mother says, "I'm sorry. It's just not possible."

Julia keeps talking, as if her mother hasn't refused. "On Broome Street there's this great little place. We'll meet there at one, okay?"

"No, no. Not at one."

"Mom," Julia says, "there is no good reason for you not to have lunch with me at one o'clock tomorrow at the Cupping Room."

She hears her mother breathing hard. She imagines the miles between them, Wall Street, the Brooklyn Bridge, the stretch of Flatbush Avenue.

"Come on," Julia says softly.

"Well," her mother says. "Well."

"Good," Julia says. Then she repeats the name and address of the restaurant again.

Her mother walks into the restaurant like an alien arriving on a new planet. She squints and bumps into things. Her eyes dance around the room, not even settling on Julia but rather observing the waitresses and the food and other customers as if they are foreign and new to her. Finally Julia goes over to her, takes her by the arm, and leads her to their table.

Even though it is April and mild weather, her mother wears a black wool coat. She refuses to take it off, and keeps it buttoned to the neck.

"Relax," Julia tells her.

Instead, her mother inspects all of the silverware, then carefully wipes each piece with her napkin.

"You know," Julia says, "it's the most normal thing in the world for a mother and daughter to have lunch together."

"Oh," her mother says, rubbing a spoon with a hard vigorous motion, "I know that. Meredith always has lunch with Jodi. Every Friday, like a date."

Meredith is her mother's agent. Julia nods. "See," she says.

Her mother relaxes a little, but when it is time for them to order, she can't decide what to have. The waitress stands, tapping her pen against her order pad, sighing loudly.

"Maybe you could come back?" Julia says to her.

"No!" her mother says. "You do it. Just order the food."

The waitress rolls her eyes. Her name tag says BeBe.

"What kind of name is BeBe?" Julia's mother asks her.

"French," the waitress says.

Julia begins to order. Once she starts, she can't seem to stop. She orders appetizers, soup, sandwiches, and an omelette. She orders juice and coffee and water.

When the waitress walks away, Julia's mother says, "I never heard of the name BeBe. Have you?"

Julia shakes her head no.

Her mother opens her purse and takes out a little notepad. Carefully she prints BEBE. FRENCH.

"Who knows?" she says. "Maybe Vicky Valentine can save a little French girl named BeBe somehow. It's good to know these things."

The food comes and fills the small round table. There is no room for the bud vase or the wine list. Julia has to move them to make room for all the food.

Her mother tastes everything and likes none of it. Still, she keeps taking small, birdlike bites from each plate, then wrinkling her nose in disgust.

"I want to ask you something," Julia says finally. "I want to know if Daddy ever played catch with me in the street. If he used to have a Princeton sweatshirt and high-top sneakers. If you used to wear pink lipstick."

"Probably," her mother says, continuing to taste and frown.

"Yes or no?"

Her mother stops, puts down her fork. "I hate that man," she says.

"I know," Julia says. "I guess I do too. Remember how he used to promise to come and get me? Or how he'd tell me I could go there?"

"How could I have been so foolish? That's what I ask myself. To have loved someone like that." She shakes her head.

"You didn't know he was going to leave you," Julia says.

"There were signs. Lipstick on his shirts. Expensive perfume on him. I didn't want to know."

Julia tries to focus on those good memories, when everything seemed clean and light.

"He used to teach you how to pitch," her mother is saying, "Sidearm. Curveball. You could do them all."

Julia feels tears in her eyes.

"Hey," her mother says, "don't get upset about it. When he left us, I spent months trying to think of what to do. That's how I came up with Vicky Valentine. A brave little girl who has a good family on Park Avenue. I thought she'd help you."

"Help me?" Julia says. "I hated her. I thought she was the daughter you wanted. Blond and cute, saving lives and solving mysteries."

Her mother smiles sadly. "There are no Vicky Valentines," she says. "I thought you knew that."

"Ma," Julia says, "it took me a long time to figure that out." Her fingers bend, start to remember something else. When you throw a curveball, she thinks, you put two fingers on the seams. You twist your wrist. You put a spin on the ball.

On is right, Julia thinks. You never know. When she put her mother in a cab home, her mother said, "I don't want to do this a lot. No offense but it's not my cup of tea. It would be nice if you came by more often though." Somehow, this makes Julia relieved and happy. There is no June Cleaver lurking in her mother. There is no Vicky Valentine lurking in herself.

She stops and buys food at Dean & DeLuca. She spends too much money on ravioli stuffed with wild mushrooms, on homemade cream sauce. She feels extravagant.

When Julia walks into the loft, she stops dead in her tracks. There is a woman dressed in a blue crushed velvet jumpsuit standing in the middle of the floor, scowling. Even though Julia is sure burglars don't dress like this, why else would a strange woman be in her apartment?

"If you move," Julia says, "I'll scream."

"Are you the woman staying here?"

Julia straightens her back. "I live here," she says. "Yes."

"Good," the woman says. "Then maybe you can tell me where all this shit came from."

"Who are you?" Julia asks.

"Holly Kaye."

The name sounds vaguely familiar, like a name she's seen in a magazine or something.

"This is my apartment," Holly Kaye says.

"Your apartment?" Julia says. Her legs start to wobble slightly.

"I came by for a few things and I find . . . clutter. Everywhere."

She has on pancake makeup, bright lipstick. And Julia thinks she is wearing a wig and false eyelashes. She wants Holly Kaye to leave, to take her few things and get out.

"I mean," Holly Kaye is saying, "you were told that this was like a temporary arrangement. I'm only in Atlantic City. I didn't relocate or anything. You're not supposed to move shit in."

She is definitely wearing a wig, Julia decides. Real hair is not that color red. Real hair moves.

"I mean," Holly Kaye says again, "I'll be back in June. You and your shit have got to go."

Julia moves into the room and starts to unload her groceries. She tries to pretend this woman isn't here. She remembers that Holly Kaye is a lounge singer working in Atlantic City. When she first moved in,

Julia had found publicity pictures of her dressed in a miniskirt and white go-go boots.

"I have a car waiting," Holly Kaye says. "I don't like this." She sweeps her arms outward. "I don't like clutter."

Julia keeps unpacking.

A horn starts to honk outside the window.

"That's Wayne," Holly Kaye says. "I could tell the agency, you know. You could lose this job."

Julia shrugs. "I'm getting my own place anyway," she says. "So I don't care if you tell them."

"A wiseass, huh?" Holly Kaye says. "Don't get too comfy."

After she leaves, Julia discovers that Holly Kaye has walked off with some of her nuts-and-bolts earrings. But this doesn't make her angry. Instead, she laughs. Then she washes the floor where Holly Kaye stood, trying to reclaim the apartment. She washes and washes until long after the sky has darkened from violet to inky blue. But something has been taken away.

Good morning, America!

"Lucy," Ashley Hayes says, "this is big. I mean big."

They are sitting in a midtown restaurant eating lunch. It is the kind of place that Lucy and Jasper used to say they would go and celebrate at when one of them became famous. "Or," Jasper used to say, "when one of us actually gets paid for our art."

Ashley Hayes, the *My Dolly* editor, wears thick black-framed glasses and a bustier under a short black jacket. She has already asked Lucy who her colorist is, and it took Lucy a few minutes to realize they were talking about hair and not illustrations.

"Coloring books, a boy dolly, a wardrobe," Ashley Hayes is saying.

They are sitting underneath a large plaster breast. Across the restaurant, on another wall, hangs a plaster nose.

Lucy nods as Ashley continues.

"A sister, paper dolls." Ashley smiles. Her lipstick is very red. Paloma Picasso red. "You are going to be rich," she says.

Lucy thinks, This is happening to someone else.

"We want it by Christmas," Ashley says. "Intense work but I know you can do it."

"Yes," Lucy says, finally speaking. "I can."

The waiter arrives and places Lucy's pumpkin ravioli in front of her. There are julienned strips of squash on top of it.

"Simplicity," Ashley says, twirling her black squid-ink spaghetti on her fork. "That's the key to the success of this. Boy Dolly. Baby Dolly. No fancy names. No fancy clothes. When you came up with that drawing, you hit on something, Lucy. That book hits the stands next month. Get ready."

Suddenly, all of Lucy's time is spent at her drawing table by the window. She has to finish the counting book for Nathaniel. She has to get to work on clothes for My Dolly and on Boy Dolly and Baby Sister Dolly. She has taped a picture on the wall above the table. It is her third-grade class picture. There she is, in the back with the tall children. And there, in the front, is Harriet Becker with her tangled dirty-blond hair. She is looking down at the floor. Her dress is too long, a faded blue checked one with puffy sleeves.

At home in Massachusetts, Lucy searched through her closet until she found this picture. She brought it into the kitchen and asked her mother whatever happened to Harriet Becker.

"That poor little girl?" her mother asked.

"Yes," Lucy said. "This one." She pointed to Harriet, standing there in the front row.

In the picture, there is a big space between Harriet and the next child, Susan Polk. No one stood close to Harriet Becker. They were afraid of lice and ringworm. When they passed her desk, they made a hissing sound like an aerosol can to kill the cooties.

Lucy's mother studied the class picture. "We used to bring the mother canned food and old clothes," she said.

"I heard something terrible happened to her," Lucy said. "To Harriet."

"Her mother drank, I think. She wasn't even grateful for the handouts."

"I heard she got hit by a car or something," Lucy said. Her finger rested on the picture, filling the space left between Harriet and Susan Polk.

Her mother shrugged. "I thought they moved to Florida. Some-place warm."

Staring at that picture, Lucy found herself wishing that Harriet Becker would look up, away from her scuffed Mary Janes and the classroom floor, into Lucy's eyes.

"He died," Lucy's mother was saying. "This Reilly boy. Drugs."

Her mother tapped the face of the boy holding the small black sign: Mrs. Williams, Grade 3.

Nathaniel Jones courts a woman the way Cary Grant or Rock Hudson wooed Doris Day in the movies. He sends flowers. He arranges romantic dinners. He sends airplane tickets and limousines and reservations in hotel suites. He makes Lucy's head spin. He has invaded her life. She can't seem to get away from him. It is the way her father courted her mother back in the forties, the way she had been raised to believe men win women's hearts.

But despite the daily bouquets of roses and the weekends at the Ritz-Carlton in Boston, Lucy feels strangely disconnected from the affair. There is something big missing between her and Nathaniel Jones, something she can't put her finger on. Julia and Katherine call her for every detail after her weekends in Boston with him. They remind her how romantic all this is. They imagine her future for her— a house on the Cape, an apartment on Beacon Hill, trips to Europe and beautiful clothes. "He's one of the most eligible bachelors around," Katherine keeps reminding her. "And he's after you."

When Lucy gets back to her own apartment though, she never thinks of Nathaniel Jones. She thinks of Harriet Becker, of her new Dolly series. She thinks of the counting book. Her Four Friends link arms. They are multiracial, dressed in vivid colors like a Benetton ad. Her Seven Seashells are nestled against pink sparkly sand. She comes up with her own idea for the number ten—Ten Tails.

She leaves two pages three-quarters blank. She colors the background blue. The top quarter looks like a brick wall, with ten tails hanging down, some dropping into the blue background. A monkey's tail. A rat's tail. A duck's tail. A horse's tail. Ten different ones, lazily swishing.

"You're a genius, babe," Nathaniel murmurs to her in the soft downy sheets of the Ritz-Carlton that Sunday morning.

He has the picture propped up against his knees. He is smoking a cigar.

"It's great. It almost looks upside down," he says. "And it deals with cultural differences and animal identification. The works."

Lucy is wearing the pastel blue silk robe he has given her. That too makes her feel like Doris Day. Or maybe Marilyn Monroe. She does not wear silk robes. She wears T-shirts or terry cloth. She does not, as she does today, sip mimosas in a hotel suite. Or eat fresh croissants from a silver basket.

"How does it feel," Nathaniel asks her, "to be there?"

Lucy stops peeling apart the fine layers of croissant. "Be where?"

He laughs and opens his arms, sends cigar ash across the sheets. "There. Here. Almost at the top."

Lucy cannot even make herself smile.

"Great," she says.

Nathaniel Jones is a man you cannot say no to. He is relentless. That's how he got to be famous. That's why his face sells Scotch. That's why he sells children's books. And Lucy, after her weekend at home with her family, gave in to him. As difficult as he is, bossy and demanding, something about him is also easy. He takes charge. He makes all the decisions. And Lucy just has to go along with him, not even think.

She flies to Boston every weekend. There is a car waiting for her. There is a hotel room and flowers and even fancy presents. She thinks that if she were in a movie, this is the part that would be a kaleidoscope of spinning images—she and Nathaniel out on the town, kissing in taxis and eating at fine restaurants, toasting each other with champagne and losing themselves in twinkling marquee lights. If this were a movie, she would fall in love with this man and lead the life women are supposed to lead, according to her mother.

But every time she returns to New York and her own apartment, she feels relieved. She puts on her faded T-shirt of the London subway system. She drinks a cold Brooklyn Beer. She doesn't even answer the phone. She just draws.

Lucy takes a leave from Whirlwind Weekends. *My Dolly* appears and suddenly nothing is the same. Stores sell out of the book, toy stores sell out of the doll. *My Dolly* is in *The New York Times*, *People* magazine. Everywhere Lucy goes, Harriet Becker's sad little face is looking at her.

She and Julia go to stores in Manhattan and hide behind stacks of Barbies and Cabbage Patch dolls, watching people buy My Dolly. Little girls hug it. Don't worry, they tell it, I'll take care of you.

"Are you rich yet?" Julia asks her.

Every day Lucy gets phone calls, reports on reorders and sales, more offers for My Dolly items.

"Almost," she tells Julia.

They are in a Toys R Us, watching a new order of My Dollys being put on the shelves.

"Does it feel as good as you thought it would?" Julia asks her.

Lucy nods. Of all the things—the contracts, Nathaniel Jones, the money—this is the thing that feels best, the most right. Having her creation out here in a store in Valley Stream, Indianapolis, San Jose. Having little girls love My Dolly.

Julia squeezes Lucy's hand. "This is so great," she whispers, as the shelves are filled with more tangle-haired dolls.

Ashley Hayes's voice on the telephone says, "*Good Morning America!* Can you believe it?"

It is another Saturday morning. Outside, the sun is warming Boston. Nathaniel Jones has four newspapers spread across the Ritz-Carlton bed.

But he looks up when Lucy repeats, "*Good Morning America*? Wow."

Her hand trembles.

"I'll FAX you the details," Ashley says. "Call everyone you know and tell them to watch you on Thursday."

When she hangs up, Nathaniel picks up the phone. "Send up a bottle of Perrier-Jouet," he says. "Hell, send two bottles."

"It's only a television show," she tells him when he hangs up.

He takes her in his arms. "You are going up, up, up, Lucy," he says.

These are the kinds of things that excite him. National television. Magazine coverage. Royalty statements.

He pushes her gently onto the bed. The newspapers crackle under her silk robe.

"I'm going to get newsprint all over this," she tells him. Sometimes, his elbows seem to stab into her. Their bodies don't fit quite right.

"Who cares?" he laughs. "I'll buy you a dozen more."

She smiles. She smiles because she is succeeding at her craft. Because she is going to be on *Good Morning America*. Because this man will buy her a dozen silk robes. Because two bottles of champagne are on their way up to her. She smiles because she should be the happiest woman in the world right now. And maybe, if she smiles hard enough, this sad part inside her will dissolve.

"What I think we should do," Nathaniel tells her as he refills her glass with champagne, "is move you up here."

"Me?" she says. "Move to Boston?"

"Right."

There is a cloud of gray-blue cigar smoke above the bed. Lucy waves her hand to disperse it.

"I don't know," she says.

But Nathaniel talks over her. "You can move in with me," he says. "You'll love living at my place."

She has been there only once. He thinks it is more romantic to spend weekends in a hotel. But one night she hosted a party with him at his brownstone. It was filled with modern art, splotches and swirls on canvases, odd-shaped furniture and shelves of awards.

"I don't know," she says again. She thinks of a life of silk robes and glitzy parties. She tries to remember what it was that she and Jasper were working for, what it was they used to plan when this day came. But she can't remember. Perhaps, she thinks, it's all this champagne that's clouding her mind.

Zing

Katherine does not go to Memphis with Spencer. Instead, she goes to Boston and spends a long weekend with Andy. She pretends, during those four days, that she is married to Andy. She tries to find out what she has missed by leaving him that day almost a year ago. While he is at the hospital making rounds, she goes to a fish market.

"My husband," she tells the man behind the counter, "likes fresh swordfish steaks."

The man has gray hair and watery blue eyes. His face is windburned to a ruddy color, his lips are cracked and chapped. As he weighs the fish, Katherine sees a gold wedding band on his finger. This man has probably been married for twenty, maybe even thirty years, Katherine thinks. She is sure no woman ever left him searching for passion. Somewhere in Boston there is a wife for him, who gives him lemons to cut the fish smell on his hands, and sleeps with him every night.

"Anything else?" he asks her in a thick Boston accent.

Katherine shakes her head. But she doesn't move. Instead, she stands at the counter and watches him.

The next customer, a middle-aged woman with her teenaged daughter, says, "Hey, Mike. How's the scrod today?"

The daughter has a poor complexion, long stringy hair. Her nose twitches against the smell of fresh fish, and she looks, bored, out the window toward the harbor.

Someone is married to this woman, Katherine thinks. She cannot imagine her marrying for passion either. And the teenager. She probably kisses boys who ride motorcycles, boys who drop out of school. Is that passion? Is that love?

"You all set here?" Mike is asking her.

"Oh," Katherine says. "Yes."

She stumbles out the door, into the bright day.

Katherine and Andy are meeting Lucy and Nathaniel for brunch at the Ritz-Carlton.

"Is Lucy the same as ever?" Andy asks while they dress. He carefully knots a red and blue striped tie.

"No," Katherine answers quickly. "She's different."

He laughs, tightens the tie. "She used to be a spitfire," he says. "Guys were terrified of her. A real wiseass."

Katherine considers this. Lucy did not have many boyfriends in school. The ones she did have were always different from the fraternity guys everyone else clamored to date. For a while she saw a graduate oceanography student. And then a guy who taught sailing.

"Was she aloof?" Katherine says.

"Aloof," Andy repeats. "I guess so. But I loved those little cartoons of hers."

"Lucinda Luckinbill," Katherine says. She brushes her hair, sprays hairspray on the bangs.

Andy pats her on the back like she's an old pal.

"Ready?" he says.

Nathaniel Jones is not nearly as handsome as Katherine imagined. He is shorter, slightly paunchier than he seems in those Scotch ads.

Lucy seems to not even notice that he is there beside her, hanging on her elbow, watching her as she talks.

"I haven't seen you in years, Doctor," Lucy says to Andy.

"That's what Katherine and I were just talking about," he says.

He glances at Katherine. It feels good to be here with him, to have these signals, she thinks. She places her hand on his thigh, and lets it rest there.

Nathaniel talks and talks. He orders champagne. "For my star," he says, hugging Lucy.

Lucy still seems not to notice him. "He's making me a drunk," she says.

They are halfway through brunch when Nathaniel finally asks Andy what kind of doctor he is. They are almost finished eating before he talks to Katherine at all. Over coffee he says, "Help me convince Lucy to move up here. With me."

Lucy groans. "Not now," she says.

In that instant Katherine suddenly likes Nathaniel. Maybe he isn't exactly rude, she decides. Maybe he's just in love. And then her good feelings about her and Andy start to fade. It looks like Lucy has met someone who adores her, who is passionate about her. She starts to wonder how Spencer is doing. But when she tries to imagine him on his pilgrimage to Graceland, she reinvents him, makes him taller, thinner, better dressed.

Later, back at his apartment, Andy says, "Lucy's just the same."

This surprises Katherine. "I see her so differently now," she says. "Is she going to marry this guy?"

Katherine shrugs. She says, "Who can figure out love?"

Andy says, "I can."

"Let's spend the entire day in bed," Katherine tells him on her last morning there. "Let's make waffles and eat them right here. Let's have sex right up until I have to catch my train."

Andy laughs and kisses the tip of her nose. "You nut," he says.

Then he gets up and in a few minutes she hears the shower running, and Schubert playing on the radio.

Instead of going straight back to New York, Katherine goes home to Connecticut for the night. Her sister Shannon picks her up at the train in her new car, a black Acura Legend. "My grown-up car," she calls it.

The big white house with the black shutters looks good when they pull into the driveway.

Katherine says, "It's so quiet here."

Shannon cuts the engine. "What?" she says. "The urbanite likes a little peace and quiet?"

Katherine doesn't answer. She gets her suitcase out of the backseat and goes inside. At first, she stands in the front foyer, and breathes in the familiar smell, like lemons and wax. She touches the desk, rubs the shiny mahogany. She knows what is kept in every drawer in that desk—postage stamps, envelopes, pens, and unsharpened pencils.

Her mother finds her there and says, "What do you need? An invitation?"

Katherine shakes her head. "Everything just looks so good."

There are canapés set up in the den. Sitting there, on the dark maroon leather couch, Katherine feels like a guest. It is the same way she feels at Meryl King's. She feels she doesn't really belong anywhere at all. She tries to picture herself living in Queens, listening to Elvis songs, eating bad Italian food but having great sex. The thought depresses her. She cannot see Spencer in this room. She cannot imagine introducing him as her husband.

Shannon is saying, "Can I tell her now?"

"Go ahead," their mother says. "Before you burst."

She stretches her hand out to Katherine. "Da-dah!" she announces.

Sparkling there on her ring finger is a large pear-shaped diamond.

Suddenly, Katherine starts to cry.

She sees the worried looks Shannon and her mother exchange.

"I'm all right," she manages to say.

"I thought you were over this," her mother is saying. "Is this about Andy still?"

Katherine looks at Shannon. "It's about me," she says. "How do you know it's right? How do you know you and Rich should get married?"

Shannon looks at her mother again.

"Honey," her mother says, "you just know."

"I don't buy that," Katherine says.

Shannon smooths the hem of her lime green sweater. She studies that instead of Katherine's face.

Katherine says to her, "You don't know either, do you?"

Shannon laughs, a short nervous laugh. "Yes, I do," she says. "We have it all planned. We booked the club and everything."

"Do you have orgasms with him?" Katherine blurts. "Do you die whenever he touches you?"

"Katherine!" her mother says.

Shannon blushes bright pink.

"There's this guy in New York," Katherine continues. "Spencer. He's a little nerdy guy. I don't think I love him, but it gets confused because the thing I didn't have with Andy, passion—"

Her mother and Shannon both stand.

"That's enough, Katherine. Honestly, you have me worried sick. I don't know what you are going to do or say next—"

"But this is important," Katherine insists.

Her mother pretends to study her Rolex watch. "We had better get a move on, girls. We have to meet your father at the club at seven."

Later, in her own bed that night, Katherine stares up at the words she wrote on the ceiling. Softly, she sings the songs to herself. "Uh . . . uh . . . uh . . . uh . . . stayin' alive. . . ."

There is a soft knock on her door.

Shannon says, "Kat?"

Katherine doesn't answer, but Shannon opens the door anyway.

She stands there, silent, a few minutes. Then she says, "No. At least, I don't think I do. You know, have them. You know. Climax."

Katherine swallows hard.

"One time," Shannon says, "I started to feel something. Something different, you know? Something great. And I didn't know what was happening, and I said, 'Rich? Rich?' And then he finished and I felt like I was left hanging in midair." She sighs. "Maybe that was one. I don't know."

Katherine doesn't answer her.

"Sometimes," Shannon says, her voice as soft and small as a child's, "I imagine going off and having a wild weekend. Having an affair with a stranger. Really feeling what it's like." She giggles. "Forget I ever said that."

"All right," Katherine says.

Shannon hesitates. "Well," she says, "goodnight."

"Goodnight."

"Kat?" she says. "Do you think I shouldn't marry Rich then?"

Katherine sighs. "No," she says. "I don't know what to think."

"Isn't it great?" Spencer asks Katherine.

She stares at it. A plastic Elvis head. It looks too lifelike, as if someone actually decapitated Elvis and placed his head on a pedestal.

"It's kind of creepy," she says.

Spencer looks hurt. He rubs Elvis's jet-black pompadour. "No," he says. "Really?"

"It's weird," she says.

Spencer laughs. "You're just not used to it," he says.

Katherine flops down on his couch. "Can you cover it up or something?" she asks him.

Spencer comes and sits beside her. "I missed you so much," he says. "How was Connecticut? How was your family?"

She feels only a little guilty about her lie. She told him she spent all the time at home.

"My sister's getting married in October, so there was a lot to discuss, and plan. You know."

He looks at her, all eager and open with his cocker spaniel look. "Did you miss me?"

"I thought about you a lot," she says.

Spencer moves his hand up her thigh, under her white summer dress, slips it into her panties. He knows exactly where to touch her. And Katherine, despite herself, feels her back arch, hears a small groan escape from her. Out of the corner of her eye, she sees Elvis, watching.

Katherine grips Spencer's wrist, stops his slow, precise movements.

"Spencer," she says. Her voice is filled with determination.

"Spencer," she says again, "I am so sorry."

He looks at her, confused. She sees a line of sweat glisten on his forehead.

What she says next surprises even herself. "I've decided to marry Andy after all," she says. "I'm going to move to Boston and marry him."

Spencer says, "But you can't. What about the ophthalmologist? What about me?"

"I'm sorry," she says again. "I want to marry Andy."

And the words feel as right as she supposes they ever will. Not one hundred percent right. Not right enough to make her soar. Not even right enough to take away that small part of her that will always feel sort of sad. Still, she knows she will walk out of here and call Andy. She will tell him she loves him. She will say, "I'm coming home."

When Katherine gets off the subway and walks back to Meryl's apartment it is still light. She wishes that she thought the city looked beautiful. She even stops and studies the Chrysler Building, all shiny and silver in the distance. But all she really sees is the garbage in the street, the two men huddled together in a corner with cardboard signs:

PLEASE HELP. WE ARE VIETNAM VETS. WE ARE HUNGRY. They each hold out ragged paper cups.

She closes her eyes and conjures a place that doesn't exist yet. A house with large rooms and great details in its woodwork. Splashes of light everywhere. A green yard with flowers and trees in bloom. She fights for this image to make her happy. But all it does is make her weary. On her way inside the building, she empties her wallet into the men's paper cups.

There is no one home in the apartment. Laurie Walker has come by and left some of her things—white nurse's uniforms hang on the door, wrapped in plastic dry-cleaner's bags, boxes with shoes and a blow-dryer and a curling iron poking out sit in one corner of the living room. Katherine goes into her new room and flops on the bed. She has to call Andy and her mother. She has to tell Meryl she is leaving. She has to notify the school that she won't be back. But she cannot move. All she can do is close her eyes. Her hand moves up her thigh. She feels her back arch slightly as her fingers move inside her underwear, searching, searching for the spot that Spencer touched.

Swimming pools, movie stars

In two weeks, Holly Kaye will be back from Atlantic City and Julia will have to move. There are a lot of apartments to house-sit for in the summer. She sits with her options spread before her on the coffee table. It is June, unseasonably cool, but sunny. She has bought a new end table. There are primitive figures cut from it—a running lion, a soaring eagle. The table is dark metal, built by a sculptor.

Julia reads the descriptions of the apartments. A two-bedroom on Washington Mews. Probably an NYU professor's, she decides. A penthouse off Fifth Avenue. Someone spending the summer at their house in the Hamptons. Another loft, not far from here. She stacks all the papers, leases, and contracts into a neat pile. She doesn't want to live in any of them. What she wants is for Holly Kaye to never return. Julia doesn't exactly wish her harm, she wishes she would just disappear. Vaporize, leaving a puddle of blue crushed velvet behind.

She paces around Holly Kaye's apartment, touching all the things she has bought. It is hard to imagine that a short time ago, she owned nothing. That she used to move from apartment to apartment in taxis, all of her belongings in a suitcase and one Hefty garbage bag. Once, on a rainy night when there were no cabs to be found, Julia moved on a crosstown bus. That's how free she was, how unencumbered.

But this feels better. And she doesn't want Holly Kaye to return and send her hurling backward, into someone else's apartment, searching the faces of strangers for comfort and excitement. She likes knowing that this couch is hers, that she has chosen these vases and pictures and rugs. She likes knowing that On will call her. That he will sleep beside her. That he cannot tell her about Shanghai or Mao Tse-tung or recite Tang poetry doesn't matter to her. She has constructed this life for herself, here on North Moore Street in this apartment. A life, Julia believes, that is better than anyone's. Better even than Vicky Valentine's.

Every day she calls Edie at the company that finds her the apartments.

"Any news from Holly Kaye?" she asks.

The answer is always no.

Holly Kaye's mail has started to arrive here again. Letters with postmarks from Reno and Las Vegas. Julia holds them up to the light, searching for good news, offers of jobs out west or a marriage proposal from someone in Tahoe. But she either can't make out the words or finds chatty, boring postcards from pianists and singers who have worked with Holly Kaye. "Good weather for this time of year," they say. "Warm and dry. We need sweaters at night."

Julia and Lucy take Katherine out to dinner as a farewell party. They go to a restaurant where stars supposedly hang out. But they don't see anyone they recognize, even though Katherine keeps thinking she sees someone famous.

"Over there," she whispers, "isn't that Diane Keaton?"

They follow her gaze. It isn't.

"Wait," she says. "I think that's Alan King."

It isn't.

"Why don't we just relax and order dinner," Lucy suggests.

But Katherine's eyes keep dancing around the room. She stares at the front door, the ladies' room, the bar.

"I want to see one famous person before I leave New York," she says, disappointed.

Julia says, "I always see them when I work at the flea market. Paul Simon. Dustin Hoffman. Polly Bergen. Everybody."

"You are so lucky," Katherine tells her.

"Hey," Julia says. "How can we forget? We're having dinner with a star. Our own Lucy Wilcox."

Lucy laughs. "Hardly."

"You've been on national TV," Katherine says. "That counts for something."

Julia agrees.

But Lucy just shakes her head.

On comes over all excited.

"We've got a recording gig in L.A." he tells Julia. "We leave in a month."

"Los Angeles?" she says. She feels terror building in her chest, rising upward.

But On doesn't notice. "This is so great," he keeps saying. "Isn't it so great?"

"Los Angeles?" Julia says again. "That's really far away. That's on the other side of the country."

She imagines all the things between here and there. Highways. The Great Lakes. Yellowstone and the Grand Canyon and the Rocky Mountains. Diners and car lots and Motel 6's. People who speak with southern accents. Families in the midwest. Ski resorts. Camping grounds. The list crowds her mind until she has to sit down and hold the arms of her new easy chair real tight.

On plays the drums on her metal coffee table, banging out a beat with his fingers. It's rock and roll, Buddy Holly or someone. Rat-a-tat-tat. Rat-a-tat-tat.

Julia focuses on the new chair. It is turquoise and pink, a pattern of triangles and circles that reminded her of *The Jetsons*. But now it reminds her of outer space, of the big expanse of sky between Los

Angeles and New York. When it is dark here, she thinks, people out there are still on the beach. They eat lunch when we eat dinner. It's worlds away.

On says, "Aren't you happy for me?"

"Well," Julia says, "personally I think Los Angeles is shallow. No culture. It's all brand-new and flimsy. All pink stucco and palm trees." She scrunches her face in distaste.

"No!" he says. He comes and sits at her feet. "It's big old convertibles. It's swimming pools and movie stars. It's fame and fortune."

Julia shrugs. She is trembling. She is clutching her new Jetsons chair so hard her knuckles are white.

"And," On adds, "it's only for a couple of months."

She shrugs again. "Whatever," she says.

Holly Kaye will be back in three days. Julia has not taken a new apartment to house-sit. Every day, another one slips away, assigned to someone else. Already the best ones are gone and her choices are narrowed down to a floor-through on St. Marks, an apartment near Columbia University, and two one-bedrooms in the East Twenties. "You moved too slowly," they tell her. "You should decide soon."

Lucy brings her empty boxes from the liquor store to help Julia pack.

Julia says, "Oh, I don't have that much stuff."

She looks around the apartment. She can't even remember it the way it was when she moved in, all empty and barren. She shows Lucy the new halogen lamp she bought. And the long pine table.

"I think I can use this as a desk," she says, rubbing its surface.

Lucy sighs. "But you need a place first," she says.

She points to the bookshelves.

"How about we start there. Load the books into these boxes."

"I can do that last," Julia tells her. "That doesn't take any time at all."

Lucy is looking around the loft too.

"Have you booked a truck or something?" she asks her. "They're hard to get in the summer, you know."

"I thought I'd do that tomorrow," Julia says, although she hasn't thought it at all.

"But you have to leave tomorrow," Lucy says.

Julia nods.

"Lucy," she says later, "it's possible that Holly Kaye won't come back."

"Really?" Lucy says. "I didn't know that. I thought her contract ended this week."

"Yes," Julia says, "but maybe she'll go somewhere else."

Lucy is growing impatient. "Like where for instance?" she asks. She stands up and paces in front of Julia, waiting for an answer.

"Like Reno," Julia says. "Like Las Vegas. Like wherever lounge singers go."

Lucy stops pacing and faces Julia. "Julia," she says, "she is not going to Las Vegas. She's coming here."

"I know," Julia says.

Lucy kneels in front of her, the way On had when he was telling her about L.A.

"I'm sorry," she says.

Julia forces a laugh. "It's only an apartment," she says. "Big deal."

When Lucy leaves, Julia stands in the middle of the loft. She is surrounded by her things. It is dark and she doesn't turn on any lights. Instead, she stands there and she shouts. She shouts her name. She shouts letters of the alphabet. She shouts her telephone number. But the words die there, in the apartment. She has filled all that space. There is no more echo.

Julia leaves the apartment. It is the middle of the night. Or, she corrects herself, it is early in the morning of the day she has to move. She walks to the bar where she had gone that first night, when she met Timothy from Australia. When her life started to change. Even though it is late, almost closing time, the bar is half full, but quiet.

Julia perches on a bar stool. When the bartender comes to take her order, she says, "Diet Coke," and looks up.

The bartender is Barry, looking as nondescript as ever. Except that he is embarrassed to see her.

"I knew you'd come in here someday," he says. His voice is very sad.

"How long have you worked here?" she asks him. Before he answers she says, "When did you get back?"

He busies himself washing glasses. He doesn't look at her when he talks.

"I never went," he tells her.

Julia suddenly wants nothing more than to believe that Barry did have a job in L.A. She wants him to have told her the truth, even though all along she knew he was lying.

"The contract fell through," she says eagerly. "Right?"

He shakes his head. He keeps washing the same glasses, over and over.

"You got something here, then," Julia says.

She too is focusing on the spray of water, on the way it trickles down the glasses like tears.

"You didn't want to go out to L.A.," she keeps talking. "Who wants to live there, right? A cultural desert."

"I wish . . ." he begins, but he doesn't say anything else.

Julia doesn't want to hear the truth. She stands up and says, "I've got to go now."

"Listen," Barry says. His fingers are growing all wrinkled like raisins. "There was no soap-opera job."

"That's all right," she says quickly. "I'm sure you're very happy here."

She walks out of the bar and grabs a taxi to On's as fast as she can.

On is awake, eating take-out fried chicken when she arrives. He is dressed in a pair of black pants and nothing else.

"I want to come with you," she tells him right away.

He fixes a plate of food for her. There is coleslaw and potato salad too.

"I want to move to L.A.," she continues. "I'll go to film school. And that's the place to do it."

On bites into a drumstick. He looks thoughtful as he chews.

"We can rent a Ryder truck and drive out there," she says. Her mind is full of all those things between here and L.A. again. But this time they are not weighing her down. Instead, they are making her excited. She has never seen any of it before. Yellowstone, she thinks. The Grand Canyon.

On says, "What about pink stucco and palm trees?"

"What about swimming pools and movie stars?" she says.

"Julia," he says, "we can drive out together. We can be together when we're out there. But I don't want to commit to something—"

"I don't want to either," she says, meaning it. "I want to go out there with you and see what happens."

He thinks about this. Then he nods.

"That sounds right," he says. "We'll just see how it goes."

Julia starts to leave, to get more boxes. She has to pack her things, get ready for Holly Kaye's return. At the door, she tells On, "We'll be eating dinner while everyone in New York is getting ready for bed."

He says, "We'll be the last ones to see the sun before it sets."

"Just think of it," she says. "Just imagine."

Whirlwind weekends

Jasper's voice on her machine says: "Hey, Miss Famous Illustrator. Miss National TV. Miss *Good Morning America*. Remember me? I knew you when."

Lucy doesn't call him back. She doesn't know what that message is supposed to mean. Has she forgotten him because of all that's happened with *My Dolly*? Is that what he thinks? Is he right?

She leaves for another weekend in Boston with Nathaniel Jones, the green message light flashing behind her.

They go to his office first. Nathaniel has a new project for her. It's another book by Fawn MacIntyre. An alphabet book.

"Same concept," he tells Lucy. "Complex ideas for kids."

Lucy says, "I'm so busy with this Dolly family. The Boy Dolly. The Baby Sister."

"A is for armadillo," Nathaniel says. "B is for baguette."

Lucy frowns. "Baguette?" she says. "Are you kidding me? What child knows the word baguette?"

"These books are very upscale," he says.

"Why not B is for brie?" she mumbles. She thinks of Jasper. Ten Tiananmen Squares, he had said. Nine Noriegas.

Nathaniel strokes her hand. "We're flexible. You know that. We didn't do ten tornadoes, did we?"

"No."

"I'm not married to baguette," he says.

But Lucy shakes her head. "I want to concentrate on My Dolly."

"Just look the thing over," Nathaniel says. "There's some great stuff."

He flips through the pages. His face brightens. He holds something up for Lucy to see.

"Quixote?" Lucy reads out loud. "Q is for Quixote?"

Nathaniel is getting excited. "You could do something very Man of La Mancha with this one," he says. "Windmills. Donkeys."

Lucy says, "Forget it."

Nathaniel holds up two hands. "Take your time. Think it over. No rush."

"Quixote," she says again.

"I love when you're difficult," he says. He kisses her cheek. "You knock me out when you get like this."

She doesn't say anything.

"So," Nathaniel says, tucking Fawn's new manuscript into Lucy's overnight bag. "What do you want to do?"

"Maybe something simple," she says. "Like going to the No Name for fresh fish."

He turns to her. "I know," he says. "I've got a real treat for you," he says. "Marblehead." His hands poke at the air with each word. "Beach. Rosalie's. The Inn by the Sea."

"A quiet dinner here would be fine," she says.

He picks up her bag. "You are going to love it up there. Just you wait."

"Lucy," Jasper's voice says on her machine, "it's me again. I really do want to see you. I want to talk. I want to see your pretty face."

She calls him back right away. She curls her toes in her sneakers, waiting for him to answer. She can feel sand in her shoes from the beach. Her skin is still tight from the sun.

When Jasper hears that it's her, she can feel his smile through the telephone wires.

"Where were you?" he asks her.

She doesn't want to tell him about Nathaniel so she says, "At the beach."

"The beach. Great."

It wasn't great, but she doesn't correct him.

"I wanted to see you before I leave," Jasper is saying.

Her hands and skin suddenly grow cold. "Leave?" she says.

"I got a part in the road show of *Singin' in the Rain*," he says. Then he adds quickly, "Not the Gene Kelly part."

Lucy sinks onto her couch. "You did?" she says. "Really?"

"Chicago, Houston, Denver. The works."

"Here we are," Lucy says. "Right where we wanted to be."

"Yeah," Jasper says.

He tells her he has rehearsals all week. Then he leaves on Monday for six months. "I want to see you first, though," he says.

They don't set up anything specific. He just says he'll call her. Lucy sits alone after they hang up and thinks about her life, this city, without Jasper in it at all. Jasper will be dancing his way across the country. Julia will be in Los Angeles. Even Katherine is gone. Lucy hugs herself tight, bends her toes and grips the tiny pebbles in her sneaker with them. She sits like that until, finally, she moves to her drawing table and begins to create a family for My Dolly.

Lucy and Julia stand on the corner in front of Lucy's apartment. Any minute now, On will arrive in the Ryder truck. He will pull up here beside them and Julia will get in and drive away. Lucy keeps watching the street, wishing he wouldn't appear at all.

"I'll be back," Julia is saying. "Listen, can you see me at Zuma Beach? Let's face it. I'm a New Yorker. I'll die out there with all that sunshine and stuff."

"They don't have delis like we do," Lucy tells her. "They don't wear black."

"Pastels," Julia says. "Can you imagine?"

"You don't look good in pastels," Lucy says.

"Or designer jogging suits," Julia says. She is watching the street too.

Julia has dyed her hair bright red. There are too many blonds out there, she told Lucy. Fake ones and real ones. Who needs to be just another pretty face? Her hair is the fakest red Lucy has ever seen. Stop sign red. Candy apple red. It makes Lucy want to cry.

"You'll make new friends out there," Lucy says softly.

"No," Julia tells her. "I won't talk to anybody. Except On. And him only sometimes."

"Promise?" Lucy asks her. And then she is crying. She is looking at her friend's bright red hair and she is crying hard.

They are both crying and hugging and don't see the Ryder truck as it comes down Broadway with On in the driver's seat. When he pulls up beside them, they finally let go.

"They don't have newsstands out there," Lucy says.

"Stop saying out there," Julia says, trying to laugh. "I feel like I'm going to outer space or something."

"You are," Lucy tells her. "What else would you call a place where everyone is blond and wears pastel jogging suits?"

"Home," Julia says. Her eyeliner and mascara have left rivers of black running down her cheeks. "Home."

Lucy nods.

"I'll see you Oscar night when you get your Academy Award for best screenplay," Lucy shouts to her as Julia climbs in the truck.

They are starting to drive away. Julia leans way out of the window. "See me?" she calls. "You'll be my date." They are almost at Houston Street. Her voice is faint. "Buy a black dress," she calls.

Lucy waves. She waves and waves until the truck is gone, completely out of sight.

•　•

Lucy agrees to work one last Whirlwind Weekend as a favor to the company. "You were one of our best guides," they tell her. It's a weekend to London and she will have two trainees with her, Lisbeth and Marnie. They are eager and fresh-faced. They look like they do soap commercials, Lucy thinks when she meets them at the airport.

Lisbeth says, "I bought both of my nieces a My Dolly last Christmas. They love them."

It still surprises Lucy when she hears things like this. She no longer watches toy stores stock their shelves with My Dolly. Now she concentrates on making a wardrobe and a family for it. She designs long dresses that look like sacks, with puffy sleeves and Peter Pan collars. They are made of faded cotton, worn corduroy.

"Everyone wants to love that poor little doll," Lisbeth is saying.

"Well," Lucy says. "Thanks."

She tells them about Whirlwind Weekends. How the people who take them are not travelers. How they are a little afraid of foreign things.

"They like things they are comfortable with," she says. "Hamburgers and pizza. Souvenirs that are not too exotic."

Marnie says, "But we can change that, right? I mean, we can expand their horizons. Show them new things."

She is a pale blond, with fair pink skin and light blue eyes. She looks like a doll herself.

"I mean," she continues, "I spent my junior year abroad. In Switzerland? And at first, I was really scared and stuff. But pretty soon I got really acclimated."

"But you had a year," Lucy says. "These people only have a weekend. You have to kind of protect them."

Lisbeth is nodding.

But Marnie frowns. "But, like with me," she says, "I ended up wanting to do everything. Lake Lucerne and fondue and Zermatt and—"

Lucy grits her teeth. "Well," she says. "If they had a year, I'm sure they'd loosen up. But in a weekend, that's a different story. You can't change a life in one weekend."

"Well," Marnie says reluctantly. "Maybe not."

Lucy reviews the itinerary with them. Even though she hasn't done a Whirlwind trip in months, the schedule feels as familiar as ever. The Medieval Manor. The tour on the double-decker bus. *Cats* and the changing of the guard and shopping at Harrods.

She explains how many dollars there are to a pound. She shows them subway maps. "And," she warns them, "be careful crossing the street. Make sure you look both ways. They drive on the left there. And people can get hurt."

For an instant, Lucy thinks about going back. About forgetting the alphabet book, the My Dolly clothes and family, forgetting all of it and doing just this—Whirlwind Weekends. She finds herself almost longing for the regularity, the certainty of them. The way they never change.

By the time they land back at Kennedy, Marnie and Lisbeth do not look as fresh-faced as they did a few days earlier. They look tired, all dark circles and dry skin. Their feet hurt and they are cranky.

"You'd think these people have never been out of New Jersey," Marnie tells Lucy.

"They haven't," Lucy says.

She gives them tips for fighting jet lag. She says, "Get some sea salt and take a bath in it." She says, "Eat turkey."

She has a good case of it herself. For a time, when she did a trip every weekend, Lucy lived in a kind of overtired fog. She was almost used to crossing time lines. But it has been a while, and she finds herself feeling like Marnie and Lisbeth—sore and tired. Both nights in the hotel in London she woke at three A.M., unable to fall back asleep. She had warned them about the possibility of that happening, and she heard them next door to her, their television on, their voices and giggles.

Lucy's tired feet drag as she makes her way from the subway to her apartment building, through the lobby and into the elevator. She had thought she would get some work done tonight. Maybe even decide about doing Fawn's book or not. It is then, as the elevator speeds her upward, that she realizes this is the first weekend that she hasn't seen Nathaniel Jones in a very long time.

She leans against the wall, realizing too that she has not missed him, or even thought about him. How, Lucy wonders, could she have considered leaving New York for a man she doesn't even think about? Nathaniel Jones is not fun, she thinks. And the thought makes her feel lighthearted. She doesn't love him. She doesn't want to move to Boston with him.

When she steps off the elevator, she has forgotten her achy feet. She feels wide-awake. She feels alive. She walks down the hall quickly toward her apartment, her suitcase bumping along behind her. But then she stops, her suitcase a beat behind her.

Lucy takes a deep breath. What she smells is this: a turkey roasting. A turkey with Grand Marnier and apricot stuffing. She puts down her duty-free bag filled with Tanqueray gin and Baileys Irish Cream. She presses her hands against the hallway wall to steady herself. Then slowly she walks toward her apartment, the smell of turkey growing stronger.

Before she can find her key and open the door, Jasper opens it and steps out.

"Hi," he says, a little shyly. "I still had my key, so. . . . "

She thinks about how good he looks, standing there like that. She thinks about how tomorrow he is leaving for six months. How nothing can be solved tonight.

He says, "The doorman told me you left in your uniform, so I figured you'd be back tonight. Then I got this crazy idea—." He motions behind him, toward the table set for two, the tulips bending in a vase, the wine poking out from an ice bucket.

"I have to admit," Jasper says, swallowing hard, "I was afraid of what I might find. You know," he adds, embarrassed, "a man's shaving gear. Or strange underwear. But then I thought, I have to chance it. I mean, sometimes you've got to take a chance. Right?"

Lucy does not know what will happen when she steps inside this door. She knows only that she is not moving to Boston. That Whirlwind Weekends are behind her. That she has a project to finish. And that for tonight at least, she will take a chance with Jasper.

"Right?" he asks again. There is hope in his eyes.

She says, "A lot can happen in six months."

"I know," he says. He steps aside to let her in.

"It smells good," she tells him. And she moves against him, presses herself close and wraps her arms around him.

"Didn't I ever tell you," Jasper whispers, "that turkey cures jet lag?"

Lucy nods. Her head rests right against his chest. She hears his heart, beating strong and steady. Lucy smiles into his shirt. She will be here alone, she thinks, and everything will be fine.

"Come on," she says. "Let's see what the night holds."

Jasper takes her by the waist and lifts her up, up into his arms like a ballerina, and jetés forward.

Ann Hood is the author of *Somewhere Off the Coast of Maine, Waiting to Vanish*, and *Three-Legged Horse*. She and her husband, writer Bob Reiss, live in Brooklyn, New York, where she is at work on a new novel.